The Village in the Mountains

David Diskin

THE VILLAGE IN THE MOUNTAINS is set in a fictional, southern European country in the middle of the twentieth century. After a brief period of democratic reform, the nation has once again become a totalitarian state under the rule of the Colonel, whose overriding creed is "Loyalty to the State, the Church, the Family".

The narrator of the book is a left-wing poet from a prominent family, whose personal story is intertwined with the political events of his birthplace. During the days of the old dictatorship he lived abroad as a fêted émigré. During the interim period of democratic reform he returned to the country. Now that the New Régime has become established, he is sent to live as an exile to the mountains in the northeast.

The village he is exiled to, Cagot—an isolated, primitive place high up in the border country—has a tragic history. Eight years earlier, four hundred pilgrims, paying homage to the statue of the Dark Virgin, were buried alive when the cave, housing the statue, collapsed. It is against this mountainous backdrop that a psychological drama is played out between the poet and the people with whom he comes into contact. There is Bernard, the manipulative, chess-playing Police Chief, to whom the poet must report every day; Isabella, the religiose brooding widow, who provides his meals in the ramshackle hotel where he is the only guest; Angela, the wife of the innkeeper; Henry, the schoolteacher; and Hubert Duval, the local aristocrat. It is Hubert who organises a fresh expedition to the cave of the Dark Virgin to see if, with the modern equipment now available, he can find a way to retrieve the bodies and provide them with a proper burial.

The journey to the cave and the ensuing events compel the poet to make a decision which will change his life forever.

DAVID DISKIN was born and brought up in the English Midlands and has spent most of his working life in Asia. He currently lives in Hong Kong where he pursues his interests in writing, natural history and photography. His novel, *The Village in the Mountains*, was Joint-Winner of the international Proverse Prize 2011.

Supported by

Hong Kong Arts Development Council

The Hong Kong Arts Development Council fully supports freedom of artistic expression. The views and opinions expressed in this project do not represent the stand of the Council.

The Village in the Mountains

David Diskin

Proverse Hong Kong

The Village in the Mountains
by David Diskin
2nd paperback edition
Published in Hong Kong by Proverse Hong Kong, January 2016
Copyright © Proverse Hong Kong, January 2016
ISBN: 978-988-8228-23-2
Printed by CreateSpace

1st published in Hong Kong by Proverse Hong Kong, 20 November 2012
Copyright © Proverse Hong Kong, 20 November 2012
ISBN 978-988-19935-9-5

1st edition Distribution (Hong Kong and worldwide):
The Chinese University Press of Hong Kong, The Chinese University of Hong Kong,
Shatin, New Territories, Hong Kong SAR.
E-mail: cup-bus@cuhk.edu.hk Web: www.chineseupress.com
Distribution (United Kingdom): Enquiries and orders to Christine Penney,
Stratford-upon-Avon, Warwickshire CV37 6DN, England.
Email: <chrisp@proversepublishing.com>
Enquiries: Proverse Hong Kong, P. O. Box 259, Tung Chung Post Office, Tung Chung,
Lantau Island, NT, Hong Kong SAR China.
E-mail: proverse@netvigator.com Web site: www.proversepublishing.com

Front cover photograph by Guillem de Plandolit. By permission of l'Arxiu Nacional
D'Andorra (National Archives of Andorra) (Fons: FGP. Ref. 206).
Cover design by Artist Hong Kong Company.
Page design by Proverse Hong Kong.

1st pbk ed
Proverse Hong Kong
            British Library Cataloguing in Publication Data
Diskin, David.
The village in the mountains.
I. Title
823.9'2-dc23

ISBN-13: 9789881993595

THE JOURNEY

They were waiting for me when I returned from my walk on the beach: three of them, all wearing the same ubiquitous grey uniform. Two of them were vague, nondescript; the third was different. Although there was no visible sign, no insignia, it was evident as soon as I saw him standing there with the others outside the cottage that he was the officer-in-charge. He was taller and thinner than his subordinates, but it was his eyes, fixed in that long, pallid face, that made the most impression on me. They were blue, unusual enough in itself for our race, but there was more to them than that; they had about them the opaque coldness of ice. They were the eyes of a man who would do the bidding of his superiors without question. I was afraid of him immediately.

"You were, of course, expecting us," he said, and gave a thin smile.

I nodded vaguely in assent. He handed me the summons. I noticed his fingers were long and delicate, pale also, in spite of the heat. As our hands touched, however, there was a hint of clamminess that seemed strangely at odds with my initial perception. I skimmed the words on the paper, the bland officialese that would reveal nothing of significance to a disinterested observer.

'You are requested to accompany ... to the capital ... to discuss your future situation.'

The authoritative signature and stamp brooked no refusal.

"Now?" I asked.

"Now," came the sardonic reply. "We will wait while you pack a bag."

The stress on the singular was obvious. I was allowed one bag and nothing more. All three of them followed me into the cottage and watched me as I began packing. The manuscript that lay on my desk was one of the first things that I thrust into the canvas bag with a casualness that was as obviously false to me as to them, trained observers.

"There will be no room for books or papers," the thin man said.

"They aren't necessary," one of the subordinates added, not without sympathy.

The thin man looked at him, and again a slight smile hovered momentarily on his lips. I felt sorry for the subordinate. He would not last long. I took the papers out of the bag, glanced down at the untidy script with its numerous deletions and corrections; then laid them back down on the wooden surface. It didn't much matter that I couldn't take them with me; the words, the stanzas – although so few compared with what I would once have written – were where they had all sprung from in the first place – in my head.

The thin man picked up the papers and flicked through them disparagingly without reading any of the poems. He put them down; then picked up the journal that was also on the desk. He opened it, and skimmed through the pages, occasionally pausing when something caught his attention. Finally, he put it back down on the table, open at the most recent entry.

"What is this?" he asked sternly, pointing at the pencil sketches and the accompanying notes.

"Shearwaters," I replied.

A few days earlier a strong northerly wind, cold and unseasonable, had brought the seabirds close to the rocky promontory that defined the southern boundary of the beach. There had been hundreds of them, gliding and veering on rigid wings, skimming the sea's surface, avoiding the rocks with a masterful ease. Amongst the Balearic shearwaters, I had spotted several of the rarer Cory's shearwaters, distinguishable by their larger size and more languid flight. My sketches depicted both species. Beneath was a list of the other birds I had observed that day; the list was an extensive one, as, apart from the seabird movement, there had also been a rich fall of migrant land birds.

"What does this say?" the thin man asked, picking an entry at random.

"Wryneck," I replied.

"And this?"

"Bee-eater. They're all birds," I informed him.

The thin man looked puzzled, as if he thought there was more to my nature notes than was immediately apparently. There wasn't. I turned and surveyed the shelves that took up the whole of one wall – the longest – in the cottage. They were crammed with books, books that I had had shipped back from England to the capital, and later transported to the cottage on the south-eastern coast. They were an inextricable part of my life.

"What will you do with them?" I asked.

"They will be taken care of," the thin man replied.

Again I nodded. I had expected nothing more.

"Pack some warm clothes," the thin man added. "You will need them where you're going to."

I didn't ask where "where" was. I just did as I was told. I packed the warmest clothes that I could find; sweaters that I had not worn for months, smelling of southern humidity; a fur-lined jacket that I had forgotten I even possessed. And all of this a charade. For I imagined, at best, dank walls, a cell illuminated by a single tungsten light. "And my field glasses?" I asked, fingering the instrument which had hung around my neck unheeded since my return.

"I can see no objection," the thin man returned wearily.

I placed them carefully in the bag, cushioning them between the musty sweaters against the possible vicissitudes of the journey. When I had finished packing my clothes, I squeezed in various toiletries; then, in keeping with the illusion that I was going on a journey with a definite destination, I considered the practical aspect of money. I went to the drawer in my desk, unlocked it, took out a bundle of notes and put them into my trouser pocket. During all of this I was conscious of the thin man's watchfulness. I half-expected a sign from him, but evidently he was not corrupt in the material sense.

"And my bank book?" I ventured, taking it out of the drawer.

"As you wish," the thin man said in the ironic way that an adult might indulge an ignorant child. As if a bank book would have any purpose where I was going!

No sooner had I placed the bank book in my bag, than the man asked with obvious impatience, "Are you ready now?"

I looked around me. In spite of what he had said I had not been expecting this; the idea that it might occur had been there, perhaps, but vague and unformulated. In my country, everyone – innocent and guilty alike – suffered from a sense of vulnerability. However, I had not been prepared. Like death, I thought, and so I grasped at significances.

From a shelf choked with bric-a-brac I took down the photograph of Maria. Dull, slightly out of focus, that photograph had, during the preceding months become very important to me. Maria's death had broken me, but it had also made me, slowly, so slowly – and I who had always considered myself so sensitive – more humane. I needed that photograph more than the rest of the contents in the bag combined, and I dreaded the thin man's refusing me the option.

He sighed, contemptuous of my sentimentality. I thrust the framed portrait into my bag. Saying nothing, he strode to the door and held it open for me. I zipped up my bag. The three men followed me out into the glare of the morning sun. I turned back, and – an exercise in futility – I locked the door behind me, pocketing the key after doing so.

"You have a reputation as a radical writer," the thin man said slowly, as if weighing every word, "yet you behave just like any other man in these circumstances."

His speech was meant to sting, yet it flattered me. I was glad to be seen as normal, glad that my minor acts of protest lacked originality. For I had been too removed from past events, praised and fêted for my words in foreign countries where I was safe, while those who had remained and lived by their beliefs – people now submerged in the anonymous waves of history – had been tortured, annihilated, by men such as this.

We got into the jeep, the thin man and one of the subordinates who acted as the driver in front, the other subordinate and myself in the back. The driver turned the key in the ignition. The engine churred into action. We pulled away from the cottage and drove along the coast, following the sweep of the beach to the headland. The driver found second gear; then we climbed upwards above the precipitous, scrub-covered cliffs. Below, the sea glittered silver-calm, yet just past dawn when I had walked on the beach, the water had shone golden.

I had learned to love the hourly transmutations of light on water, but now, cramped in the back of the jeep, I longed to leave the flat horizon, the sense of endlessly receding space, behind me. It promised freedom, while the reality of my situation pressed in on me, physically as it were, for the first time.

We began our descent to the fishing village, which glared white and spartan, in a cove below. I glimpsed the familiar exterior of the sea-front bar. At that time in the morning it would be empty. I envisaged Alfred, portly and dour, wiping glasses behind the simple, wooden counter; the chairs neatly arranged around the vacant tables; the chess pieces lined up in readiness for the lunchtime games. As we drove along the quayside I recognised Joseph – he was, as usual, bare to the waist, his skin tanned, sagging with age – at work on the nets strewn across the promenade. He looked up from his mending and saw me behind the glass. I saw the frown of puzzlement on his brown forehead. He had a slow mind; there was, with him, a pronounced gap between perception and understanding. We would have been virtually out of the village before he would have grasped the fact that I was being taken away, perhaps for good. And when, in the bar, the chairs had been scraped out of their regular patterns, when the chess pieces had advanced and retreated, when moist circles had formed on the table-tops, I saw him pondering openly, in his slow, but strangely powerful way: "They took him away ... in a jeep ... just like that. It is happening again."

And Alfred, the pragmatist, or the cynic, depending on one's viewpoint, would say: "You carry on. You stick to your fishing and your family. You keep your nose clean. That's what's important. Then you'll be left alone to live out your life the way you choose."

Alfred had always been aloof with me, had made it obvious that I did not really belong. Up to a point, of course, he was right. Yet who was it who told me that his son had been – what was the word in vogue at the time? – 'displaced', if I recall correctly? Perhaps it had been Joseph, who, over a game of chess, would, apropos of nothing, comment upon the hidden side of the villagers' past. The suddenness of the remarks hinted at senility, and I did wonder about their truthfulness but there had always been other sources to confirm their accuracy. After a while it had occurred to me that the revelations were especially meant for me; they were a way of bringing me to understanding, of letting the outsider in, and I had begun to look at Joseph in a different light. Yet I was never quite certain, for there was something enigmatic about Joseph: he eluded easy definition.

Anyway, I had slowly learned that behind Alfred's surly manner there lurked something tragic. He too had been touched by the unstable years.

Soon Alfred, Joseph, the bar, the village were gone. We passed the salt lagoon where flamingos shimmered pink in the morning sun; then headed inland towards the hills where orange groves straddled hillside terraces. We criss-crossed the beds of rocky streams, going over rickety bridges that jolted the jeep up and down, causing me to clutch the bag on my lap tightly.

It took two hours to reach the provincial capital – a town of four hundred thousand people known for its old quarter centred upon the Gothic cathedral, and also for the resistance that its inhabitants had shown when the Military had taken over twelve years before, and the Old Régime, as it is now known, was established. The official history had minimised the significance of the reaction, but the memory had continued to simmer beneath the surface of things. It had been here, within the cathedral precincts, so Joseph had said, that Alfred's son had been taken and led away.

Army headquarters lay in the modern part of the town. The building I was taken to was a grey concrete block. Once inside the thin man took me down grey corridors through doors that had to be unlocked then locked behind me, until we came to the cell.

"Your train leaves late this evening," he informed me. "You will remain here until it is time."

He left me. The door screamed shut. The key grated in the lock.

In my adolescence I had, in certain poems of bad faith, romanticised the prisoner's lot. Yet, up until that moment, I had never actually been imprisoned. The cell was bare-walled and cramped, furnished with a single bed and a chamber pot, the only light coming through a single barred window set high in one wall. I lay down on the discoloured mattress and closed my eyes to the scene. But my other senses defined the picture. There was a strong smell of urine. Somewhere water dripped. My skin began to itch as I thought of bedbugs. I opened my eyes again. In one corner the thin filaments of a spider's web shimmered in the light. On the wall next to the bed, in shadow, was a large, circular stain, its colour more prominent at the periphery. I did not know what the stain was, but I thought of blood, and could not rid my mind of the image.

I stood up, paced up and down the cell, sat down again. If that was a foretaste of what was in store for me ... I glimpsed momentarily the burden of time, dripping away second by second, with no stimulus to make one forget except what lay inside one's own mind. What had Michael told me after the

Old Régime had collapsed and the amnesty had taken effect, after I had returned, and he had been released? "Boredom is the worst thing. The futility of a life with no creative outlet."

"The torture?"

"They left me alone. For people like you and I the lack of stimulus – the deprivation – is torture enough."

Yet he had survived those silent years, and had, on his release, begun writing again.

"My will sustained me," he had written in an article in one of those magazines that had sprung up, Phoenix-like, out of the ashes of the democratic past. But it was clear that although his will had not been broken it had been irrevocably bent. The deprivation had had its effect, all the more subtle for Michael's not being able to recognise it. His writings – the novels and the factual analyses of what had occurred in our country – that were published in the interim period were too lax, too verbose, too repetitive. He was, in truth, a mere shadow of the writer whose incisive prose had aroused the wrath of the Military after they had seized power.

He had become harmless, as I had become harmless. Yet they had still taken me away from my coastal obscurity and put me inside that cell, where I could not dismiss the notion that the night-train to the capital was a fictitious entity and that I had, in fact, already reached my destination.

I looked at the stain on the wall again, again thought of blood, again of Michael. I had, long ago, acknowledged my own cowardice. Given the choice, I knew, that like Michael, I too would opt for the deprivation, the long, slow bending of the will rather than the strategically placed electrodes, because I knew that the latter would break me almost immediately. Then I visualised the thin man – the neat features, the blue eyes, and knew that with him I would have no chance. Not that it would be – could be – of any importance to the New Régime if I were broken. It was just that the thin man would enjoy it, reinforcing his contempt of me, bolstering his sense of egotistical superiority.

Or so I believed. I was, in fact, wrong. The thin man had a greater awareness of human nature than I had credited him with. He knew he had no need for violence. He had registered the failure in me, and had deliberately put me into that cell so that I would torture myself with my own imaginative wonderings. In this he was more representative of the New Régime than I had imagined.

I only realised this after I had been taken back along the grey corridors to the Military Commander's office.

"I really must apologise," he said immediately, beckoning me to sit down. "You are a guest of the Government, not a prisoner."

I responded to the Commander's gesture, and sat down on the chair facing him across the dark, mahogany desk. I stared at the intricate pattern of grain, as the Commander toyed with a glass paper-weight, one of several that stood on the wooden surface. Apart from these collector's items and a solitary ashtray, the desk was empty.

I looked up at the Commander. He was everything that the thin man was not: round-faced, grey-haired, bespectacled. The avuncular image was familiar to me. I had seen his photograph in the provincial newspapers, had heard the villagers talk about him. The people of the south-eastern province had a reputation for disdaining authority. The reputation was not without foundation, yet in the coastal village they had spoken of this man with grudging respect.

He had been given control of the province three years after the Military had seized power, and so had lacked the stigma of association with the initial repression. His predecessor had been hated, for he had crushed the liberals with a brutality that had extended far beyond the needs of the moment, and the oppression had continued during the three years that the man had remained in power. In the end, he had been assassinated by a disturbed relative of one of his victims. It was after this that the present Commander had been brought in. He had had the assassin executed immediately. The execution had been a public affair, and although no one had been compelled to attend, a large crowd had gathered to watch the firing squad perform its task.

This public execution had achieved a certain infamy. It was virtually unique in the recent history of the province, indeed of the country as a whole. Usually, the killings that went on – and during the nine years that the Old Régime held sway, the numbers unofficially extended into the hundreds – were carried out in secret, in darkened rooms or in deep forests, so that the victims disappeared, were buried in unmarked graves. Everyone knew of these killings; it was part of the Military's strategy that the people should know, even while tangible proof was denied them.

The Commander would have none of that. He allowed the public to witness the event. They saw the assassin walk to his death; they saw his naked torso and could verify that he hadn't been tortured beforehand; they saw the priest give him the last rites. Although it was evident that the Commander was making an example of the assassin, it was acknowledged, at first quietly, but later more openly, that this was morally preferable to the fate of los desaparecidos, for los desaparecidos lacked the finality of death. Without the actuality of a corpse, people could still cling to the thin fibres of hope, yet such unfulfilled hope was cancerous; it devoured the spirit, and became ultimately a torment in itself. The Commander seemed to recognise that, and either from a sense of humanity, or perhaps from political expediency, found it unacceptable.

It was this man that I now faced across the desk. "You say I am a guest of the Government," I began.

"That is what I gather from the dispatches I have received." He opened a drawer, took out a file and placed it on the desk in front of him. He extracted a piece of paper from the folder, and continued," It says you are to be escorted to the capital – gives the date by which you should arrive – and states explicitly that you are to be treated with the courtesy that your status demands."

"I have not been treated very courteously so far."

"I have apologised for that." He gave an amiable smile and gestured vaguely with his left hand. "The officer is over-zealous in his duties."

"And what will happen to me when I reach the capital?" I asked.

The Commander leaned forward slightly and placed his hands palm downwards on the desk. "I don't really know," he said. "Do you smoke?" he asked, and brought out from somewhere, from the same drawer as the file, I supposed, a cigarette box. I had given up long ago, but it seemed somehow churlish to refuse at that particular moment, so I took one of the cigarettes from the wooden box – the carved design on the lid was, I noticed, exquisite. The Commander took one himself; then snapped the lid shut. He lit the cigarettes. Blue smoke drifted on the air between us.

"From what I can gather," he said slowly, almost ponderously, "from other cases, you will be sent somewhere..."

"Abroad?" I asked, uncertain of what lay in store for me.

"No, I don't think so. The Government recognises that people like you are more trouble abroad than they are at home. They prefer these days to put people into internal exile."

"How can you be exiled in your own country?" I asked. The question was a genuine one. I had spent nine years abroad and during that time had yearned for my country with an ache like adolescent love. To me internal exile was a contradiction in terms.

"I only repeat what I have heard, and I do not even know this officially," the Commander responded.

"But you are a Commander."

He exhaled smoke from his mouth, and looked at me thoughtfully. When he finally spoke, it was with a kind of austere sadness, "Things are changing. There is new blood coming in. You have only yourselves to blame, of course. It was liberals like you that helped to create an atmosphere where individuality was everything, and what was the result?"

I waited silently for him to tell me.

"Pornography; drugs; moral anarchy. And worse, you have helped to create men like Thomas."

"Thomas?"

"The officer who arrested you."

"He is a creation of the Régime," I protested. "What have I to do with him?"

"He is a reaction to what occurred in the 'interim period', as your journalist friends care to call it."

"But our country has always bred people like him," I argued and was surprised by the strength of my reaction. I had not thought about such matters for a long time, had consciously renounced such concerns after Maria's death. The time-worn controversies had paled into insignificance next to that. Yet something in the Commander's words raised old ghosts. They thrust me back to my earlier years, those years of exile abroad. "It is the Régime that allows them their particular perverse fulfilment. You cannot implicate me in that," I said.

The Commander sighed. "It is of no importance," he said, suddenly appearing tired, worn down, by the whole political business. "But believe me," he added, forcibly arousing himself, "in spite of people like Thomas, the New Régime is different. The Colonel doesn't want to go back to the old days. There were too many deaths, too much blood. You are proof enough of that. It would be a simple matter for him to remove you if he wanted to."

He stubbed out his cigarette end in an ashtray; then settled back in his chair with the air of a man at the end of his tenure, waiting for retirement.

There was a sharp knock at the door. The Commander looked at his watch; then shouted, "Come in."

Two men entered, dressed in the same grey uniforms as my escorts earlier in the day. One of them put my bag down on the floor at the side of my chair. "It is time to go to the station," the Commander said to me. "These men will accompany you to the capital."

I stood up and picked up my bag. I nodded to the Commander – he nodded in return – then followed the two officers out of the room. Outside it was dusk; the streets seemed still, suspended under a magenta-coloured sky. We drove along the wide boulevard that encircled the town. This time the two military personnel sat together in the front of the jeep; I was alone in the back. Through the open window the trees lining the road blossomed white under the street lamps; the scent of the flowers hung softly on the still air. And at regular intervals, under the same lights, policemen stood in pairs, pistols prominent in the holsters on their hips. They appeared unreal, spectral almost, yet even in the democratic years, when I was a mere child, I recalled that the police and the military – the uniform was so similar, that they seemed to be one and the same – had always been a pervasive part of the street environment. That I noticed them so much now was due, evidently, to my state of mind. I had been leading a life with a regular, limited rhythm. I had consciously avoided any external stimuli that might break that rhythm. The day's events had changed all of that. The thin man, the hours in the prison cell, had had a greater effect on me than I had been aware of during my interview with the Commander. I was physically tired but my mind was stimulated and would not be stilled.

So, just as the police began to take on an unnatural significance, so, during the ensuing journey, did other phenomena. The station, for example: the cavernous roof with its web of girders, the clouds of steam rising from the hissing locomotives, the whistles, the bustling people – all seemed slightly distanced from me, yet vivid, imbued with a meaning that evaded definition, as in that dream-state between waking and sleeping.

I was ushered onto the train by the two men who accompanied me. They were both rather silent, rather morose. I sensed they were contemptuous of me; in their eyes poetry, literature in general, would be regarded, not as the Commander would have it, as politically suspect, but as effete. It was a peasant's reaction, and perhaps there was some truth in it, for hadn't we all been so easily crushed, removed or forced into exile? It was the less-educated with the guns – like my two guards, but on the other side of the political divide – who had offered the greatest resistance, who had fought on in the old quarter of this, the provincial capital. True, we had given voice to the underlying beliefs, made eloquent what they could not coherently express, yet without us the resistance would still have occurred. And what effect had all those words, all those lectures abroad had, other than satisfying one's own ego? What had I, and André, and others like us – the émigrés – really achieved?

I sat in a private compartment, the uniformed men opposite me, as the train chugged out of the station. Once the platform had receded, we plunged into a dark tunnel. My ears buzzed. In the window I watched my reflection watching myself – my eyes small and shrunken, my forehead glistening red, the redness extending to my exposed crown where the hair had started to recede. The hair that remained, at the sides and the back of my head, and the thin layer on top, had turned grey, as had my moustache and my beard.

"You look so distinguished," Maria had once said, in her half-ironic, half-serious way.

"Like a poet," I had replied, adopting the ironic tone.

"Like a statesman," she had replied.

Now I no longer knew what my face revealed. We emerged from the tunnel. I forced a yawn and my ears popped. Outside the lights of the town failed to eradicate my image in the glass. The guards noticed me staring and one of them made a joke that I did not catch. The other laughed. Then they both lit cigarettes before going out into the corridor and sliding the door shut behind them.

"This is what my country has created," I thought. "So why did I return?"

If I had not returned, Maria would still be alive.

POEMS OF LOVE AND DEATH, I had written on the title page of the manuscript. At once so pretentious, and yet so near to what I needed to express. And very much of my country. I had, at last, been breaking away from my accidie. And the thin man, after I had taken the papers back out of my bag, had flicked through the pages, scanning the lines. "There will be no room for books and papers."

Exposed. I felt old, as my country was old. The guards, I noticed, had finished their cigarettes, but they remained standing outside in the corridor. It was going to be a long night, for although we had a private compartment, it was not a sleeping berth.

We had left the provincial capital behind, and were now out in the countryside; there was a conspicuous lack of lights, and the dark silhouettes of hills and trees stood out against a slightly paler sky. I made them out by staring through my reflection, yet it took only a slight change of focus to obliterate the external world, and I would be face to face with myself again.

I looked through myself again and focussed on the solitary light of what I took to be a cottage, suspended in the darkness. The track curved across the landscape in a huge arc, for the light remained static, visible in the same position for twenty minutes. The guards re-entered the compartment, saw the light, as I saw it, through the reflections in the glass, and crossed themselves. The gesture puzzled me before I realised that the light marked not a cottage but a shrine, one of the many that dotted the countryside, even in the most isolated places. This one was of particular significance. I vaguely recalled reading somewhere how the line had been deliberately laid down in that huge curve to keep the shrine visible to travellers, while not intruding upon the sanctity of the Virgin symbolically depicted within. Another example of my country's conservatism, I thought, taken to the limits of absurdity. For religion was deeply engrained in the national psyche. My guards had made the sign of the cross, not out of any high spiritual feeling, but merely as a reflex action, a ritual act of obedience learned from their black-robed mothers who lived by the Old Régime's motto: 'Loyalty to the State, the Church, the Family.'

One of the guards dimmed the lights. Then they settled down, one at each end of the couch opposite me, and began to doze. I closed my eyes and did the same. Sleep did not come easily. My body was tired, but my mind remained active, as if I had taken a stimulant. Faces floated across the surface of my closed eyelids: André's, the thin man's, Maria's; then the Commander's – open-mouthed, speaking, but this time his voice was admonitory, mocking.

"You brought her back here. You murdered her."

"No," I muttered; then came to consciousness.

The guard opposite stared at me with annoyance. I had disturbed him. I looked away. The regular rhythm of the train, the darkness etched with the faint silhouettes of trees outside, soothed me a little. But it was not enough. I felt the need for movement. "Do you have a cigarette?" I asked the guard.

He hesitated a moment; then looked towards his partner who had not been awakened by my troubled dream. He shrugged his shoulders; then reached into his pocket, extracted a packet of cigarettes and offered me one. I took it and bent down to the flame of his burning match. Then I stood up to go outside.

"Where ...?" the guard began, suddenly suspicious, unsure of himself without his companion's support.

"Just outside." I indicated the place in the corridor where the guards had stood earlier.

Before he could object further, I stepped over the legs of the sleeping man, opened the door and entered the corridor. No one else was there. I opened the small sliding windows that were on a level with my face. Chill air rushed in, smelling of the smoke spewing from the engine. Clouds of grey steam swirled by. I inhaled deeply on the cigarette. It tasted acrid, as had the one I had smoked in the Commander's office, but then I had not been especially aware of how much I disliked it. Now, undistracted, I would have ground it under my foot had it not been for the fact that it had been my reason for getting out of the compartment for a while. So I continued to smoke, but slowly, only occasionally putting the tip to my lips to satisfy the guard who, I sensed, was observing me closely.

When I had finished I went back to my seat and closed my eyes again. This time I slept, only waking when the train came to a standstill with a jolt. I yawned and looked at the dully illuminated platforms outside. They were thronged with people huddled together in family groups, sprawling untidily over the concrete. Most of the children were asleep, but the majority of the adults seemed to be awake, keeping a watchful eye on the baggage that defined the territorial boundary of their particular group.

The sense of unreality returned to me. Who were these people, their faces for the most part lost in shadow, so that only the whites of their eyes stood out? Where were they going? Our train remained stationary for thirty minutes, as did the one, a virtual mirror image of our own that stood on the opposite platform. Yet the people occupying the floor space did not move. I didn't understand, but the vision of those people trapped in a kind of purgatory, forever doomed to spend the nights swathed in blankets on the cold concrete has stayed with me.

"Where are these people going?" I asked my guard who, like me, was looking avidly out of the window.

His purpose, however, was of a more practical nature. He opened the window as a man pushing a trolley containing two steel urns went by, calling "Coffee! Tea!"

"Coffee" the guard cried out after the man had gone past. The man turned, nodded; then took the few paces backwards to the window. As he had passed it had struck me that there was something odd about him, but it was only when he was close to, turning a tap so that the dark liquid drained out of the urn, that I saw he had no left hand. His arm terminated in a rounded stump.

"Only one?" the man asked roughly.

"One for me as well," I interposed.

The man went through the motions again.

"Where are all of these people going?" I asked him, since the soldier had ignored my question.

The man looked up at me with a quizzical expression on his stubbly face. "South," he said, and handed me the plastic cup. I paid for my drink and for the guard's as well. The latter thanked me curtly, with no real pretence at gratitude.

"Your friend is a heavy sleeper," I said, referring to his companion who was still sprawled across the seat, snoring gently. The guard merely grunted in reply; then stared into his coffee cup, indicating that my attempts at conversation were unwelcome. This irked me. I wanted to know what the hawker had meant by his cryptic "south", what symbolism lay beyond the directional word.

I learned later that the people haunting the platform at the station had been pilgrims waiting for the special government-appointed locomotive to take them south, virtually as far south as one could go in our country, into the arid, semi-desert regions to the place where twelve years previously a young girl had supposedly had direct communication with the Virgin Mary. At the time, thousands of people had flocked to the site to see the girl, who, as mediator between the Madonna and the people, was reputed to be in possession of healing powers. This had been during the first months of the Old Régime, and the Military had stressed the occurrence in the media, tying it in with their conservative moral vision. However, after the first few years of pilgrimage, familiarity had begun to breed not contempt but indifference. The media had turned to other things, the number of pilgrims had decreased as the sought for miracles had not occurred, and the Military had become preoccupied with its own failures. In the final years of the Old Régime the pilgrimage had ceased to exist. The girl, by this time a rather dull woman in her late twenties, unmarried, virginal, shrunken into herself, seemed to have succumbed to the pressure of spiritual self-doubt. She no longer had visions. And then, no sooner had the Colonel come to power, but the whole thing had been revived. The impetus behind the revival had been a photo-essay in the magazine 'Insight', one of the numerous weekly journals that had been initiated under the Old Régime in the time of my exile, dedicated to sensational photo-stories that appealed to the public without offending the ruling class.

It was in the mountains that I had read the article, in a copy of the magazine that Isabella had left lying around the hotel. I remember it vividly: the title 'O my God, why hast thou forsaken me?'; the lurid double page photo-spread of the woman cloaked in black, her back to the camera, lifting outstretched arms to a storm-blue sky, the kind of sky that is still, but electric with tension, before rain. And then on the following page – and I don't know how the photographer had achieved the effect – the woman was facing the camera, her face no longer hooded but uplifted, illuminated in a manner that recalled the luminosity of a painting by El Greco, while beyond a yellow streak of lightning hurtled across the angry sky. The picture, however cinematically contrived it appeared, spoke of epiphany, the rediscovery of the woman's numinous experiences.

So the pilgrimage was reborn. The Colonel himself sponsored the numerous journeys to the south. Extra trains were laid on, at subsidised prices, to cater for the pilgrims' spiritual needs.

It was the other guard, the one with the capacity for trouble-free sleep, who put me right about my lost souls on the platform – this when the eastern sky had turned pale, the moon had all but gone, and my reflection in the window had diminished. I had simply described the situation to him, and asked him what it meant. He had answered plainly, and as he spoke I knew that I should have realised at the time, as I should have known immediately about the shrine I had seen from the train. Religion was important to my countrymen, but it had never been to me. My parents had been professedly religious, but they were rich, of the city. Going to church was to them the equivalent of going to the opera; socially, it was necessary to be seen, to share the sphere, morally and artistically, of one's equals. Through them I had learnt nothing about the reality of the peasant, as I had learnt nothing through the radical circle in which I had moved at the university in my student days. Most of my peers came from the same privileged background as myself, and those who didn't, those working class people who had somehow gotten into the system, were, by and large, from the urban areas too. The peasantry were excluded from our perspective, and yet they constituted the majority of the people in the country. So in exile abroad, lecturing, writing my poems, I had perpetuated the myth of oppression, of the strong feeding on the weak, of democracy being crushed under the heels of the Military; as all of us in exile, albeit from different angles, had.

And, as far as we were concerned, as representatives of a larger radical group many of whom had remained behind and had suffered in the homeland, at that time we had been correct. But, as representatives of the population en masse, we had, I believe – and it had taken me a long time to accept the truth of this – been out of touch. Agriculture, not industry, was where the soul of the country lay. We had not taken that simple fact into account. For all our convictions, all our sense of being right, we had, ultimately, been wrong. The peasants had no use for our liberalism. The Military and the Colonel had recognised that fact, and they had been successful. The peasants respected authority, whether in the form of God or Government. The Government had allied itself with the Creator, whereas we had been agnostics, or worse, atheists.

The country had got the government that it deserved. It had been during the last two years – in my solitary existence on the coast – that I had slowly, against my will, come to that conclusion. I had resigned myself to the fact, as I had resigned myself to the agonising reality of Maria's death. Yet understanding, as opposed to acceptance, still eluded me. I was out of touch with the land that had created me.

This feeling of alienation was not relieved by the sight of the city – the capital, my birthplace, – rising like a mirage in the distance out of the monotonous flatness of the plain. A misty grey aura surrounded the buildings – the blocks of high-rise apartments, dwellings of workers on the edge of the urban sprawl – but the aura was man-created: pollution from the factories that had created the wealth to which I owed my education, my creativity. Under that atmospheric layer were streets teeming with all of the emotional excesses, good and bad, that constituted humanity. "A poet's dream", I had once called it in my poem 'The City', meaning any city, but it had been my birthplace that I had had in mind. An example of my romanticism. Eight years after I had written the poem, people – too many people – whom I had respected had been plucked from the civilised streets (the tree-lined boulevards had been symbolic of control, of calm) and brutally murdered in the name of 'the State, the Church, the Family.' And all too recently those same streets had taken Maria away from me. After her death I had sworn never to return. Yet the Colonel had compelled me. I was, for the moment, no longer my own man.

The plain was grey, naked. Deep furrows made strange patterns across its flat surface. Even at that early hour, tractors were extending the pattern – and not only tractors; the occasional ox, its back sunken under the pressure of the plough, could be seen traversing the smaller fields led by its sullen master.

Only the odd raised mound disrupted the monotony; crumbling watchtowers stood on their slight crests, reminders of an age as barbaric as our own. And always, as the track twisted and turned for reasons only its designers could know of, the city drew nearer, as if it were moving towards us, to seize us in its grasp, to swallow us whole. My guards, both now wide awake, smoking, so early, their first cigarettes of the day, did not see the city's malevolence. They were, like children, enraptured. Children who saw the city, ultimately so foreign to them, as a source of ... of what? I suppose of release from the rural restrictions that, even in a provincial capital, governed their lives. This city, the real city, offered them the satisfaction of anonymity. I could see them chafing at the bit with the desire to experience the streets. And I saw the glint of a steel blade, the pierced flesh, the crimson flow – another facet of the city's multifaceted reality. But this they would not have been thinking of. Theirs was a simplistic vision, the peasant's vision.

The fields gave way to brickworks and haphazardly constructed shacks, the shanty towns clinging like parasites to the edge of the city proper. Then came the apartment blocks, tall, grey, lifeless concrete structures, row upon row of them, with patches of grass in between, thrown in as an afterthought to relieve the architectural dullness of it all. This modern growth, the result of modern notions imbibed whole from the more progressive European centres without thought for our own particular heritage – and this, ironically, from the conservative Military régime – depressed me. When I had been a child the buildings had not existed. Then, going south on the train, we had passed through slums before entering the countryside – the flat fields now overlain by concrete – but the slums had had, in a demonic way, an organic vitality of their own. The dark, squat houses, the grimy faces of the children, the cheeky smiles and gestures as the train went by held a perverse attraction for me. But these concrete erections spoke of nothing but sterility. Even the sun, now bathing them in the pink glow of its dawn rays, could not transmute them into something beyond themselves. Dawn was a magical time, but these constructions were beyond redemption.

And out of this landscape, quickly, yet paradoxically, as if suspended in a dream, a stone came floating and thudded against the window. The guard opposite me, who was staring intently out of the window, did not see the missile thrown from the foot of the embankment by an adolescent hand. He recoiled abruptly at the contact of stone and glass, and held his hand to his cheek, frightened that the contact might have extended to that of glass and flesh.

"What was that?" he asked nervously.

"I don't know," his partner replied disingenuously. "A bird?"

"A stone," I said, enlightening them. "Someone threw a stone at the train."

"The window could have broken," the guard opposite me said, and on his face I saw the slow realisation, the fumbling imaginative grasp of what the result would have been if that had occurred.

"But why?" the other guard wondered aloud, and then looked at me accusingly, as if I were somehow to blame.

"The fact that it was this window is purely arbitrary," I stated. "They just wanted to hit the train."

"A game?" my accuser suggested.

"A game," I replied.

We moved closer to the centre of the city. Dark, high walls hid all but the tops of the buildings from view, and then suddenly we were in a tunnel. There was a screech of brakes, a change in the engine's rhythm, and we came to a halt in the cavernous space of the central station.

The two guards became tense. They stood up, smoothed out their crumpled uniforms as best they could, and ushered me out of the carriage onto the platform with an assumed authoritative briskness. The air was cold and seemed, in spite of the steam hissing from the locomotive that obscured the red buffers that marked the end of the line, to be imbued with a harsh clarity. I carried my bag, and led them – after all, this was familiar territory to me – from the platform into the main area of the station, a rectangular space of ticket booths, a cafeteria and a newspaper stall. The two guards looked around them, shivering a little, as if unable to decide on their next move. "A taxi?" I suggested facetiously, but before they could respond to that, a man in military uniform approached us, confirmed my identity, and led us outside to a waiting jeep.

As we drove through the streets it soon became obvious to me that I was being taken, not to Army Headquarters, as I had imagined, but to the Secretariat from where the Colonel had ruled the country for the past fifteen months. Once there the guards who had accompanied me from the provincial capital left me without a word. Two other guards, armed with rifles that seemed more ceremonial than dangerous, escorted me through a maze of corridors to a large stylish waiting room, whose only occupant was a male secretary. He sat at an over-sized oaken desk.

"Please sit down," the man said with formal politeness.

I did as I was asked, and rested my bag on my knees. The man arranged some papers on his desk – for show, I thought – before walking over to the doors, made of the same immaculately polished oak as the table, at the far end of the room. He knocked and entered, pulling the doors to behind him. He re-emerged a few minutes later and showed me into the room.

"You do, of course, remember me?" the man who greeted me said, as I stood facing him across a desk identical to the one in the outer office.

I was tired and unsettled but I forced myself to concentrate. The man was indeed familiar to me.

"You look surprised," he said, misinterpreting my fatigued reaction.

"No. I knew that you were the Colonel," I replied.

The man looked at me, his chin supported on his right hand in such a way that his forefinger obscured his mouth, and hid most of his silver-grey moustache. "Sit down," he said, less politely than his secretary had done.

I did so. I looked at him as he looked at me – coldly. I had not seen him face to face for over twenty years.

"You have aged a lot," he said. "Events have affected you." The latter sentence had the upward intonation of a question.

"I have not been myself recently," I responded. "Still, I daresay you are aware of that."

"Yes." He allowed himself a faint smile. "I know about your wife's death – a tragic incident, I'm sure. But that was some time ago, wasn't it?"

"Two years," I said, only telling him what he already knew.

"Quite. Anyway, I haven't had you brought here to talk about that. It is your father ..."

"My father?"

"Yes. You know he had a stroke?"

"Yes, I heard," I said.

"He is seriously ill. He doesn't have long to live, and he knows it. That is why he asked me to speak to you."

"He knows I am here then?" I asked.

The Colonel nodded. "He wants you to have dinner with him tonight."

"My father has spoken to me only once in the past fifteen years," I said. "I can see no reason for him to break the silence now."

The Colonel coughed briefly. "The day after tomorrow you will be sent far away from here, to the mountains," – he paused momentarily to allow the implication of his remark to sink in – " and it is highly unlikely that you will ever see your father alive again. I am indebted to your father ..." – here I detected a note of bitterness in his voice – "and I am doing this because of our relationship. Do you understand me?" His final question was harsh, pointed.

"Yes," I replied.

"Then you will go?"

"Do I have a choice?"

"I cannot force you to go," he responded, "but I think it would be wise for you to hear what he has to say. Don't you?"

I agreed to go, but this out of a sense of compulsion, in spite of what the Colonel had said, rather than from compassion or curiosity. Then I started to ask him about the mountains, but he held up his hand and stopped me.

"Tomorrow! You will be brought to me again tomorrow. Now, my men will take you to a hotel so you can have breakfast and rest after your journey."

I looked at him; at the bald, rounded head; at the round face with those narrow eyes suggestive of the Orient; at the squat nose. The moustache, perhaps an effort at bestowing a certain distinction upon himself, could not disguise his physical ugliness. When I had been a child he had been a frequent visitor to my father's house. "The Troll", my sister and I had called him behind his back, "the Troll who gobbled up people going over the bridge," and by projecting our childhood reading onto him we had unconsciously been exorcising our fear of the man who was, at the time, our father's friend. For, in spite of the man's generosity with presents, in spite of his endearments, we had been repelled by him. As children we had sensed the coldness in the man's soul. And I sensed it now, and was still disturbed by him, even this far from my childhood days.

I was relieved to get out of the room and to be taken, as he had said, to a hotel, to a room with a view over the square that was the historical centre of the city. To wait. For I was not allowed to leave the hotel until the appointed hour when I was to dine with my father. So I breakfasted, slept a while and spent the afternoon sitting on the balcony, basking in the sun.

I thought of my father, of my mother. They had both disassociated themselves from me fifteen years before. Initially, they had dismissed the poems and the political stance of my university years as being a matter of youthful indulgence, something to be put up with until I had matured and adopted their conservative ways, but when I had begun to write articles for "The Review" – articles which attracted the attention of the upper echelons of society because of my name – then their patience turned to outrage. Egotists both, they took my attacks on the Church and the increasingly influential Army as a personal affront. They disinherited me and I was forbidden to enter the home of my birth.

All of the years I was in exile abroad, I had had no contact with them. Then the amnesty was declared and I had returned to the capital with my wife. Many of the returned émigrés and released prisoners, myself included, frequented the theatre, the opera , the ballet; this not merely out of intellectual interest, but also as an expression of our right, so long denied, to be there. It had been an informative experience at such cultural events to witness the cold stares of those who had supported the Régime, the deliberate failure to acknowledge old acquaintances, family snubbing family, sometimes, it seemed to me, as much from a sense of guilt as from antipathy; after all, those who had stayed had *los desaparecidos* on their consciences.

It had been at the opera, in the chandelier-lit foyer, that I had encountered my parents for the first time since I had been forced into exile. "What's the matter?" Maria had asked, sensing the sudden tension in me.

"My mother and father," I had replied.

We all stared at one another, four people enmeshed in a silent drama while the buzz of voices went on around us. Both of my parents had naturally aged, but it was my mother that compelled my attention. She had always been strong and decisive, a cultivated socialite. In her youth – I had seen daguerreotypes – she had been beautiful, the typical dark-eyed, olive-skinned beauty of our race. But now, she was a withered creature. Her bracelets dangled from thin, wrinkled wrists. The necklace failed to conceal the sagging flesh. She was, I saw, seriously ill. It was only her will that held her firm, her attendance at the opera a forced refutation of what she must have known to be inevitable.

My father led her away without speaking. The old sanction still remained.

It was Maria who, two months later, told me that my mother had died. I was not without compassion; the image of the fragile, old woman at the opera had stayed with me. So I went to the church and remained at the back during the service, and at the burial – I remember it was winter; the ground was frozen, solid underfoot; people's breath rose in clouds on the static air – I stayed some distance from the mourners. I slipped away without speaking to anyone before the ceremony had finished.

The following summer Maria had been stabbed by an unknown assailant in the Old Quarter of the city. The attacker had taken her handbag and left her bleeding in the cobbled street. The blade had pierced her heart. She died virtually immediately.

After the event my father came to see me. In the cramped space of my apartment, he seemed awkward, diminished. His coming obviously caused him great difficulty.

"I am genuinely sorry," he said to me. "She was a good woman."

Then he went on to confess that Maria had been to see him not long after the encounter at the opera in an attempt to bring us together again. She hadn't succeeded – pride on both of our parts would have made that impossible – but something in her spirit had appealed to my father, and a tenuous link had been established between them. It was because of this link, although I didn't know it at the time, that Maria had been able to bring me news of my mother's death.

"You came to the funeral," he said. "That was good of you. I cannot attend Maria's, but I will think of her. My presence here ..." He faltered, and gestured vaguely with his hands, on which the blue veins were so prominent. It was the closest he could get to expressing sympathy. He had left without saying anymore. I had had no contact with him since then.

So when I saw him that evening, after my visit to the Colonel, I was shocked by his appearance. When he had visited me he had been thinner, more worn than I had expected, but now his face was gaunt, shrunken, the hollowness of his cheekbones gave his face the appearance of a death mask. The stroke had left him paralysed from the waist down.

My father's physical appearance mirrored his mental state. He was distracted, unable to concentrate for any length of time. We ate dinner, for the most part in silence – that is, I ate dinner; my father barely touched his food, although he did drink the wine with an almost obscene voraciousness for an old man. And this was deliberate, an act of will to give him the gift of speech, as wine often gives me the gift of creation, no matter how much that what is created has to be revised in the sober light of the day. But for him there would be no time for revision.

It was after the meal, when we sat before a burning coal fire – he was in his wheelchair; I was on a sofa that smelt of senility – that he began to really speak to me, fuelled by the alcohol. His voice was hoarse. It was a great physical effort for him to express himself. "I am dying," he said, sipping his brandy," as I am sure that the Colonel told you. I am frightened. I admit it. Your mother's death," he continued, faltering. "Everything confuses me. But that's because I am old. My mind ..."

I drank my brandy and waited for him to continue.

He began to cough. His gnarled hand clutched an handkerchief, held it to his mouth. I glimpsed a clot of blood-stained phlegm. When his coughing fit had subsided, he folded the handkerchief to conceal its contents, and held it on his lap. His fingers toyed with it as he continued to speak. "When you are so close to death," he said slowly, "you see things from a different perspective. – What happened between us? I can't change history, but I can make amends."

"What do you mean?" I asked.

He sucked air in through his mouth." I spoke to the editor of 'The Nation' recently – Ernest Lille. Perhaps you remember him?"

I shook my head. Lille's name was familiar to me, but he had only risen to journalistic prominence – as an apologist for the Military – during my years in exile. My father's memory was failing him.

"It doesn't matter," my father said. "The point is, he is looking for a new assistant."

The Nation was little more than a pro-Government mouthpiece. I thought for a while, looked at my father looking at me. His shrivelled face was an enigma, but I saw a certain recognition there that I had never seen before.

"Can I ask – you don't really expect me to accept such an offer, do you?"

My father raised his eyes, and looked me full in the face. He said nothing, merely gave an ironic smile. His smile vanished abruptly." The Colonel is a dangerous man," he began.

"He said he was indebted to you."

"He hates me, and he hates you even more."

"But why? You were friends," I reminded him. "I remember meals at home, at the same table."

"He used me. He clawed his way up through the Intelligence services and seized the opportunities when they came."

"The opportunities?"

"I thought he was what was necessary at the time."

My father was becoming alive, animated, more as I remembered him many years before when I was a student and we used to argue violently about politics. He had, however, never spoken so venomously as he did now, and still I did not understand.

"What do you mean he used you? After all, you were just an industrialist."

"We used each other. At the time I didn't realise his true potential. I never imagined him at the head of the Government."

My father was being deliberately evasive. There was in his words a suggestion of dark secrets, of deeper complicity with the machinations of the Old Régime than I had previously suspected.

"He resented me for my money, my culture, my connections, but there was something else that accentuated his resentment. He had a son, born shortly after you."

The information surprised me. I could recollect no mention of a wife or child, nor could I at that moment, having so recently met with the Colonel again, associate him with a woman. It was power that inspired him, not sex.

"The son was a cretin," my father continued. "The Colonel disowned him and his mother, obliterated them both from his life. The boy died prematurely in a mental home. I have no idea what became of her. You see, you were the same age. You grew up healthy and successful. You were a constant reminder of his failure. The fact still gnaws at him."

So much for fidelity to the concept of "The Family", I thought to myself.

"So you must be careful. He allowed me to see you – to make the offer. So the debt is cancelled."

"But you knew I would never accept," I protested.

"It was all I had to offer," he said. There was such a look of resignation on my father's face, of acquiescence to some superior reality, that I pitied him without knowing quite why.

"I am to be sent to the mountains," I said.

"Yes, to Cagot."

So my father knew more than I did apparently.

"The name means nothing to me," I said.

"It is a village," my father said. "That is all."

Yet so much seemed to lay unspoken behind his casual remark, that I pressed him further. "But why there? Why not ...?"

My father suddenly looked puzzled, lost, as if comprehension had failed him. "I don't know," he murmured. "All I know is that the village is called Cagot. I am tired now. I need to rest."

"But," I began to press him; then checked myself. The conversation had exhausted him. He waved his hand in an ineffectual gesture, unable, even if he had wanted, to continue.

As if on cue, the servant who had served us dinner suddenly reappeared, and said politely but firmly, "I'm afraid it's time for your father to rest. I'm sure you understand."

I got up to leave like an obedient schoolboy. "Think about the offer," my father suddenly said from the depth of his fatigue.

I followed as the servant wheeled him to the front door and I squeezed his hand, ridged with blue veins, before I left. He was still clutching his handkerchief. He said nothing further. I never saw him alive again.

I was taken back to the hotel. Two relief guards were waiting for me in the lobby to escort me up to my room.

"Can I have a drink in the bar?" I asked.

"We have strict orders," one of them replied. But there is nothing to stop you from having drinks sent to your room."

So I sat in the room with a bottle of cold white wine on the table in front of me and a cigarette smoking in the ashtray – the urge to smoke had crept upon me again, and I saw no point in resisting. The night chill crept through the badly insulated windows; I had not turned on the ancient-looking radiators, for I knew that the dry heat they emitted would give me a headache. Also, I wanted to feel the cold, needed to feel it like a wilful child indulging himself in some vaguely improper activity.

I was drunk of course, as I had been drunk every evening for the past two years, and as I had been drunk most nights before I had met Maria. She had been my own interim period. However, I was not drunk in the sense that I was crude or violent or out of control; perhaps intoxicated is a more appropriate word. Without a certain degree of intoxication I couldn't sleep; without it I found it difficult to write. My poetry had always come to me most easily in the wine-stimulated hours of evening. Morning provided the sober hours for criticism and revision, even, at times, for outright rejection of what had seemed so eloquent the night before. A reversal in time of what the Irish poet had written: "Or the day's vanity, the night's remorse".

But the same sentiments exactly. The hours of darkness had always been the most valuable to me. Then I had burned, untrammelled by self-consciousness. That night, however, I was not in a creative mood. I kept thinking about the meeting with my father, thought of him as an old man losing touch with the reality that to a certain extent – and apparently to a greater extent than I had realised – he had helped to create. There had been something ominous in his speech, some hint of undefined threat, and it was true, I considered, as I drank more and more wine, that there was something threatening about the Colonel, which went beyond my childhood memory of him.

Still, I felt that my father was being somewhat histrionic. As the Commander of the south-eastern province had said, if the Régime had meant me harm, I could have been taken out and disposed of at any time, killed quietly on the coast, my body carried away on the ebbing tide to feed the fish. It was with this in mind that I began to think more seriously about the offer my father had made to me. 'The Nation' was a prestigious paper; working for it would bring me close to the mainstream of political life in the country, and it occurred to me that perhaps there I could have an ameliorating effect.

That night I slept fitfully, going over the pros and cons in my mind, although all the while aware that I was deluding myself, playing a game. The self-betrayal would be too great. Besides, I suspected the Colonel had allowed my father to make the offer with the expectation that I would reject it. He would surely have prevented me from taking up the post if I had responded positively.

I awoke in the morning to the sound of youthful voices chanting in unison. I draped a bathrobe around me and stepped out onto the balcony to see what was happening. The hotel took up one side of a normally quiet, cobbled square; opposite was a Government building that housed the Education Ministry. A crowd of several hundred students had gathered in front of the Ministry. The placards they carried indicated that they were protesting against the seizure of certain pamphlets from the University, and the arrest of two students connected with the pamphlets. I knew nothing about this; for the last two years I had disassociated myself from political events, but I did recall vividly how the University had been filled with a new spirit, a new intellectual and moral energy during the period of 'new democratisation', as the students rather turgidly called the interim period. What I was seeing, I assumed, was a reaction against the recent wave of suppression instigated under the Colonel.

A woman – I recognised her immediately – moved forward onto the steps that led up to the entrance of the grey building, and faced the crowd. The crowd fell silent as she began to speak through a megaphone. I could not make out her words clearly, but the vibrancy of the rhetoric, half calculated, half emotional, was tangible on the cold morning air. The performance was typical of Alicia. (So was her appearance: the loose sweater, the jeans, the unkempt hair – now with strands of grey in it – all deliberately unfeminine). No one else I knew had such an intense effect on a crowd as she did. The students chanted when she wanted them to chant, became quiet when she lowered her voice, and then, when she had got their full attention, she became suddenly strident in her open condemnation of the Colonel. Those words I heard clearly enough before they were consumed by the different, more ominous sound of boots running, clacking on stone. Alicia's voice froze. The students began to look nervously around them. I could sense their fear, as the volume of the noise increased, and it became evident what was going to happen.

The students didn't run until the soldiers had burst into the square; they simply stood there, like confused children in need of guidance. It was Alicia who prompted them into action by screaming through the megaphone. The warning came too late. The soldiers came at them from three corners of the square, their faces covered by dark visors, their batons heavy in their hands. They used the weapons indiscriminately, hitting the students until they fell, beating them as they lay helpless upon the ground. The apparent randomness of the attack was, however, illusory; the action had been well planned. The soldiers' arrival from three corners of the square had provided the students with only one exit – along the narrow street that led away from the right hand side of the Ministry. Those students who had not already been caught up in the onslaught took it. I watched as the soldiers in the square did not pursue them but formed a line across the end of the street. They waited with military discipline, until someone gave a clear order to advance. At first I did not understand as the soldiers disappeared from view, leaving me staring at the blood-spattered square that was now suddenly full of black military vehicles into which the remaining soldiers were dragging their beaten victims, amongst them Alicia. The vehicles were driven away. The soldiers stood together in small groups smoking cigarettes.

An unnatural silence descended on the square. This was dispelled by the arrival of more of the black vans, which pulled up and formed a neat line on the cobblestones. The drivers got out, chatted with the soldiers; accepted cigarettes from them. This interlude, almost dreamlike in its ordinariness in comparison with what I had just witnessed, was broken by the return of the soldiers carrying, dragging, kicking the students who had tried to flee. Many of them had been savagely attacked; blood streamed from foreheads; limbs hung limply; many were unconscious. Still I did not understand, until I realised that the number of soldiers now swarming into the square had increased considerably. Then, I visualised it all – the students taking the only available exit, running scared; the sense of relief when those at the front thought they had evaded the military (forgetful, temporarily, of the fate of their peers left behind), only to find that relief turn to fear again when they saw the soldiers in front of them, blocking their path; then the students turning in retreat to see the soldiers from the square slowly advancing on them, the realisation that they were trapped in a deliberately created funnel from which there was no means of escape.

But there was something more than this. I stood on the balcony, observing the episode from beginning to end, until the last student had been carted away, until the soldier in charge had dismissed his men and only his solitary jeep remained in the square below. Before he got into the jeep he suddenly looked up at me, and smiled. I looked at him coldly, but after he had gone I felt unnerved. I could not rid myself of the notion that the look, the smile had been premeditated, just as the breaking up of the demonstration had been carefully planned beforehand. The idea seemed absurd, but I felt in some vague way that I was being manipulated, that the fact I had been there to witness the events was not simply a matter of coincidence. After all, I knew Alicia.

Alicia had been one of the first exiles I had come into contact with in London. Her controlled madness had been evident from the start, but then she had had her reasons. Her husband had been a classical pianist of renown well beyond our country's borders. His genius was universally acknowledged, but not only was he a great musician, he was also, and this was unusual given his profession, a committed and active leftist who used his artistic fame to promote his political views. Alicia had been a student, much younger than he when they had met and married. She had told me about the passionate nature of their affair. I had known him vaguely, as we had moved in the same cultural sphere, and I had envied him. There had been something larger than life about him, from his size – he was well over six feet – to his almost demonic musical ability. His mere presence in a room charged the atmosphere.

As such, he was a ready target for the Military. He was imprisoned. In his cell, the soldiers, anonymous to this day, smashed his hands against the stone floor with their rifle butts until they were a pulped mass and then shot him in the head. Alicia, prompted by her friends, had fled abroad. Her sense of disgust, her hatred and her desire for revenge had made her a formidable critic of the Régime. In the lecture theatres, in the street marches – those long trails of students and workers in alien cities – she rose to the fore, and, in a sense, usurped my position.

I had been in London attending a conference, when the coup had occurred. At that time I had a reputation as a radical journalist, critical of the recent activities of the Military, fearful for my country's future. In the event, I was seen as having had my finger on the pulse of the country, even if the suddenness and brutality of the takeover had surprised me. I was also a poet, and because I was from a foreign country, especially a foreign country experiencing repression of a particularly unsavoury kind, my status was enhanced by the fact. I was the voice of the opposition in exile, until Alicia came along.

I was always at the forefront of the demonstrations that took place in the major university and industrial centres of Britain. At first, at the demonstrations I attended, I read poems I had written for the occasion. They were simple, rhetorical, they told of events that I had not personally witnessed. Nevertheless, they worked. They had a strong emotional appeal, and I loved to stand on a rostrum before my audience, the microphones perched at mouth-level, reading in my native tongue while someone at my side followed with an English translation. It was these events that fed my vanity, made me the golden boy of the literati and, more importantly, of the media.

My status as a celebrity began to take precedence over my work. The poems that I had written about events in my own country were translated into English and sold well, but I wrote less and less, drank more and more, and went through a bevy of women – the kind that hang upon the famous, hoping, by a process of osmosis, for their own brief moment of recognition.

In spite of my poetry, my approach to politics was fundamentally prosaic, rational. Essentially I was a moderate, seeking balance and fairness in my articles. The Military Régime, because of what it stood for, because of what it did, was abhorrent to me and I made that plain. My opposition was total, but at meetings and demonstrations, attended mainly by

British students, that flared up in response to the crisis I also sought out reasons for the coup, and in doing so gave voice to my feeling that some blame had to be attached to the weak democratic governments that had preceded it. Selfishness, trade union agitation, a failure to read the signs, had played a part. And I said so. And the students listened, but impatiently; it wasn't what they wanted to hear.

It was Alicia who gave them that. She was a far more romantic figure than I was. Her husband's death had about it the aura of martyrdom, so she was listened to with what amounted to reverence from the beginning of her sweep through the free countries. She was more than up to the role that had been thrust upon her. Like her dead husband, she was larger than life, a natural actress with a command of several languages. She knew how to sway the crowd, to imbue them with the hatred that she felt within herself, to make them chant against the perpetrators of the coup, and then to bring them to silence with the minute of mourning at the end of her diatribe. She was magnificent, and desirable, and dangerous.

For a while we had been lovers. For me, she was an enigma. I had never known a woman who burned so intensely before. Why she was drawn towards me is less easy to say; partly, I imagine, because I was a poet; partly because I was the central focus of the opposition abroad; and partly because, as she once remarked, "Your ego is as strong as mine."

This, at the time, may have been true. However, we were ultimately incompatible. We came together with a nervous energy, a kind of struggle for domination which left us both exhausted, yet strangely dissatisfied. Our love-making lacked mutuality, it lacked tenderness.

Our relationship was, necessarily, brief-lived. It ended in bitterness, a terrible scene of mutual recrimination, which spilled over into the political sphere. We began to compete for the loyalty of the exiles, in what became an ignominious battle of wills. My womanising, my hedonism, told against me. Alicia condemned me for my "dilettantism", as she liked to call it, and there was malice in her condemnation. She moved to limit my influence, saw me as an enemy to the true cause. – "A son of the bourgeoisie who could return whenever he chooses, but life is too pleasurable here," she had said on the radio when the interviewer had enquired about the tension that seemed to exist amongst the radicals in exile. – Her voice was influential; her attacks had the effect they were meant to have.

"He no longer believes," she would say; then quote the lines from my poem 'Another Country', which had been published in a British literary magazine two years after the coup had occurred:

> I wrote of blood
> but the blood flowed,
> congealed, in another country.
> I was not there.

"Bourgeois literary life has softened him."

"Bourgeois" became one of her commonest critical words. She resented my background, while at the same time keeping the details of her own background deliberately vague, hinting at unhappiness and deprivation. I later learned, in fact, that her parents had been relatively prosperous farmers who owned their own land – not quite the image that Alicia wanted to project. However, there was truth in some of her criticisms, even if her motives were of dubious provenance. I began to feel that I had corrupted myself, not so much, at the time, because of my hedonistic activities, but because of the poems I had written to please the crowd. The students, who had previously applauded me, began, under the influence of Alicia to turn against me. For the first time I saw them for what they were – youths in search of a cause which their own secure backgrounds had denied them. And I saw this because I felt that I had been acting in much the same way. My poems had been fictions – I had painted in words the knockings on the door, the stench of fear, the stench of blood, the unyielding brutality of the soldiers, but they had not come from direct experience, which was perhaps not so important; I do not deny the imagination its due. What was important was that these moral, political poems were acts of bad faith. They were written not so much in response to the terrible events that had taken place in my country, but with an eye on the exposure that they would bring to me. Through them, I had actively sought the fame that I desired at the time.

In this respect, Alicia and I were soul mates. She had been right when she had compared the relative strength of our egos. Fortunately 'Another Country', which Alicia condemned, saying that it revealed a vacillation in my commitment to the cause, marked a new phase in my creative life. It was my poetic viewpoint, not my political one, which was beginning to change. I had in the past, I realised, 'played' at poetry, but now poetry consumed me; it became all important.

The following year I left the English capital, and rented a cottage on the coast of East Anglia where the flat land of marshes and saline pools merged naturally into the flatness of the sea. During that hot, still summer, poems came like angels to me, poems like nothing I had written before, tight with the tension between the concrete and the abstract, the sensual and the detached.

There was something hallucinatory about those few months of my life, a sense of happiness in my own solitude that I have never experienced since, and I doubt that I am ever likely to experience again. I slept in late, revised during the afternoon what I had written the previous night. Then in the late afternoon I walked the marshes equipped with a pair of field-glasses and an ornithological field-guide, observing the birds that frequented the area. In the evening, fuelled by the wine that I had had sent up from London, I would begin to write, continuing until the early hours of the morning. August turned to September, September to October. I watched as the summering birds disappeared, as the wading birds, so difficult to differentiate from one another, passed through the marshes on their journey from Siberia to Africa. I heard from my bed, the calls of the geese carried across the darkness on the biting wind. The seasonal change marked a change in myself. The poems were more or less completed. What had been necessary solitude suddenly took on the tinge of loneliness.

Then, in late autumn, the wind became elemental in its force, and one day, when gales and high tides coincided, the waves breached the barrier of the shingle bank and swept across the low-lying fields, inundating my living room and kitchen, bringing with them the damp, cloying smell of seaweed. I had not minded this overmuch. It gave my mind something practical to focus on. It also brought me release from a person I disliked, and gave me instead someone I was to love.

For, although a feeling of loneliness had begun to encroach upon me, I had not, for the weeks that preceded the flood, been alone. My publishers had decided to print a bilingual edition of the poems written that summer, and so they had sent a translator to stay with me to do the English version of the poems. Unfortunately, Hugh Carradon and I had not got on well together. I had been so absorbed in my work that I had not noticed the defects in the cottage, or, if I had noticed them, they had struck me as being of little importance. Hugh, however, had spotted them from the beginning. "My dear man," he said, "how can you possibly create such wonderful poetry living in this ... this hovel?"

"I like it here," I responded bluntly, speaking in my own language, laying down the terms of our relationship.

He smiled at this, but it was the disdainful smile of a man who understood.

"Quite," he said in English, adding, "but do you have a room for me?"

I had, but not one that would suit. Nevertheless, he stayed for three weeks in all, which was something for such a fastidious man. Those three weeks, after the summer solitude, were full of unspoken tension. The man irritated me; I disliked his accent, his clothes, his manner. His presence made me ill at ease. The tension was accentuated by the fact that we disagreed about the way certain parts of my poems should be translated. My command of the English language was, inevitably, not on the same level as his – but neither was his command of my mother tongue as proficient as mine, a fact which he refused to acknowledge. So we found ourselves at loggerheads, arguing over minor points of diction for the sake of arguing.

Fortunately, the flood had driven him away. "I can't possibly stay here under such conditions," he had complained, a comical figure as he stood in his pyjamas in the living room of the cottage, with the salt water swirling around his ankles. And he had packed his sodden bags, and somehow got his car started and driven along the partially submerged road through the darkness to the village and south on the road to London.

Then I had felt sorry for him, and also grudgingly admired him for undertaking the journey under such adverse conditions. The flood was, of course, an excuse. It made things easy. Without it, we would have parted under far less acceptable circumstances.

The next day, after clearing up the mess with the help of the villagers who had rallied around, I phoned Sally Winterton, my editor, and requested another translator. When she wavered at the idea, I became more adamant, acting the petulant author, except I was not acting. There was no way I could possibly work with Hugh again. She conceded, promised me someone more suited to my temperament.

Maria arrived within the week. Why Maria hadn't been assigned to me in the first place I didn't know – until Sally later confessed that she had suggested Maria from the beginning, but had been over-ridden by one of the directors at the publishing house.

"Why?" I had asked at the time, which was in fact at my wedding reception. 'I think he was attracted to Maria himself, in a protective, paternalistic way. He was worried that you might" – and here she weighed her words diplomatically – "might not keep the relationship on just a professional level."

"Well, obviously he was right," I retorted, with somewhat heavy irony.

"I don't think this was quite what he had in mind either," she said and smiled.

I could see what she had meant about the director's protective attitude, however, even while I was responding sarcastically. Maria had about her, at least on initial

46

acquaintance, a kind of shy vulnerability. For me, however, this only enhanced her physical attractiveness – and she was very attractive. The short blonde hair, the translucent blue eyes, the boyish figure, which only appeared boyish because of the casual sweater and jeans that she habitually wore, were what struck me when she arrived at the cottage in a taxi, taken from the station in the town twenty miles inland from the coastal village.

She spoke, quietly, diffidently as she introduced herself, as I carried her single bag into the cottage. Then, once inside, having observed her surroundings, said more volubly, "So this is where you write your poems?" I thought I detected praise in her words, but there was also something in the way she said them that reminded me of Hugh Carradon's first words.

"Hugh thought it was a hovel," I said.

"It smells strange," she responded and sniffed the air.

"The flood," I offered in explanation.

"Flood?"

"Didn't Sally tell you that the sea flooded the cottage?"

"No, she didn't. This was all arranged so quickly over the telephone. So that was why Hugh left?"

"Not really. We had our differences."

"Yes, you would."

And we, I thought, would we have our differences too? I saw that the initial impression she gave of shyness, was, if not exactly erroneous, certainly a good deal away from the total truth. Her last words seemed to contain within them an assumption that I didn't quite like, as though she were defining the terms of our relationship, dispensing with the normal rules of polite discourse, which even Hugh, as an Englishman, had more or less adhered to.

Hugh had, of course, been totally English. A natural linguist, he had studied the language of my country at Oxford, and then, backed financially by rich and generous parents, spent two years travelling as whim took him around the country, absorbing its language and culture into his consciousness. He had written a book about his experiences, which had been well received at the time – this well before the foundation of the Old Régime – when my country was regarded as very much a beautiful, if strangely primitive place, an adjunct to Europe, rather than being quite of Europe itself.

Hugh had given me a copy of the book from what must have been a dwindling personal stock, as the work had been long out of print. I did not like it much; reading it I felt that I was viewing my country through distorted eyes. It was too cheerful, too youthful, too English a vision, if that is not contradictory. It spoke of my countrymen's passion, yet there was absolutely no hint of the darker side of that passion, the potential for brutality which is inherent in our race. Quite clearly, Hugh did not see it. Fastidious even in his youth, he wrote of the sacrifice of the bulls with dislike, but analysed it in terms of the need for romance and colour and spectacle – all of which was true – but he never seemed to grasp the fact that it also satisfied deeper, more perverse needs.

Maria, on the other, hand had some of my country's blood in her. She told me over dinner on that first day – a meal that she had insisted on preparing herself – how her English father had been a diplomat in my country for a brief period, how he had married a local woman there, how she had been a peripatetic child, taken from country to country on the diplomatic circuit. She had been brought up bilingually on her mother's insistence.

She had also spent some time each year back in the mother's homeland, so she was fluent in both of her parents' languages, as well as competent in two or three others because of her youthful travels.

"And where is home now?" I asked her, after she had told me all of this.

She raised the glass of wine to her lips, sipped the deep red liquid – the wine was strong, full-bodied; it came from our country – and said, with a melancholy inflexion, "I don't know. I've had so many homes that nowhere seems like home anymore."

"And your parents?"

"They got divorced a long time ago. My mother went back home. She's dead now. My father retired three years ago. He bought a house in Cornwall, in the town where he was born. I'm not sure why; he hardly knows a soul there anymore."

"And you – I mean where do you live?"

She looked at me, a searching look that suggested I was prying. "In London," she answered, and offered nothing more.

I felt obliged to respect her privacy. Our relationship was meant to be a professional one – writer and translator – and, in spite of the publishing director's fears, I had always, when it came to my art, tried to maintain a strict distinction between the professional and the personal.

I soon discovered that there was a sympathy between us when it came to the poetry. Hugh and I had argued about the word, the phrase, the rendering of the rhythm in the translated versions; there had been no flow of understanding. With Maria that did not arise; she seemed to know what I was trying to convey through my art, and could reproduce that, as effectively as I thought anyone could, into English. It was not just a matter of linguistic sensibility, it was also a matter of poetic sensibility. Occasionally, she would even question my use of a word or phrase in the native language. I listened to her, sometimes acted upon her doubt, sometimes not, but I always talked through my decision with her. She made me consider my art more closely, more editor than translator at times.

We worked hard on the poems, beginning early in the morning after breakfast – Maria was an early riser, and unhesitatingly imposed her own working rhythm on me – and going through, with a break for lunch, until late afternoon. She preferred to forget about the poetry in the evening, and dragged me down to the public house in the village, where she drank beer and played darts against the locals. She was surprisingly good, and the regulars took to her quickly. I had always felt myself an outsider in the village, which was of my own making since my working rhythm had been at odds with the social rhythm of the village. But now with the poems completed – the translation was secondary – I unwound, and enjoyed myself, although my dart playing was more of an amusement to the villagers than anything else, and this to a large extent because of the contrast I made with Maria.

"Where did you learn to play darts?" I asked her.

"A misspent youth," she replied, and, as was her way, left it at that.

At first I thought she was being deliberately enigmatic and this irritated me, but it gradually occurred to me that her evasions were a form of defence. Against what, I couldn't say, and the barrier she erected was so effective that I didn't try to penetrate it. I took her seriously because of the way that she dealt with my poems, whereas with someone else I might have treated our relationship more in the way of a game and try to break down her defensive walls.

Autumn drifted into winter. At the weekends Maria disappeared to London, leaving on Friday evening, returning on Monday morning, with a regularity that testified to her professionalism. Saturdays and Sundays left me at a loss. The poems were finished. My current period of creativity had come to an end. I felt deflated, on edge. There was nothing unusual in this; it was the way I normally felt on the completion of a project, yet I realised I didn't feel this way during the week when Maria was with me. I missed her company.

I wandered the marshes on those long weekends, watched the ducks wing their way low over the yellow reeds; saw the geese fly inland from over the sea in high chevrons, heading for the fields inland. At night I heard the curlews bubbling, the penetrating whistle of drake wigeon, the hollow honking of the geese. I felt more and more unfulfilled. And I wrote a love poem to Maria, the one that began:

> Days begin to taste of winter now,
> Bitter to the palate's edge,
> And the wind parodies laughter.

I sat up all one Sunday night, drinking until I could write no more, forcing my emotions into the purity of form, objectifying the subjective to bring me relief. I didn't finish until gone four that night. Drunkenness and exhaustion forced me to bed. I awoke, still fully clothed, towards midday, and stumbled out into what passed for the sitting room to find Maria already there. The previous night's papers were strewn on the table in front of her, apart from the finished version, which she held in her hand. I glanced down, and through blurred eyes read, or perhaps remembered, the final lines:

> Till the time that will again be ours –
> The time when you and I are we.

She turned around. "God, you look awful," she said. "Would you like me to make you a coffee?"

She went into the kitchen, which even now smelled faintly of the sea. She filled the kettle and came back into the sitting room while the water heated up.

"I see you're writing again?" she said, with a hint of irony in her voice. "Is this to be part of the book?"

"No. The book is finished. Besides, the tone of this poem is different. It wouldn't fit in." Then I turned on her, provocatively. "Don't you agree?"

"Yes," she said, and smiled. It was a smile that matched the irony in her voice, yet it was not without warmth. "This seems very personal; the poems in the book are a lot cooler, a lot more analytical."

"Less involved?"

"No, I'm not saying that, but the involvement is with the nature of poetry itself – the disparity between reality and visions of reality. This is a straightforward love poem, isn't it? Or am I missing something?"

"I don't know. It came to me when I was drunk last night."

"It didn't just come," she admonished me. "I've seen the amount of paper on the desk. I suppose I've never realised before the sweat that ..."

"It was a lot easier than most," I interrupted.

The kettle began to whistle. I followed Maria through into the kitchen. She turned off the gas, and poured the water into the mugs, adding sugar – we each took one teaspoonful – and milk.

"It's funny," she continued," but it never occurred to me that there was a woman in your life. You seem so self-contained here, so independent. It makes me feel that my presence is intrusive."

I looked at her, directly into those blue eyes of hers, trying to penetrate them to see if she was being disingenuous. She turned her eyes away. I felt at a loss, like the gawky self-conscious teenager that I had once been, rather than the licentious egotist that Alicia had made me out to be.

"No, you're not being intrusive," I assured her quietly. "I appreciate your being here very much."

"Good," she said. "I'm glad. I'll go and unpack; then perhaps we can do a little work before lunch."

She took her coffee-mug and disappeared upstairs to her room. I remained in the kitchen in my crumpled clothes, gazing through the wide windows across the level fields to the shingle bank, watching the gulls squabble over the marsh. Maria came back downstairs, holding a black file under her arm. She sat down at the table opposite me. I noticed that she had brushed her hair.

"I spoke to Sally over the weekend, showed her the manuscripts so far. She was very pleased. She reckoned, and I agreed with her, that three more weeks should do it."

"That sounds right to me," I agreed without commitment.

Maria picked up on the tone of my response, scrutinised my features. "Is anything the matter?" she asked. "I mean, if you don't want to do this now, we can always do it this afternoon – or when you're in the mood."

"I'm sorry," I said. "No, please carry on."

This she did. "Sally has shown the translations we've done already to Tim. He's full of praise, apparently, but he has made a few suggestions."

The habitual professional relationship was re-established. She outlined the language consultant's suggestions. Some she agreed with, some she disagreed with, and always she could offer rational justification for her responses. She wanted my opinion, but that morning, I conceded almost every point she made. It just didn't seem to be of any great importance whether a particular adjective should be rendered as' calm', 'placid' or 'tranquil'. Maria soon recognised my mood was not conducive to the task in hand. The last thing she wanted was to be told that she was always right. She felt that decisions had to be justified, and could not be justified without taking the various other possibilities into account. Usually I was responsive to that need; that Monday I was not.

She looked at her watch. 'Why don't we go to the pub for lunch?" she said. I shrugged. It was part of my creed, and she knew it, that I didn't drink at lunchtime, but this time I made an exception. There was no point in continuing the way we were; it would only compound the frustrations that we were both aware existed. So I agreed.

We put on our coats, and walked along the muddy track to the road that led into the village. We passed the windmill that had long since ceased to function as such, being now someone's home, and came to the beginning of the village proper, which consisted of a string of picturesque, white-washed cottages, some of them optimistically advertising 'Vacancies' or 'Bed and Breakfast' signs in their downstairs windows.

"Who on earth do they expect to be coming here at this time of year?" I asked rhetorically.

"I'm here," Maria retorted, with amused intonation.

"That poem," I began; then felt awkward and faltered.

"Yes?"

We were passing the local post-office. An old lady, fragile-looking in the autumnal air, came out of the door. She smiled at us, then hobbled away.

"It was meant for you," I confessed.

Maria stopped walking. Her hands were thrust deep into the pockets of her black duffel coat, the kind that a student might wear.

"I'm sorry," she said. "I didn't realise ..."

I sensed then that she was not telling the truth, which did not stop me from feeling exposed and vulnerable. I looked at the post-office window, saw my reflection merging with the stationery and sweets, but could not quite recognise myself.

Maria linked her arm through mine. "Come on. I think we both need a drink," she said.

We headed towards the pub, picking our way along the narrow, mud-spattered pavement. "Why are so many pubs called 'The Red Lion'," I asked, in my native language as we turned the corner and saw the pub sign in front of us. "'The Black Bull' or 'The White Swan' I understand; bulls are black, swans are white, and they're both English animals. But a lion isn't really red, and I don't grasp the English connection."

Maria, understanding, gave a subdued laugh. "I have no idea," she said in English. "It doesn't matter."

Then she stopped, and looked at me, a look that exists for me now as tangibly as it did then. "It's all right," she said, "it's all right."

And it was. She was acknowledging the connection between us, the connection that I didn't know existed as far as she was concerned until that moment in that grey, wet street, under that grey monotonous sky.

We drank our fill at the pub, ate a ploughman's lunch, played darts, and returned to the cottage through streets and fields that seemed to glow with a benevolent essence – a result of the alcohol and our mood. That afternoon we became lovers. Later came the marriage, the years of fulfilment, the eventual return to the capital that we both knew so well. Then her death.

A sudden knock on the door disrupted my thoughts. I left the balcony, went inside and opened the door. A guard confronted me. "I have orders to take you to the Secretariat," he said firmly.

I got dressed; then followed him down to the hotel entrance, to the waiting jeep. We drove through the sunlit streets. It was a spacious city, old-fashioned and elegant in the centre with its classical buildings and its wide boulevards, and the spring sunshine illuminated the buds on the trees with a clarity that hinted at optimistic renewal. The girls in the streets wore light, pastel-coloured dresses; most of the men had dispensed with their jackets and had rolled up their shirt sleeves. There was a sense of youth and vitality about the city, and again the Irish poet's words came back to me:

That is no country for old men....

Yet old men ruled the city and they allowed youth their freedom when it did not interfere with their power, but crushed it if it dared not to conform to the role they demanded of it, as I had witnessed that morning. Acceptance, now as it had been twelve years before, was the keynote. And the majority accepted. Otherwise the Colonel could not have crushed the burgeoning democracy of the interim period so easily.

We pulled up outside the Secretariat building. As on the previous day, I was taken by two armed guards – I had no idea whether they were the same guards or not – to the waiting room, to the same secretary – this man I remembered – sitting at the same oaken desk. This time I examined the man more closely. There was little to him. He was the archetype of the faceless bureaucrat: clean-shaven, smart, well-dressed, an innocuous family man who you would pass in the street without paying him any particular attention." A decent man," as my mother would have said, and meant it. But this was inaccurate. I looked at the man looking at me, and detected in him the consciousness of his own position. He stood between the Colonel and the outside world, and that gave him power – illusory, I thought, as he was easily replaceable – but his belief in his own indispensability was obvious in his cold, supercilious manner. He was not just a product of my particular country; I had seen such men – so alike that they were, to my mind, interchangeable entities, functionaries, not individuals – in every country I had been to: at the airports, the railway stations, in offices that as a foreigner in exile I had had to visit to obtain the appropriate papers. I could not take such people seriously, yet I knew how irritating they could be.

The man kept me waiting for a few minutes, while he signed some papers – this ritual I was accustomed to – and then showed me into the Colonel's office.

The Colonel was standing at the window, smoking a fat cigar; the slanting rays of the sun highlighted the bald dome of his head, the squat curve of the nose. The smoke rose in pale blue wisps on the sunbeams. He was like some cartoon figure, the caricature of a penny-ante dictator, but ultimately, of course, he wasn't in the least comical; quite the opposite, in fact.

"Sit down," he ordered, barely glancing at me.

I did as I was told. He remained where he was, standing impassively before the window, sucking on his cigar and exhaling the smoke in perfectly formed rings. "A fine morning," he said, suddenly breaking the silence he had himself imposed." This city is so often dull and grey, but when the sun shines – well, then things happen."

He turned and looked me directly in the eye, or so I felt. I couldn't see his features clearly as he was now a silhouette, a dark outline only, against the vitreous daylight. "You spoke with your father?" he suddenly asked.

"Yes," I said, and no more.

"I understood he was to make you an offer?"

"Yes, he did."

"And?"

"I refused, of course."

The Colonel allowed himself, or so I thought, as he was still in silhouette, a thin smile of gratified expectation. Then he moved away from the window, came towards the desk and stubbed out the remains of his cigar in an ashtray. His eyes pierced mine. "I didn't expect you to do otherwise, but your father felt that it was a gesture that had to be made."

I returned his stare, refusing to be intimidated. "So now you are no longer in his debt," I said.

"I will always be in his debt," he replied quietly, "but that is beside the point as far as you are concerned. You have made your decision."

He went behind the desk, and took out a black file from a drawer invisible to me. I looked at his fingers. They were Troll's fingers – and this literally so to my sister and I when we had been children, for the Colonel was physically deformed. His fingers were short and squat because they lacked a joint; there were only two horizontal creases on each finger between the palm and the nail instead of the usual three. To me they were peasant's fingers, crude, of the earth. I thought of what my father had told me about the man's mongol child; saw in it the result of genetic deficiency passed down through the father. And I wondered if the Colonel, with his raw intelligence, had seen something of himself reflected in his child's eyes.

He sat down opposite me and opened the file. He began to speak, like a judge pronouncing sentence. "You will be taken by train to Rona and from there you will be transported to the village of Cagot. The village will be your home for an indefinite period of time. You will be responsible to the Police Chief of the village and you will have to report to him on a daily basis. Other than that you will be free to pass the time as you choose, although any documents or letters that you wish to post out of the village will have to be submitted to the Police Chief beforehand, so that he can see that there is nothing unsuitable in them."

"Why all of this?" I asked.

"Would you prefer the alternative?" he replied.

"But it all seems so futile," I said. "You know I went to the coast to be left alone. I no longer have an interest in politics."

The Colonel shrugged. "Yet you have begun to write again."

"Personal work. Literary work."

The Colonel gave a short, animal laugh. "You have already been a traitor to your country once. I don't believe people change. Still, you are lucky. In the past if you had returned, you would have been …dealt with, but now we are far more humane."

Now I laughed – a short, sardonic laugh – and saw the glint of irritation in the man's eyes. "And what will you do to the students who were beaten and arrested this morning?" I asked, angered by his professions of humanity.

"That is hardly an apolitical question," he retorted.

I said nothing, wondering if he would deny any knowledge of the events I had witnessed from the hotel balcony. He didn't. "The demonstration was illegal. It had not been cleared by the authorities. The people involved were fully aware of that fact, so they must accept the consequences of their actions. They will be imprisoned for a day or two to teach them respect for the law. You see, that is our country's problem – there is no respect for the law." He tapped his desk with the shortened forefinger of his left hand.

I looked at the Colonel, but said nothing to provoke him further. He stood up. "My secretary will inform you of the arrangements that have been made," he said. I was being dismissed. "There are things ..."

"Yes?" I asked, and waited for him to continue.

"It doesn't matter. Go!" he commanded.

I stood up, and looked at him. "Still the Troll," I thought. "Still the Troll!"

Maybe the Colonel was right that people never really change. Maybe he had deliberately provoked me to prove his point. About him, I had no doubt. He had graduated from the Military Academy with honours, and had entered the Intelligence Services immediately afterwards. He had, covertly, been a potent force in enabling the Old Régime to come to power. His agents had infiltrated the trade unions and student bodies, enabling him to build up a comprehensive series of files on people who were regarded as 'subversives'. It was these people who had swiftly 'disappeared' after the Military had seized power.

Under the Old Régime promotion swiftly followed promotion. He was instrumental in weeding out any members of Civil Intelligence who showed signs of doubt about the dictatorship. They too were brutally dealt with. Yet, strangely, blame was never really laid at his door. The blood always seemed to be on other people's hands. This was, in part, because he had publicly spoken out, in opposition to some of the Military rulers of the time, against interference with exiles abroad. So when an assassin was killed in Paris by the bomb intended for his victim – my old friend André, in fact, who was one of the most vehement opponents of the Military – the Colonel was vindicated, and he denounced the scheme as a fiasco.

He was a cunning player of the game. He was ambitious, but cautious. To him, the excesses of the Military Régime had been morally justifiable, but he was sensitive to the Régime's failures as well. Economically, the twelve years of the Régime had been a disaster. Inflation soared out of control. Unemployment reached a record level. The country fell deeply into debt to foreign banks, banks that had their headquarters in cities where the exiles were a powerful and influential presence. There was international pressure on the country to initiate reforms. In the event, the Military undertook to reform itself. An internal, secretive coup ousted those who were first and second in the governing hierarchy. A general amnesty was declared, prisoners were released and the Press was allowed to function freely once again. Exiled citizens, myself included, returned from abroad to take part in the 'new democratisation'. The Military, however, still retained power, insisting that it was necessary for them to maintain order until a democratic system of government could be brought into being. The Colonel became Head of Intelligence during this period – a reward for his role in the internal coup – and took it upon himself to monitor the liberalisation process and to prepare files on the returning émigrés. This only became known later, for the Colonel, as befitted an operator in the Intelligence services, remained very much a figure in the background.

There were calls for trials of those who had committed crimes against the populace in the Military takeover and its aftermath. Some high officials were implicated in the killings and the torture; others were known to be corrupt, having lined their own pockets with state money. And it is true that several prosecutions were successfully made, and the necessary penalties exacted. However, they were scapegoats, people seen as dispensable by the Military still in power. Other offenders – and scores of names come to mind – were not brought to trial, or, if they were, had their cases dismissed out of hand. Many of them are part of the current Régime.

It is clear, in retrospect, that there was no intention on the part of the vast majority of the Military to allow democracy to function freely again. After two years of lies and evasions, the people took to the streets of the capital in what was perhaps the largest demonstration ever to be held in the city. The march turned violent, provoked, it has been said, by agents provocateurs planted in the crowd. Many people were injured, property was destroyed and shops were looted. The Military declared a State of Emergency. From the confusion of those few days, the Colonel had emerged as the undisputed head of the Government. He appeared on public platforms. His speeches were broadcast over the radio, reported in the newspapers. There was no doubt about his message. The country had shown itself unready for democracy. Strong government was necessary, and he would provide it. Press freedom was suspended. Many people were temporarily imprisoned. Some intellectuals were put under house arrest. The brief years of freedom became known as the interim period. I had returned at the beginning, but had played little part in the events that led up to the foundation of the New Régime. Maria had been killed not long after our return, and I had retreated to the coast. I read books, went for long walks, began compiling detailed notes about the natural history of the area. I had no radio, and I seldom read a newspaper, except for the odd one that had been discarded in the bar.

The villagers themselves were more political, but worn down by memories. Most of the young people had left to seek work elsewhere, so it was an old man's village. It was the events of twelve years before that were real to them. If they referred to the new democratic pulse in the country, it was with a kind of sardonic scepticism. "They won't let it happen," Alfred would say from behind his wooden counter. "They like power too much. You won't see a civilian government in this country, not for a long time yet." And that seemed to be the general opinion of the village, which went on about its business – some fishing, a little farming – and preferred to let the country go on about its own.

Now I was going to another village, but this time in the mountains. The train pulled out of the railway station before dawn on the following day and headed east. It was only when we had left the city behind, that the sun rose – a huge red ball above the monotonous flatness of the meseta. I turned away from the sun and looked backwards; I could see nothing but barren, hedgeless fields until the track curved, and the capital came back into view, and behind that, to the north-west, I made out the serrated edges of the central mountains glowing pink in the dawn light. The city too had a pink aura around it, and distance made it at that moment appear beautiful to me, a beauty, however, that was tinged with a sense of loss.

The train went through a cutting. When it re-emerged the city had gone. I didn't look back again.

I had the compartment to myself. This time there were no guards, no evidence that my journey was involuntary. An army official had escorted me to the station, and had waited on the platform until the train had departed. He had even lifted his arm in a vague gesture of farewell, and I had nodded in return. I would be met at Rona, the eastern railhead at the base of the great mountain range that separated our country from its neighbour. Until then I would be free – free to get off at any of the intermediate stations if I felt like it. But I wouldn't, and the Colonel knew that I wouldn't. I had nowhere else to go.

I had, in fact, been treated very equably. After my interview with the Colonel I had spoken to his secretary, and then been escorted by a pleasant, young officer to the city centre to take care of the practical details relevant to my exile. We had visited my bank and arranged that my money be transferred to Rona. Cagot itself had no bank, and I would not be allowed to visit Rona myself, but army personnel were always going to and fro between the village and the town, and there would be no problem about my receiving the money.

After I had withdrawn a substantial amount of the money from the bank to see me through the early weeks – and because I knew my country, knew that in spite of good intentions, bureaucratic incompetence was rife – I was driven to the city's main shopping area.

"You will need suitable clothes," the young officer told me.

"Boots, a heavy coat, thick woollen socks. At this time of the year there may still be snow on the ground."

I followed his recommendations, allowed him to help me choose the necessary clothes. "And is there anything else you will need?" he asked.

"Paper, pens, pencils – and books," I replied. "Lots of books."

"What kind of books?"

"Novels, poetry, some philosophy, books on the natural history of the mountains."

The officer thought for a while, stroking his neat moustache with the forefinger of his right hand, while thin lines formed on his forehead.

"Is there a problem?" I asked.

"I have to report back after our shopping expedition," he informed me, "to the Colonel himself. I am not sure that he would approve."

"Then why don't you consult the Colonel beforehand?" I suggested. "Contact him now and see what he has to say."

The officer considered my proposal. "It doesn't matter," he said and smiled. "Which bookshop would you like to go to?"

I told him. We went to the shop, and I bought enough books to fill a medium-sized suitcase. The officer seemed amused by the volume. "I never realised that people in our country read so much," he said ironically.

"They don't," I retorted, then stopped myself from continuing in the same sarcastic vein. The officer was being helpful; it would have been impolitic of me to antagonise him.

"Where to now?" he asked, in a slightly less amiable manner.

"A stationer's," I replied.

We went to a shop I knew within a stone's throw of the bookshop, and I bought notebooks, reams of paper and the writing instruments I required.

"So now we are finished," he said.

"One more thing," I said, "if it's no trouble. I need a bag to carry the books in."

So I went and bought the extra suitcase; this officer made no stipulation about the number of bags I was allowed to take with me. I was then driven back to my hotel.

"Your train leaves early tomorrow," the officer informed me. "We will pick you up at five o'clock in the morning." It was this officer who had seen me off at the station.

I looked out of the window again. Now there were meadows dotted with coarse-haired sheep, but the grass was spartan, rough, more like weeds than pastureland. We passed through a village of low grey, stone houses that dotted the hill rising up abruptly out of the plain. The only building that stood out as different, dominating the village, was the church. It was built of the same grey stone, but its size, its hanging buttresses, its towering steeple suggested more a cathedral than a church. The only other construction of comparable height was the grain silo next to the railway line at the edge of the village.

And so it went on: barren fields stretching to the level horizon across the parched land, the view only disrupted by the occasional village, an isolated entity dominated by its church and silo, so much so that each village seemed to be a simulacrum of the one that had preceded it.

I took out a cigarette from the packet I had bought at the station, lit it and stepped out into the corridor to stretch my legs. The passageway was empty. I walked down it to the door of the carriage. I was in first class. Some of the compartments were empty, and there was never more than a solitary individual in those compartments that were occupied. Privilege bought privacy. At the door, I pulled down the window, and ignoring the warning sign, rested my elbows on the base of the window and poked my head out of the train. The air, mixed with the sooty smell of smoke, rushed across my face, turned my cigarette to instant ash. The train was going around a bend, and, as the first-class compartment was at the front of the train, I could see all of the other carriages curving behind me. They appeared to be crowded. There were bodies, faces, jammed at all of the windows and doors, gazing out across the landscape. Seeing nothing, I thought, just gazing upon the emptiness.

I stepped back inside out of the wind, and lit another cigarette. As I did so, woman stepped out of the compartment nearest to the door and brushed past me. I glimpsed the fur coat, the woman's dark hair, inhaled the sweet-smelling perfume. I heard the lavatory door close behind her, then later, the rush of water as the toilet was flushed. She reappeared, but did not go back into her compartment. Instead, she leaned out of the window where I was standing, forcing me to stand back a little to avoid touching her. I looked at the grey and white coat that curved taut around her spine, the blue-black hair that hung over her collar, concealing her face. I smelled her perfume again. It suggested money, connections. I drew on the filter of my cigarette and blew the smoke into the air.

The woman pulled herself erect, and turned to me. "I'm sorry to bother you," she said, "but would you mind if I asked for a cigarette. I thought I had some, but when I looked in my bag ..."

I looked at her. As a teenager, and in her twenties, she would have been beautiful, but the wrinkles around her dark eyes and at the corners of her mouth indicated that her youth had begun to desert her. I took the packet out of my coat pocket and held it out to her. When I gave her a light, she curved both of her hands up around the match. Her nails were long, immaculately manicured, painted red.

"Where are you going?" I asked out of politeness.

"To Chavonne," she replied. "My brother is getting married tomorrow. I have to be there."

"And your husband?" I asked, looking at the wedding ring on her finger. She puffed on her cigarette; then raised her eyes to meet mine. She smiled. "He is a very busy man. He would like to attend, of course, but ..."

"Of course," I said, a little flippantly. "What does he do?"

"He is a bank manager," she replied. She mentioned one of the most prestigious banks in the capital, but her words were spoken matter-of-factly, not to impress.

"A pillar of the community," I suggested.

"Quite," she said, and raised her eyebrows.

"And what do you do?" she asked.

"I'm a poet," I replied.

She laughed. "That's not a job," she said. "A novelist, a painter, a musician – then, yes, but a poet?"

"Why not?" I asked, becoming intrigued with the woman.

"Money," she said. "Surely a poet can't live on his poetry alone?"

"No, I suppose not," I agreed.

"Then how do you live?" she insisted.

"Frugally," I replied.

"You're teasing me," she retorted. "I don't believe you're a poet at all."

Suddenly, the train plunged into a tunnel. The lights in the corridor flickered; then came on fully. Smoke billowed through the window, so I raised the sash.

"Well, you can buy my books in the bookshops," I said. "Or at least you could a year ago."

On my shopping expedition the previous afternoon, I had checked the poetry shelves in the bookshop; my works hadn't been there, although as far as I knew they hadn't been officially banned.

"Aaah," she said as realisation dawned. She finished her cigarette, and threw the stub on the floor, grinding it beneath her heel. "And where are you going now?" she asked.

"To Cagot," I replied.

"Where?"

"Cagot," I repeated.

"Yes, I heard you. But where's Cagot?"

"I'm not really sure," I replied. "It's in the mountains, somewhere east of Rona."

"To write your poems?" she suggested.

"No," I replied.

"But why else would a poet go to the mountains?"

"Because he has no choice."

She smoothed her hair back from her face with her right hand, and looked at me. A frown etched her brow. "You are being punished?" she said, in what sounded more like a statement than a question.

"I suppose you could describe it like that, yes."

"Why?

"I was a liberal. I campaigned against the Old Régime, wrote poems and articles they didn't like."

"And against the Colonel?"

"Nothing. But men like that have long memories – about certain things, anyway."

"My husband supports the Colonel," she said.

"Most businessmen do; that's the way it is in this country. And you? Do you support the Colonel?"

"I do as my husband does."

"In everything?"

She looked directly into my face and smiled. A man walking down the corridor glanced curiously at us as he passed by. "We're in the way here," she said quietly. "Why don't we go into my compartment?"

I followed her, closing the door behind me, then pulled down the dark curtains so that we could not be seen from the corridor. The woman turned, feigned surprise, "I didn't ..."

"Yes, you did," I said.

I had not had a woman since Maria's death, had not considered the possibility, nor had anyone, until that moment, made advances towards me. The village on the coast had been one of old women, as well as old men. Yet I had not forgotten how to interpret the signs, the subtle gestures that indicated the hidden pulse beneath the surface conversation. This woman was deliberately seducing me. I did not consider her motives, did not at that moment care, for I suddenly felt a desperate need for the contact of flesh against flesh.

And it was like that, an act of desperation. There was no foreplay, no tender discovery of her body's secrets. I thrust her down onto the coarse material of the seat, raised her skirt, pulled down her tights and panties. She undid my trousers, and then I was in her, thrusting into her vagina as she pressed her feet against the seat opposite to maintain her balance. I came quickly, violently, and having came let my body weigh heavily against hers, as if to crush the demons of dissatisfaction that seemed to hang on the air between us. The woman continued moving her thighs, willing herself to orgasm, which she attained just before my penis, now flaccid, slipped out of her.

"Thank you," she whispered, and held onto me tightly, but there was nothing behind her words or gesture. They were mechanical, and I sensed her desire for me to be gone, as I knew that I too wanted to go. We stood up and rearranged our clothes in the cramped space.

Outside, the land had begun to undulate; low hills relieved the flatness of the horizon. The woman broke the embarrassing silence. "I don't normally ..."

"Neither do I," I assured her.

She raised the covers over the door. The corridor was empty. She slid the door along the groove in the floor. A blast of chill air swept into the heated compartment. Then she held her hand out for me to shake it. Her action amused and puzzled me. It seemed too polite, inappropriate after what had just occurred. "Good luck," she said.

I squeezed her hand. "And you," I said.

"I don't even know your name?" she suddenly said after I had stepped out into the corridor.

I told her, but she gave no sign of recognition. "And you?" I asked, because it was expected.

"Maria," she said, and smiled.

I looked at her.

"Is anything the matter?" she asked, seeing the expression that passed across my face. I hardly heard her words, but there was something about the way that they were said that didn't correspond, a vague suggestion of hardness and cynicism.

I dismissed the idea; life was full of contingencies, of coincidences that had no significance. "I'm fine," I said. "Enjoy the wedding."

"The wedding? Of course!" She closed the door behind me.

I returned to my compartment, and began to read one of the books that I had bought on the previous day – a translation of Kafka's *Das Schloss* – but I felt restless. I could not concentrate on the prose; the situations, the words eluded me, so that at the end of a page I had little idea of what I had read. My mind was on other things. I felt guilty. I felt that I had betrayed my murdered wife. I felt the lust burning in me still, so much so that had the woman entered my compartment, I would have taken her again.

Outside the sun was hard and bright; the sky a cloudless, opaque blue, so harsh, so penetrating, it was unbearable. I turned my eyes away, put my book down on the seat and stepped out into the corridor. I decided to go to the restaurant car for a cup of coffee. On the way I passed the woman's compartment, and glanced inside. She was sitting next to the window, writing something in a small notebook. She did not raise her eyes as I passed.

I sat at a stained table and drank my coffee. There were only two other people in the carriage, an old man and a woman, huddled together in one corner silently drinking brandy. I paid no attention to them, but watched the land begin to change through the smeared glass of the window. A thin wedge of river caught the sun and glittered silver in the distance. The perspective was erroneous, for I knew the river was wide, of considerable importance given the general aridity of the central plain. The landscape became one of numerous irrigation channels flowing alongside cultivated fields, which, although seemingly unproductive now, would in season yield up maize, sugar beet, and various fruits.

We passed village after village, small centres only a few kilometres apart, with larger towns interspersed between them. The river came closer, meandered back and forth across the flood plain so that sometimes it was on the left, sometimes on the right of the railway track. The train clattered across steel bridges, losing its regular rhythm in a metallic rush of air. Kestrels hovered at regular intervals along the side of the track.

"May I join you?" the woman asked.

I had not seen her enter the carriage, not noticed her buy the coffee at the small counter. In fact, in observing the landscape, I had forgotten about her altogether. But now she was standing in front of me. She had disposed of her fur coat. I looked at the plain black sweater, the plain black skirt – the skirt I had not long before hoisted above her pale thighs – and thought that such apparent plainness had been deliberately chosen to enhance her sexuality.

"Of course," I replied, although in truth, I would have much preferred to have been left alone.

The woman sensed my reluctance." It would be rather odd," she said, as she sat down opposite me, "if I sat down at another table and we ignored each other – given what has happened."

"True," I agreed.

Neither of us spoke for a while.

"I shall be getting off soon," she said, breaking the silence.

And I thought of Chavonne – the central town, almost a city, which was the hub of the cultivated floodplain. I had never stopped there, had always passed through, as I was passing through now, on my way to other destinations. Now it took on a different reality.

"Are you from Chavonne?" I asked the woman.

"No," she answered," I was born in the south. My parents moved to the capital when I was a child. I was five years old at the time."

"And your brother?"

"My brother?"

"The one who is getting married."

"He lives in the capital as well. His fiancée comes from Chavonne. It was her family's wish that she be married in her birthplace."

"Didn't your parents mind?"

"Why should they?" she said. "It's traditional for the bride to have her way in such matters – you ought to know that."

The old couple in the corner stood up and made their way slowly out of the compartment.

"Anyway," the woman continued," my parents are dead."

The woman took a packet of cigarettes out of her handbag, and offered me one. I accepted.

"I thought you didn't have any cigarettes," I said, as she leaned over and flicked the wheel on her lighter with her thumb, making a blue flame appear.

"I was mistaken," she said. "I found them a while ago."

She inhaled deeply, and blew the smoke out of her mouth in a steady stream, pursing her lips as she did so. Her lipstick was red, unsmudged. I had not kissed her.

"What I don't understand," she said abruptly, then paused before carrying on, "is what is stopping you from getting off the train."

"What do you mean?" I asked, and stared down at the dregs in my coffee cup

"You said you were being punished, sent to ..."

"Cagot," I reminded her.

"Yes, Cagot. But you seem to be accepting it as if you've given up the fight. I mean, is there anyone on the train with you – a guard, a soldier?"

"No," I admitted.

"Well, then there is nothing to stop you from disappearing."

"It is part of the agreement," I said, and shrugged my shoulders. "Too many people have disappeared. I have no desire to disappear."

I looked out of the window for a moment, and saw nothing. "Anyway, what is it to you?" I asked.

"Nothing," she replied, and raised her coffee cup to her lips, observing me questioningly.

"This is my country," I began to explain. "I have already spent too many years away in exile. Now, all I long for is a little peace."

"In a village you've never been to, remote, isolated, kilometres from where you were born?"

"And where was I born?"

"In the capital, I presume. Didn't you say?"

"No."

She flicked her hair away from her eyes, and puffed on her cigarette. I gazed out of the window at the multiplicity of curving tracks, the stationary locomotives, the railway sheds, the train idly shunting a covered wagon into a siding – all of which marked the approach of Chavonne.

She stood up and said, "I must go and get my bags."

I stood up with her, unwilling to leave my own bags unattended while we were in the station. I followed her down the narrow corridors. Our progress was impeded by people moving out of their compartments, luggage in tow, in what seemed a nervous anticipation of arrival, as if they were afraid of missing their stop. The woman treated them with a patrician disdain, scolding them when they got in her way. I saw their reaction, the damming thoughts revealed in their dark eyes, yet no one retaliated verbally, and they all moved out of the way quickly enough

The train came to a halt at the platform. I helped her down with her baggage, and waited as she hailed a porter.

"Goodbye," she said, as she turned to me. "What did you say you're name was again?"

I repeated my name.

"I shall look out for your poetry," she said.

I watched her walk down the busy platform; then returned to my compartment to check on my belongings. Everything was as I had left it on the overhead racks. *Das Schloss* was still open, spine downwards, on the small table adjacent to the window. I sat down and began to read where I had left off, but I remembered nothing of what I had read previously, so I closed the book, deciding to begin the novel again when I was in the mood, and stared out of the window.

An old man with a walking stick came slowly down the platform, carrying a single black briefcase. It was the briefcase, along with the dark overcoat, and the silvery grey hair and beard that gave him a distinguished, professorial air. I searched my memory to see if I could place him, but came up with nothing. Perhaps he just looked as though he should have been familiar to me. Still, I sensed that he would come into my compartment, and he did. He slid the door open, and inspected the ticket he held in his hand.

"This is Compartment E, isn't it?" he inquired. "I booked a window seat." His voice was a little hoarse, but his words were clear, concise.

"Yes," I said, and pointed to the seat opposite my own.

He sat down, and placed his briefcase on the unoccupied seat next to him.

"Ah, Kafka," he said, as he noticed my book on the table. "A much over-rated writer, don't you think? Just chasing his own neurotic tail, and offering no way out of the circumambulation. And they call him a moral writer!"

"I don't know," I answered. "I haven't started the novel yet." Which was more or less true, but I had once read *Die Verwandlung* and had recognised the truths in it. However, I had no desire to get involved in an intellectual disagreement with my newly acquired travelling companion.

"Take my advice," he continued. "Don't bother! Read something more worthwhile."

"And what would you recommend?" I asked, concealing my amusement.

"Some of our own national literature ..." And he went on to name several writers, some of whom were dead, some of whom were still alive, but they all had one thing in common; they were all traditionalists, little known outside of our own country.

"But the people you have mentioned are" – I struggled to find the word to express my opinions without being too harsh – "innocuous. They are competent writers, but they don't transcend the national boundary."

The old man looked at me. Light glistened in his eyes, giving him an amused, ironic expression. "Perhaps you should read your Kafka after all," he suggested.

"Oh, I shall," I said, and picked up the book again in order to bring the conversation to a close.

There was a shrill whistle from the platform; the train gave a sudden lurch forward, remained motionless for a few seconds, then in a hissing cloud of steam began to move slowly out of the station.

A few pages later I happened to glance up over the edge of my book just as the old man was reaching into his overcoat pocket – in spite of the heat in the compartment, he had kept his coat on. He took out a small silver flask, unscrewed the top and took a long swig of whatever liquid was inside.

"Brandy," he said on noticing that I was watching him." I feel that I have reached an age where I can indulge without having to make excuses for myself. Would you like some?"

I made a polite refusal. The man took another drink of the brandy; then screwed the top back on. He didn't put the flask back in his pocket, but cradled it between his hands, gently stroking its worn surface with his thumbs. "Where are you off to?" he asked, forcing me into conversation.

"To Cagot – in the mountains," I replied.

"For your health, I suppose?"

"Do people go to Cagot for their health?" I said; then asked him where he was going before he could respond to my initial question.

"Esmée," he informed me.

Esmée with its seven hundred thousand people, and its two cathedrals, was the major city between the capital and the mountains. It was an industrial centre, our country's violent history having eradicated whatever past glory it may once have had. I had never been there, but I knew that it did have a university, and a respected one at that.

"You work at the university there?" I enquired.

He shook his head and laughed. "No, but you are not the first person who has mistaken me for a professor. I am retired now, but I used to be a government official – "part of our country's slothful bureaucracy." The ironic remark was a quotation from somewhere. – I couldn't place it exactly.

"And you?" he asked me.

"I'm a writer," I told him, seeing no reason to lie.

"I see," he said, and thought for a while. "Recently returned from abroad I imagine."

"Not so recently."

"Within the last three years, then," he said, clearly pleased with his own percipience.

"I couldn't return before," I stated bluntly.

"I daresay not," the old man said, and, having unscrewed the top again, took another drink – this time, a longer one – from his flask.

I looked out of the window. We had left the floodplain behind. The vista had reverted to one of barren fields, dull and monotonous under a sky which had now lost its fierce blueness and become watery, diffused. A line of pastel grey hills loomed in the distance.

"What do you write?" the old man suddenly asked. "Novels? Short stories?"

"I'm a poet," I said.

"I've never read much poetry," he said. "A good novel is more in my line."

I smiled at him.

"I doubt I've even heard of you," he continued, and raised his eyebrows questioningly.

"I doubt it as well," I replied, and maintained a teasing silence before finally telling him my name. The man nodded in recognition.

"I remember your early works, the satirical ones," he said. "They were in the newspapers. They created quite a stir at the time."

I was flattered in spite of myself. "That was a long time ago," I said.

"Yes, it was. To be honest, I thought you were dead."

"Why?"

"The silence."

The man, like so many educated people in my country who had experienced the Old Régime, was out of touch. He remembered me solely from my juvenilia. The novelists he liked were bland, reactionary. His ignorance was not entirely his own fault. The strict censorship imposed by the Military had deprived the country of radical, innovative art. All but a minute amount of what mattered over the preceding fifteen years had been written and published abroad. True, there had been a welcome resurgence during the interim period; books previously banned had flooded into the country, but the country had not had time to absorb the wealth of new material before the Colonel had begun to clamp down again. Even on the coast, rumours of what was happening filtered through, rumours of books disappearing from shelves as swiftly as they had appeared, of new, radical publishing houses being forced to close. The nation was becoming culturally dispossessed once more.

It was not surprising that the old man only knew of my youthful poems. My public, political poems written during the early months of my exile – those poems that brought me such high regard, made me a celebrity in a foreign land – had naturally been banned. They were published once the Old Régime had collapsed, and this against my better judgement, for those poems no longer meant anything to me; I had personally disowned them.

I did, however, manage to persuade the publisher to rename the collection 'Poems from Exile', rather than use the more lurid title 'Blood on Their Hands', which is how the book had first appeared in England and other European countries. My later work, the work that had begun with 'Another Country' and had continued during that summer and autumn on the bleak English coast, the work that had given me Maria, was also published, but was less well received. It was denser, terser, less easy to understand being, as it was, a personal exploration of the relationship between life and art. And people weren't really interested. It didn't express the mood of the moment, the release from a conservative, repressive government that people felt they could now openly condemn. My earlier poems, on the other hand, fitted the bill.

Still, those initial days back in the capital had been good for me. I liked the controversy, I enjoyed being amongst my own people again, even those who were critical of my work. And there were a handful of critics who saw 'Another Country' as a significant development, a kind of poetic maturing that augured well for the future of poetry in our country.

Then Maria was killed and the Colonel took over and everything turned sour.

"Are you still writing," the old man said, disrupting my thoughts.

"My work was taken away from me," I replied provokingly to see how he would respond.

He shrugged his thin shoulders, put his flask back into his overcoat pocket, then looked vaguely out of the window.

"I suppose they have their reasons," he said quietly.

"And what might they be?"

"I'm an old man," he said. "I'm out of touch, but I've seen the magazines on the news-stands in Esmée – the filth; I've seen the university students and the way they behave, with no respect for people or property."

The old man, made loquacious by the brandy, carried on speaking, but I let his words drift by me. I didn't have to listen closely. It was the usual conservative argument, the same argument, more or less, that I had heard from the Commander of the south–eastern province two days previously.

When he had finished I excused myself and went to the restaurant car for lunch. It was early, so I had the carriage to myself. I ordered steak and a bottle of wine. The steak came tough, overdone, but the wine was strong and good.

Gradually, other people came into the carriage to eat; fortunately the old man was not amongst them. I was glad to be alone, glad that the wine soothed me as I watched the landscape change through smudged glass. We were now in the range of hills that I had noticed earlier, except that they were more mountains than hills, part of the chain that traversed the land from north to south. Because they created a natural barrier, communication routes had been channelled through three or four narrow valleys. The train was steaming through one of those valleys as I fought with my steak. The line ran parallel to a road, both of which criss-crossed a swollen river over bridges spaced at irregular intervals. There was little traffic on the road, little evidence that the valley was inhabited at all. Trees lined the riverbank, their branches bare and exposed apart from the few that were just beginning to bud.

The valley sides rising steeply above the river were covered in tussocky grass, providing meagre food for the goats that clambered precariously on isolated crags. I glimpsed a bird of prey, a buzzard or an eagle, soaring high in the distance.

When I returned to my compartment, flushed with wine, the old man was reading a newspaper, 'The Nation' I noticed, and smiled to myself. I sat down, closed my eyes and dozed, and then fell into a deep sleep. By the time I woke up we had left the wild valley far behind; now the view was reminiscent of the meseta around the capital, flat, stark, with the horizon like a sea-horizon, straight and uninterrupted, the land itself redolent of the sea, strangely beautiful in its apparent barrenness.

"It's funny," the old man said, seeing me absorbing the landscape, "on the one side you have an empty land, nothing for miles but grass and sheep, and on the other you have some of the most fertile land in the country."

He moved his head to indicate the other side of the train. He was right; the railway seemed magically to act as a dividing line. I could see through the window of the compartment door, then through the window of the carriage exterior itself, acre upon acre of fields, the dark, rich soil traversed by neat plough lines, watered by rotating sprays that glittered when the afternoon sun broke through the clouds. The fields passed, gave way to orchards, then the orchards gave way to fields once more. But when I turned back to the window where my elbow rested nothing had changed; there was the same emptiness, the same almost unbearable sense of limitless space; even the clouds seemed lower there, darker, as if they were trying to prevent the sun from touching the land.

"You dreamed while you slept," the old man said. "You called out – 'Maria' I think it was."

"I don't remember," I said, and picked up my book to shut out the old man and the schizophrenic landscape.

An hour later we arrived at Esmée, the old man's destination. I waited until he had gotten off the train and gone down the platform, before I got off myself to stretch my legs. I bought some cigarettes from a kiosk on the platform, and smoked one outside the carriage, only climbing back in when the guard blew his whistle to announce the continuation of the journey.

Many people had left the train at Esmée, but few had gotten on, so I had the compartment to myself for the last leg of the journey to Rona. It took three hours, but seemed longer, largely I suppose because the train was climbing up towards the mountains and was forced to go slowly because of the gradient. The sky had changed to a monotonous shade of grey, and we had not been long in the foothills before it began to rain heavily. The lights came on in the compartment, and the rain ran in thick streaks across the window, obscuring the land, which had turned rugged, and which became rockier, wilder still, the nearer we drew to Rona.

It was dark when the train steamed into the station. When I got off I realised how few people were left on the train. The platform was quiet and very cold; I had to search in my bag for the scarf that the officer who had accompanied me on my shopping expedition had recommended I buy. I draped it around my neck, and then picked up my bag and my suitcase again. I gave my ticket in at the barrier, and stepped out past a simple ticket office and cramped waiting room into the street. No one was waiting for me. I sighed and retreated to the waiting room, which was cold and empty. I lit a cigarette and sat down on one of the hard wooden benches.

A few minutes later a man opened the door, a railway worker judging by his uniform, and gave me a puzzled look. "There are no more trains until tomorrow," he said. A bunch of keys jangled in his hand.

"Someone is meeting me," I said.

"So you've just come in then?"

"Yes," I replied.

The man stood there hesitantly; then looked at his watch. "I'm supposed to lock the door now," he said.

"They shouldn't be long," I said.

"Who?"

"Whoever it is who is coming to pick me up."

The man went away. I lit another cigarette, and had virtually finished it when the man returned, and said, "Here he is."

The person he was addressing came in behind him. He was a soldier in uniform, and was young, barely out of school, I thought. He spoke my name with a questioning intonation. I nodded.

"Please come with me," he said.

I picked up my bags – the soldier offered no assistance – and left the waiting room. The railway worker turned off the lights and locked the door behind him. I followed the soldier to the street, where a jeep was parked. He helped me put my bags in the back, and then suggested that I sit in the front. I did so. He sat in the driver's seat and started the ignition.

"Only one of you?" I said. "I've come to expect two."

"There will be two tomorrow," he retorted quickly. "We drew straws to see who would pick you up tonight. I lost."

"I'm sorry," I said, but the soldier ignored my sarcasm." Where are we going?" I asked.

"A hotel," he answered in a subdued voice.

Rona was built on a hill. We drove through total darkness for a kilometre, before the lights from the town appeared above us. The soldier put the jeep into low gear, and accelerated as we climbed up a narrow street between rows of buildings, many of which were in darkness. The street twisted and turned as we ascended through the lifeless town. We came to a halt outside a three storey building, which had little to distinguish it from its neighbours apart from a small sign on the wall indicating rooms were available.

The hotel must have been somebody's idea of a joke; true, the sign outside advertised rooms for rent, but it omitted to say by the hour. "It's all that is available," the soldier explained inside my room, seeing displeasure on my face as I surveyed the soiled bed, and the thin partitions that served as walls. To one side a woman cleared her throat, hawking her phlegm, I imagined, into a wash-basin exactly the same as the one in the corner of my room; to the other, there was the creaking of old bedsprings, the muffled sounds of lovemaking.

"You know this hotel well?" I enquired.

"I am just following orders," he replied.

"Of course," I said.

"A jeep will come for you at eight o'clock in the morning," the soldier informed me before he left.

I spent a miserable night in that room. The hotel had no dining facilities – "People don't come here for food," the receptionist told me humourlessly – and I had no energy to explore the dark, steep streets in search of a restaurant. So I lay on the bed in the darkness, listening to the acts of bloodless passion taking place around me. After ten o'clock the noises ceased, but the silence that followed was even worse. I couldn't sleep, so turned on the light and picked up Kafka's novel; I read a few lines; then abandoned it. I switched off the light again, and closed my eyes. Maria appeared before me unbidden, as did the Colonel, whose face loomed threateningly behind my wife's. I turned over on my side, and willed them to vanish.

It seemed that I had only just fallen asleep when there was a knocking on the door. I forced my eyes open and glanced at my watch. It was eight fifteen. I pulled on my pants and trousers and opened the door. Two soldiers stood there, as young as the one who had met me at the station.

"We have come to take you to Cagot," the taller of the two said.

"Give me ten minutes to get ready," I said. "Then you can take me for breakfast on the way." I closed the door in their faces before they could respond. I washed my hands and face in the plug-less washbasin and finished dressing, then carried my bags down the uncarpeted stairs. The soldiers were talking and laughing to the receptionist, but became serious when they saw me.

"The jeep's parked just outside," the taller soldier said.

I went out while the soldiers exchanged a few more words with the clerk. I waited for them to come out." I would like some breakfast before we go," I reiterated.

"We are late already," the shorter soldier began.

"I didn't have any dinner," I interrupted him, "and I'm hungry."

"Okay," the other soldier conceded. "We wouldn't want you to pass out on us, would we? Get in the jeep and we'll go to a café I know on the other side of the town."

The shorter soldier drove through the streets to the crest of the hill, which was dominated by a castle, its walls rising sheer above the red-tiled roofs of the town. The soldier constantly worked the brake as we descended. We stopped at the edge of the town, where the land began to flatten out; the taller man pointed to a café. "There you are," he said. "The best coffee in town!"

"He's prejudiced," the other put in. "It's his father's café."

The breakfast was good. I ate fresh, heavily-buttered rolls and drank lots of the strong, black coffee recommended by the soldier. Then we drove to Cagot, four hours away along a winding precipitous road, high up in the mountains.

THE VILLAGE

H ow to describe the village?
Well, there were three village idiots instead of the usual one, a fact indicative of the inbred insularity of the people in this region. They formed their own little group, and were often to be seen together perched like three strange birds on the wall in front of the inn which served as the nerve-centre of the village. Generally, they were left unmolested; occasionally they were taunted by the village youths who seemed to have too much idle time on their hands, but if the mockery ever threatened to get out of hand, then the men – short, stocky, slow in their movements – would intervene and send the youths on their way.

The idiots were there on the wall when the jeep pulled up outside the inn on the day of my arrival.

"A drink first," the soldiers said, as they turned off the ignition and got out of the vehicle, leaving me alone, feeling stupid in the back.

I watched them stride briskly through the snow into the low brick building, noticed the eroded sign above the door that indicated, almost indiscernibly, that the building was indeed an inn, saw the smoke spiralling into the leaden sky from the chimney on the roof. I got out of the jeep to stretch my legs. The cold air struck me immediately, made me shiver, but it smelled fresh and clean. I heard the rushing of water from the nearby river. Across the valley green conifers coated with snow spread up the mountain slopes, then stopped abruptly, so that above them there were only the grey, jagged peaks, dripping snow themselves. Then I noticed the silence. No vehicles made their way up the valley. I could hear no birds. Only the invisible river rushing against invisible rocks intruded, but intrusion is the wrong word, for the river seemed naturally at one with the quietness of the village, so that the sound was like silence itself.

Then a bell rang, a dissonant encroachment on the natural scene. I looked around for the source of the noise and paid attention to the idiots for the first time. They sat on the wall in front of the inn side by side, so close that their bodies touched. They all had the same expression of grinning mischief, as if they realised my situation and were taunting me because of it. The one closest to me held a bell at arms length in front of him, and tinkled it again when he saw that he had got my attention.

"Bell," he said, in a deep yet strangely abstracted voice.

"Bell," the two others chorused and looked at me with the same abstract expression.

"Ting-a-ling," I sang out.

"Ting-a-ling," all three of them replied in unison.

"I am sorry," a voice, bouncy and jovial, disrupted our game. "These soldiers are ignorant fellows. Please, please come into the inn and have a drink with us. I don't know what they were thinking of, leaving you out here all by yourself."

The speaker took my arm and led me towards the door of the inn. I allowed myself to be escorted without question. I was bemused by my situation. First there had been the soldiers who had abandoned me without a thought, and then there had been the idiots and their bells, and now there was this comical figure, short, squat and loquacious, dressed in an official grey uniform, guiding me as he wished.

"I am so glad that you have arrived," he said. "It is so... so tiresome here for a man of sensibility. You play chess? You must play chess. I can see it. I am so starved here. You can play chess, can't you?" he repeated beseechingly.

"I can, but not very well."

"Never mind! There is plenty of time," the man assured me.

We stopped outside the sturdy door of the building. The man still held onto my coat at the elbow. "You are the poet aren't, you?"

"Yes," I said.

"That's good, so good," the man continued. "This place is starved of culture. I am looking forward to having some intellectual company for a change."

"And who are you?" I asked directly.

"Bernard," he said." You can call me Bernard."

Then he held out his hand so that I had no choice but to shake it. His grip was firm, muscular.

He opened the door. "Come in. Come in. It is pleasant inside, even if the people are nothing but peasants."

We entered the room. The bar was crowded – this at one o'clock in the afternoon – and the atmosphere was oppressive because of the pipe-smoke and cigarette-smoke that swirled in a multitude of patterns under the low ceiling. The wooden beams hung just above my head; I looked up and noticed the whorls and knots traced across their surface. The hum of voices wound down, lapsed into unnatural silence; then started up again. My presence had had an impact; I had been noticed, and then almost instantly become part of the landscape, neither accepted nor rejected, simply there.

I had been expected, of course, but the lack of interest, either emotional or intellectual, shown by the villagers left me feeling disoriented. I touched the wooden counter of the bar, which was as intricately patterned as the beams, to assure myself that it was solid, tangible.

"Philip! Philip!" my companion called to the barman. "Please – a drink for my friend."

The barman, a lanky, pale faced individual, smiled at me. "Yes?" he asked and looked me in the eye

"A brandy," Bernard said before I could reply. "A brandy. I am sure that my friend would like a brandy. Am I not right?" He turned to me with an expression that reminded me of the dog that my sister and I had had as a pet when we were children.

"A brandy," I conceded, to please the man.

Here there were no bottles with nozzles attached to carefully measure out the liquid as I had become accustomed to abroad, and as was now fashionable in the capital and other urban centres. No, here it was the same as in the coastal village where the barman took the bottle from beneath the bar, and poured as much or as little into the glass as the mood took him. This barman filled my glass close to the brim; then poured a similar amount into Bernard's glass. Another glass appeared on the table – the barman's own – and he filled that in the same way. Then he proffered a toast. "Welcome," he said slowly, hesitantly, taking care over every word, "to our little ... village. I trust you...will be happy here."

"Welcome," Bernard echoed, and raised his glass.

"Thank you," I responded, and clinked my glass first against Bernard's, then against the barman's. I watched as Bernard put the glass to his lips and consumed the brandy in one swig; the barman followed suit. Then both of them looked at me, clearly expecting me to do the same. Momentarily, I felt the urge to disappoint them, but the desire faded as soon as it had arisen. I complied. I drank the brandy in one gulp, felt it burn my throat; it was so harsh, so rough that it nearly brought tears to my eyes, but I fought against any revelation of weakness. The glasses were swiftly refilled. Another toast was made. We all downed the brandy as before.

"Another," Bernard demanded, with a hint of provocation, as he slammed down his glass on the bar.

"And ... for you?" the barman asked, looking at me with the same disconcerting directness as before, a mannerism that contrasted with his disconnected speech.

"Why not?" I replied. "And yourself?"

The barman shrugged his fragile shoulders. He too could not refuse. The three glasses were replenished. This time I made the toast. "To the Motherland," I said as I raised my glass.

"The Motherland," Bernard agreed, while observing me closely as if to determine the level of my sincerity. The barman merely snorted and had finished his brandy, the third in the space of ten minutes, before Bernard and I had even put our glasses to our lips.

"Hey Philip, how about some service over here?" I heard a voice say, and the barman went down the other end of the bar to do his job.

"Ah, Philip, Philip," Bernard muttered in a tone of nostalgic reverie. "I've never known a man who can drink brandy the way that he can. Yet I've never seen him drunk, you know. Never."

Bernard slapped his hand down onto the bar's wooden surface to emphasise his point. I picked up my glass and drank the contents in one go, to prove that I too was a capable drinker. But I was only fooling myself. My throat burned; my head throbbed and the bar began to take on a slightly distorted quality. Bernard fingered his glass without actually raising it to his lips.

"Another one?" he said after I had finished mine.

"I would like a beer," I said, forcing myself to speak coherently.

"A beer!" Bernard shouted to the woman who had suddenly appeared behind the bar. Philip, I noticed, was lost in a cloud of smoke down the far end of the room.

"But you never drink beer, Bernard!" the woman exclaimed.

"It's for my friend."

I looked at the barmaid. She was tall, lithe, in her early thirties. Her dark hair curled down to her shoulders, but didn't conceal the large gold earrings that dangled from her lobes. Her skin was dark, which, along with her facial features – the strong nose, the full lips – indicated there was a gypsy element in her blood.

"So you must be the poet," she said, as she pulled down on the handle visible behind the bar. I heard the beer run into the glass, watched her as she put the glass on the wooden surface of the counter in front of me.

"Yes," I responded. "And you are?"

"Angela," she answered.

"Philip's good wife," Bernard interposed. "They run the inn together."

She had green eyes, I noticed before she went off to serve another customer, luminous green eyes. Then I knew that I had drunk too much too quickly.

"Where's the toilet?" I asked Bernard.

"What?"

I repeated my question. He gave me directions. I managed to make my way to the lavatory, which was at the back of the inn. The urinal was a trough in the open air; a wall which came up to my chest provided modesty. I peed, while gazing at the scenery around me through an alcoholic haze. As I zipped myself up, I noticed that icicles, beautiful in their form and transparency, hung down from the metal pipe that traversed the upper edge of the stained urinal. I touched one, felt its cold smoothness, but, brittle, it snapped off in my hand. I let it fall, down amongst the refuse that clogged the trough.

The cold air sobered me up a little. I went back into the bar, and found Bernard in conversation with the two soldiers who had driven me up from Rona.

"Ah, here he is," Bernard said, and put his arm around my shoulder. "We thought for a moment you were trying to escape."

The soldiers laughed at the joke.

"Now why would I want to escape?" I said.

"No reason," he said. "I have it on good authority that you came here more or less willingly. Is that right?"

"Is that in my file?" I enquired.

"File?"

"I assume you have a file on me."

"Why do you assume that?" Bernard asked, feigning innocence.

"You are the Police Chief," I said without hesitation. "It's only natural that you have records on me."

Bernard gave a raucous laugh and patted me on the back. "I see that little escapes your attention," he said. "I never once mentioned ..."

"No, you didn't," I interrupted. "So you had to be the Police Chief. That seems logical enough."

My comments only seemed to make the man merrier.

"You are going to make a fine chess companion," he said.

"But right now I would like to be taken to wherever it is I'm staying."

"Living," the Police Chief corrected me. "These men will take you to the hotel," he said, referring to the soldiers. "By the way, you have to report to me at the police-station at seven in the evening," he added casually, as if it were an afterthought.

"What?"

He repeated what he had just said. "I'm afraid that is the rule. It's a mere formality, and I shall have the chess set and a bottle of brandy waiting. But it's part of my job, one of the conditions of your living here."

"Are there any other conditions I should know about?

"You are a free agent in and around the village. Do as you please, within reason, of course. All you have to do as far as I am concerned is report to me at the police-station at seven every evening and at nine every morning."

"So that you know I haven't gone a-roaming?"

"I don't make the rules," he said; then added, "Yes; but at least it gives me something to do. A man could die of boredom in this place. Or become an alcoholic. No stimulation."

The bar seemed stimulating enough to me. I looked around before leaving with the soldiers. Philip was standing at one end of the counter, a glass in his hand brimful with brandy, talking to two swarthy locals. His wife was wiping recently washed glasses with a towel, scanning the bar as she did so, mistress of all that she surveyed. Her eyes met mine, and she smiled, a smile that I was not quite sure how to interpret, although anywhere else I would have taken it to be sensual in nature. Dominoes clattered at several tables. In one corner several men were raucously betting over a game of nine-pins. Behind me four old women were playing cards together. Apart from Angela they were the only women in the bar. Such a male predominance was not unusual in my country. There were bars in the old, working class quarter of the capital that were just like this. But now it struck me, gave me some idea of the kind of society I was in.

The soldiers escorted me out of the inn. The three idiots were still there on the wall – the one with the bell rang it as soon as I appeared, and the other two sang 'ting-a-ling' in their strange voices – but there was no sign of the jeep.

"No need to worry," one of the soldiers assured me – I realised then that he was as drunk as I was – "your belongings have already been taken to the hotel."

The hotel was, in fact, just around the corner, opposite the church on the main road through the village. We walked down the middle of the black road. Sunlight glared off its damp surface, glared off the banks of snow piled up on either side of the cleared tarmac.

I had half-noticed the hotel when we had driven into the village. Its size, and ostentation – at least for such a remote mountain village – meant that, willy-nilly, it forced itself into one's field of vision. Now, I looked at it more closely as we approached. A worn sign indicated that it was the 'Grand Hotel.' It was a ramshackle, Gothic structure, four storeys high. The wood was dark and weathered; many of the windows were sealed, and on the upper floors, where the boarding-up seemed to have been executed spasmodically, several windows were little more than black holes surrounded by jagged fringes of glass. The door into the hotel creaked on its hinges when one of the soldiers pushed it. I followed them into the large, gloomy lobby – little sunlight penetrated the inside because of the wood nailed tight across the windows. The sepulchral feel of the interior was enhanced by the swathes of white cloth, stained and dust-covered, that were strewn over the hotel furniture.

"The off-season?" I suggested, but the soldiers paid no heed.

The reception desk was bare and empty. Hooks with numbers on them were fixed onto the wall behind the desk, but no keys hung there. However, the wooden counter, I noticed had been recently polished, its reflective sheen, catching the light from somewhere, in benign contrast to the general dilapidation. There was a bell on the counter. I pressed it, and listened to the metallic echo as the sound bounced off the dull walls.

We waited. No one spoke. My guards seemed strangely subdued after the raucous atmosphere of the inn. Impatiently, one of them rang the bell again. Then we heard footsteps tapping hollowly along an invisible corridor.

"A ghost?" I whispered, knowing that, to an extent, it was the continuing effect of the brandy that made me taunt the soldiers. They did not appreciate my sense of humour; indeed the way they waited in anticipation as the footsteps drew closer made me think that they had not seen the joke at all.

The relief on their faces was visible when the woman, solid and fleshly, came around the corner that was hidden in gloom, at one end of the lobby.

"I was expecting you earlier," she scolded the soldiers peremptorily. "I was told you would be here at one o'clock."

"We were delayed," one of the soldiers interrupted.

"Yes, in the inn no doubt," she continued in the same forceful manner, sniffing the air tellingly as she did so. "Well, I prepared lunch for you, but I doubt that it's worth eating now."

"No, no," the soldiers said not quite in unison, in repentant voices, "we would like to ..."

"And you?" she turned to me for the first time, without mellowing her tone in the slightest. "Are you hungry as well?"

"No," I said and looked at her.

She held my gaze.

"But I would like a beer."

"It's my job to provide food, not beer," she informed me bluntly.

"But I thought this was a hotel," I said.

"Not anymore," she replied. "At least, you are the only guest."

"So you can't provide me with a beer?"

She wavered. The soldiers watched as this woman and I set about defining our relationship. I half expected her to refuse, and pictured myself walking out of the door, back to the inn to have my little victory and to provoke her at the same time.

"If you eat the food I've prepared for you," she said, "then I might be able to find something for you to drink with it."

"Might?"

"Yes," she answered.

"Very well," I laughed. "You've persuaded me."

She didn't laugh, didn't even smile, although of course I was drunk, as she was fully aware, and she was as sober as a stone. She led us to the corner from where she had appeared. To the right, a long corridor led to the back of the hotel; to the left was a door with a sign on it that indicated it was a restaurant. She pushed the door open for us, and we entered.

The restaurant, unlike the lobby, was light and clean. The windows were curtained, unboarded; all of the tables were covered by white tablecloths. A door at one end led directly to the street outside. We sat at the only table that was laid, and waited silently while the woman disappeared into an adjoining room. She returned immediately carrying a tray that contained chunks of bread, and a large bowl of stew, which, in spite of what she had said, was hot and steaming.

She put the tray on the table. We served ourselves. The soldiers ate voraciously, their appetites enhanced by the alcohol. I was not hungry, but ate to please the woman and also because the stew, thick with potatoes and tender chunks of lamb, was delicious. The woman watched me for a while, before going back into the kitchen and returning with three glasses and three bottles of beer.

"You're an angel," I said, and the soldiers, guzzling their food, mumbled in agreement with me.

"Mmmm," the woman grunted at the sentiment, and set about opening the bottles for us. Her hands were short and strong; I noticed the calluses on the fingers, the dull gold wedding ring, the lines of engrained dirt across her palms.

"What is your name?" I asked.

"Isabella," she replied.

"And you work here?"

"Yes," she replied in the same direct tone. "It's my job to feed you. That's all. The beer you have to pay for. You have to look after your room, light your own fire ..."

"Wash my own clothes?" I asked, tongue-in-cheek.

"I daresay we can come to some arrangement," she said. "Now, if you'll excuse me, I have things to do. Call me when you've finished and I'll show you your room."

She disappeared through the door that led to the corridor and the lobby. The soldiers and I finished the stew and drank our beer – strong ale with a thick, creamy head.

"She's a good cook," I said to the soldiers.

"The best," the taller soldier answered. "She used to run this restaurant in the days when the hotel was open –still does when there are special functions."

"Doesn't the hotel open in season?" I asked.

"No more. Not enough custom."

I felt a little discomfited at the thought of being the only guest in such a large building. "But it must have thrived once," I protested. "A place this size."

"We don't know anything about that," the other soldier interrupted. "We're not from these parts. You'll have to ask the Police Chief."

"Or Isabella," I suggested.

The soldier shrugged his shoulders, as if to indicate that Isabella would be about as forthcoming as he had been.

We finished our beers. The taller soldier went to the door, opened it, and called out Isabella's name. "We're leaving now," he said when she eventually appeared. "We'll leave him in your hands."

"Follow me," she ordered curtly.

She strode up the long corridor, expecting me to do as she had said. Saying nothing, I accompanied the soldiers back into the lobby.

"What are you ...?" the shorter soldier began to ask.

"My bags," I responded. "They were left there." I pointed to where they lay on the worn carpet in front of the reception desk. I picked them up and headed back towards the corridor. I heard the door that led out of the hotel swing on its hinges before it closed behind the soldiers with a desultory click.

Isabella was waiting for me, her back propped against the wall, at the end of the narrow passageway. When I reached her, she turned her back without speaking. Immediately ahead of us was a door. Isabella unlocked it and handed me the key. "This is your room," she said. "The bathroom is there," she continued, indicating a door more or less opposite mine. Dinner is at six."

"A little early," I suggested.

"You have to report to the Police Chief at seven. And besides, I don't want to be here until all hours of the night."

"You don't live here then?" I asked.

"My house is in the village," she replied; then continued with the practical details. "Breakfast is at eight."

"Because I have to report to the Police Chief at nine," I interrupted.

"And lunch is usually at half past twelve," she said, ignoring my comment. "If you intend to miss meals for any reason" – and I could see that she was thinking of the inn – "then I would be grateful if you could inform me beforehand."

"And if I need you for anything between meals?"

"Then you could try the housekeeper's room."

"Where's that?"

"The door next to the kitchen," she said, and pointed back down the corridor. "Is there anything else?" she asked, her tone indicating that she expected there not to be.

"Six o'clock, you said?"

"Yes."

"Thank you."

I entered the room and locked the door behind me. The room smelt enclosed and dank. I put my bags down and opened the large French windows to let in some air. The windows led out onto a balcony that was, at that time of day, bathed in sunlight. I stepped out and, resting my hands on a metal rail which, despite the sun, was cold to the touch, breathed in the scene before me.

The valley floor was covered with snow, except where the river rushed, a cold steely blue cutting through the sparkling whiteness. The lower slopes of the mountains below the conifers were a patchwork quilt of white, brown, and grey, where the fertile earth vied with the snow for dominance. To the right a wooden bridge spanned the river. I could only make out three buildings on the other side. The one upstream beyond the bridge was evidently a school. I heard a bell ring, sharp and distinct in the clear air, a counterpoint to the regular rushing of the river water, and thought I heard children's voices, laughing, singing, although that may have just been the sound of the river. The building directly opposite the hotel was single-storied with a line of regular windows along its side, giving it an official look, but the snow curved up and clung to its sides and no effort had been made to clear a path so I guessed that the building was not often used. (I later learned that it was the meeting hall for the village council. I had been correct; it was, indeed, rarely used.) The other building, way over to my left, was made of concrete, and had no visible windows.

That one piqued my curiosity, and I saw it was accessible as two men in overalls emerged from its hidden interior and walked along the slushy path beside the river. I watched them walk past the meeting hall and head towards the bridge that would bring them across the river.

Something compelled me to observe the men more closely, so I went back into the room, rummaged in my bag and took out my field glasses. I quickly returned to the balcony and focussed my binoculars on the men. They were both short and swarthy, but it was not their physical features, which were unexceptional enough, that aroused my interest; it was their overalls. The original colour of these had clearly been white, but now that whiteness only formed a canvas for a foregrounding of abstract, spattered patterns. These patterns stood out against that landscape of white snow, green trees, and grey river, because they had been painted in a vibrant red, the colour of blood.

I turned and forced the building the men had come from into my field of view. I could make out little that I had not been able to discern with the naked eye. The building was bunker-shaped, windowless, made of ochre-coloured concrete. I scanned the area around it. A stream flowed down from the mountains just beyond the building and joined the main river. I noticed it, had moved past it before it struck me that there was something unusual about the stream. The landscape blurred as I moved back to focus on the tributary. I realised immediately what had attracted my attention; the stream flowed the same colour as the men's aprons, a deep crimson.

Perhaps it was the alcohol stimulating an already disoriented consciousness – the events of the preceding days, after the quietude of the coastal village, had, it is obvious when I re-read what I have written so far in this account, taken their toll – that caused morbid images to come to my mind. I felt, as I had felt on a number of occasions since my journey had begun, that the external world was, in some vague way, antagonistic towards me, playing tricks on me, toying with me.

I had to exorcise the images – images akin to those found in a painting by Bosch – from my consciousness. I left the hotel, having carefully closed the French windows, and locked the door. A track just past the hotel led off the main road across the fields towards the bridge. I took it, and felt water and sludge ooze into my shoes. The two men with blood spattered overalls acknowledged me amicably as we passed. I hurried on, crossed the stone bridge, and took the muddy path that ran alongside the riverbank. Sweating and breathless, I came to the dun-coloured building, and heard the high-pitched squealing of pigs being slaughtered. A sign at the entrance to the building, which was at the side that faced away from the river towards the mountains, announced that this was the village abattoir.

I continued on to the stream; then paused to catch my breath and regain control of my emotions. I laughed aloud at my own stupidity, my singular failure to realise that the building couldn't have been anything else but a slaughterhouse. Beneath me, the animal blood was disgorged from a pipe into the swollen stream, discolouring it and the river it flowed into, until the force of the current managed to dissipate it. In spite of my laughter, I couldn't help myself; the blood, the noise of the animals in their death-throes behind me, the ceaseless roaring of the water pressed in on me, grating across my nerves, causing me to feel faint and sick. I retched violently, felt the sweat in my armpits and on my forehead, as I steadied myself by holding on to the branch of a nearby tree.

The waves of nausea eventually passed. I stood there next to the stream beside the abattoir, clinging to a naked branch feeling embarrassed and foolish. I looked around to see if I had been observed; there was no one walking along the riverside track; no one had emerged from the building. My behaviour had gone unwitnessed, or so I thought, until I glanced across the river and noticed the figure perched on the observation tower adjacent to the police-station. The rotund, uniformed man had both of his hands raised to his eyes; it was a posture familiar to me, and although I could not make them out at such a distance, I knew that Bernard was holding a pair of field glasses, and I also knew that they were focussed directly at me.

I let him know that I had seen him by unzipping my trousers and relieving myself, my urine streaming in a golden arc, melting and staining the pure white snow.

I made myself decent and walked slowly back to the hotel, still drunk, but a little more at ease since I had vomited. On the bridge, I paused for a while and scanned the rocks in the river. I heard a sharp ticking call behind me, and looked up as a grey wagtail, its body a slender vibrant yellow, flew over my head, and continued jerkily downstream.

Once back in my room, I took off my coat and shoes, lay on the bed and pulled the eiderdown over me. I went to sleep almost immediately.

I was awakened by a knocking on the door, which at first merged with the dream I was having; its persistence, however, dispelled the dream and roused me to consciousness. The room was in darkness, although a faint crepuscular glow outlined the furniture. I stumbled to my feet, shouted that I was coming, and made my way out of the bedroom into the sitting room, bumping against a chair in the unfamiliar territory. I pressed an electric light switch, but nothing happened. I made out the shapes of oil lamps hanging from hooks on the wall, but I couldn't remember where I had put my matches, and it occurred to me, for some reason, that I had not had a cigarette since my arrival in the village.

I opened the door. Isabella stood there, her face etched with impatience. "It is gone six o'clock," she said. "Your dinner is getting cold."

"My dinner?"

"Yes, I told you. Six o'clock. Don't you remember?"

"It has been a long day," I said.

"You must report to the Police Chief at seven," she said.

"Must I?"

"Those are the rules. It is best ..."

"Yes," I interrupted her, "Look, at the moment I'm not hungry, but I would like a pot of strong, black coffee. Could you possibly ...?"

The woman raised her eyebrows and sighed.

My head throbbed. My throat was like sandpaper. My body felt unclean, unwashed. "The coffee!" I demanded, on the verge of losing my temper.

The woman looked at me defiantly, but I was a man, and because my country was the way that it was, I guessed that my will would take precedence over hers.

"And the lights aren't working," I complained.

"There is no electricity," she said. "The generator was removed seven years ago."

"Then I will need some matches," I said in the same demanding tone. "To light the lamps and the fire."

"Here you are," she said, stiffly handing me a box of matches from a pocket in her apron.

"Is there hot water in the bathroom?" I asked, this time ameliorating my tone.

"I lit the boiler half an hour ago," she stated.

"Thank you," I said.

She shrugged. "Do you want milk with your coffee?" she asked.

I smiled, hoping to provoke her to respond in kind. She didn't.

"No," I said. "Just black, no sugar!"

"Here or in the restaurant?"

"Here, please. I'll take a shower while you make it."

"We don't have showers," she informed me scathingly. "It's a bath or nothing."

"I suppose that will have to do, then."

"Yes, it will," she said; then left me, although the spirit of her antagonism continued to haunt the empty corridor.

I closed the door behind her. After lighting the lamps and getting the fire going, I opened the suitcase that contained my clothes and took out a towel and dressing-gown. I undressed, and once naked began to shiver in the cold room; goose-pimples distorted my flesh. Quickly, I draped my dressing-gown around me – but it was thin, bought for the coastal village in the south-east, so here it provided decency, not warmth – and took my toilet bag and towel across the corridor into the bathroom.

The bathroom was communal, institutional. There was a line of urinals, a line of cubicles each with its own toilet and bath. Some of the doors to the cubicles were missing, and others hung limply from broken hinges. The enamel baths were stained brown. Most of the plugs were missing. I eventually managed to find one cubicle where the door closed and where the bath had a plug. I turned on the taps, and the water spurted out a chocolate brown. I pulled out the plug and watched the brown water drain away; eventually the pipes flushed clean, the mucky liquid became clear and steam filled the cubicle. I tested the temperature of the water with my foot; then slid into the hot bath.

The heat soothed me. I soaped myself; then relaxed. I thought about the hotel: the spacious restaurant, this bathroom, now decayed and decrepit, but once, presumably, ultra-modern for this village that boasted three idiots. "Who used to come to the mountains?" I wondered. I imagined hunters, fishermen, honeymoon couples, but I could not see how such people would ever fill that rambling building.

There was a sharp knock on the cubicle door.

"Yes?" I called out.

It was Isabella. "Your coffee is ready," she said, "but your door is locked." Her voice was still resonant with impatience.

"One moment," I said. I stepped out of the bath and draped my towel around me. I had put the door key in my toilet bag. I took it out and opened the cubicle door; warped and uneven, the base of the door scraped jarringly, leaving a grey scar on the tiles.

Isabella held out her hand for the key. "There is no need to lock your door," she said.

I thought of the village on the southern coast, thought of the coastal village in England. Many times in those places I had been lax, had left windows open, doors unlocked, yet I had lost nothing. Here, I had locked the door behind me automatically. I handed her the key. "I prefer it that way," I said.

She went away. I dried myself as the water in the bath drained away with a loud gurgling sound. Back in my room, a tray containing a cup, a coffee-pot and a bowl of sugar had been placed on the desk that stood in the corner of the sitting-room. I poured the coffee into the cup; then took it across to the sofa in front of the fire which was now blazing away, but casting only a small semi-circle of warmth. I drank the coffee quickly, and glanced at my watch. It was already twenty to seven.

I put on clean clothes and ate my dinner hurriedly in the restaurant before going out to keep my appointment with Bernard.

The moon was full; the village seemed transformed, magical almost, as the moonlight bounced off the frozen snow, casting a halo around the buildings. The mountains themselves were visible, their outlines sharp, their peaks blue-white against a spangled sky. I halted a few steps from the hotel, at the junction where the church faced the inn. What struck me, apart from the lunar beauty, was the silence of the place. The church seemed deserted, forlorn, abandoned as the hotel was abandoned. Orange lights emanated from the windows of the inn, suggestive of the conviviality I had experienced earlier that day (although it seemed like the distant past to me), but I could hear nothing, no chattering voices, no clinking of glasses, nothing. There were no people in the streets. The idiots, presumably, had long since gone to their respective homes.

I resisted the temptation to enter the inn and continued along the street in the direction of the police station. I had to tread carefully; the snow that had thawed during the day, forming rivulets across the tarmac, had now turned to sparkling ice. My shoes were worn thin at the soles – I should have put my new boots on – and more than once I slipped and had to struggle to maintain my balance. Like a drunkard, I thought, but I was sober by then.

The street was lined on either side with houses made of stone, most of them narrow, but three-storeys high. The ground floor of the buildings, I noticed, often served as a shop, the signs outside being legible in the moonlight. I passed a butcher's, a general store, a doctor's surgery, all more or less, apart from the signs, indistinguishable from one another. The police station disrupted the pattern. This building, although made of the same grey stone, was long and rectangular; it had only one storey, and was windowless. The only light visible from within crept out around the edges of the closed, solid door. To the side, the metallic watch-tower pierced the darkness like some abstract, silver-grey phallic representation.

I knocked on the door and turned the handle without waiting for a reply. The door refused to budge; it was locked from the inside.

"Who's there?" a voice rose from inside.

I said nothing, my curiosity aroused.

"Who's there?" the voice repeated.

I waited. The door was unbolted and opened a little; then a face – young, thin and unsure – appeared in the narrow aperture.

"Don't you have a voice?" the man, more like a boy than a man, asked sarcastically.

"I was told to report to Bernard," I told him.

"Bernard?"

"The Police Chief," I said.

"His quarters are next door," he informed me.

"Which way?" I asked.

The young man hesitated; then opened the door wider and stepped out onto the verandah. "There," he said, pointing to the wooden cabin next to the checkpoint. The barrier at the checkpoint was down, I saw, and two guards sat together in the booth playing cards.

"Thank you," I said to him.

I heard the bolts jangle behind me as I walked over to the Police Chief's cabin, and knocked on the door.

"Come in," the familiar voice boomed from within.

I pushed against the wood and the door swung open immediately.

"Ah, there you are," Bernard said. "I was beginning to think you'd forgotten our arrangement."

"You thought I'd run away?" I asked ironically.

"Hardly," he smiled at me. "Where is there to run to?" The question was rhetorical, and I could not, on the spur of the moment, think of a suitable reply.

I looked around the room. It gave the impression of cosiness. At one end sofa and chairs were arranged around a blazing fire. Bernard sat in one of the armchairs at right angles to the fire, bent over a chessboard positioned on a small table in front of him. Another armchair, exactly the same as the one he was sitting in, stood on the other side of the table. On another small table positioned on Bernard's left was a bottle of brandy, a half-filled glass, a packet of cigars, an ashtray and a box of matches. A similar table had been placed next to the empty chair, but that held only an empty ashtray.

The door I had come through marked a kind of demarcation zone; on one side was the scene I have just described, on the other, on a slightly raised platform, was a dining table and chairs. A closed door exactly opposite the one I had entered led, I presumed, out to the kitchen. Another door, half ajar, connected to a small bedroom.

All in all, although somewhat cramped and lacking in certain features – there were, for instance, no bookshelves or books in evidence – the room was suggestive of contented domesticity, reminiscent of a painting by one of the Dutch masters. I am not sure quite why I got this impression. After all, the man clearly lived here alone, and although he had removed his jacket, his shirt and trousers were still government regulation, the uniform of a policeman. Perhaps it was because of the warm, mellow shadows cast by the fire and the oil lamps on the walls; perhaps because of the studied concentration on his face, partially obscured by smoke from his cigar, as he pondered the chess problem he had set himself; perhaps because of the photographs perched on the mantelpiece that I noticed as I sat down, at his invitation, in the armchair opposite him.

"Would you like a brandy?" he asked me doubtfully.

"Yes," I responded without hesitation.

"So you have recovered from this lunchtime?"

"Recovered?"

"I'm sorry. I thought for some reason that you had drunk too much, had perhaps regretted ..."

"No," I stated firmly, evincing a certain amount of surprise. "Whatever made you think that?"

The Police-chief shrugged his shoulders, "Just an impression."

He stood up and went to a wooden cabinet which stood next to the wall behind his chair. He returned with a brandy glass and half-filled it from the bottle on the side-table; then poured a little into his own glass before handing me my drink.

Still standing, while I was seated, he proposed a toast. "To your new life here in the village," he said. "May it be a pleasant one."

I raised my glass and sipped my brandy in response. Unlike in the inn, this was smooth and warm, chosen by a man who, however buffoonish he appeared, was discerning in his tastes.

"One thing," he said, as he put his glass back down on the table, "I almost forgot. We'd best get the formalities out of the way before we continue."

He went back to the cabinet and from a drawer in its base extracted a thick, leather-bound ledger. He handed it to me. I opened it. My name was written in capital letters on the first page. The following pages had been divided neatly into columns; one for the date, one for the time, one for my signature and one for the Police-chief's confirmatory signature. "You must sign here," he said, and pointed to the first blank entry in the column titled 'GUEST SIGNATURE'.

"Do you have a pen?" I enquired.

"Of course," the Police-chief replied, and then looked perplexedly around the room. "Can you see my jacket anywhere?" he asked.

"It's on the chair over there," I said, pointing in the direction of the dining table. He walked across the room to the table, picked up his jacket and fumbled around in the pockets without result.

"I seem to have mislaid it," he said. "Are you sure you don't have one? I somehow expect poets to always ..."

"I haven't unpacked yet," I informed him abruptly. "I normally carry one."

"Yes, of course." He put his jacket back down on the bed; then walked back across the room to the mantelpiece. A few framed photographs littered its otherwise bare surface. They were all black and white: most of them were tinged brown with age. There were individual portraits of a man and a woman, whom I assumed to be his mother and father as the same people stood behind two boys and a girl in a family portrait. It was not difficult to spot the young Bernard in that picture, for even at that age – about ten, I surmised – he already had the stocky frame and the round, podgy face that were characteristic of him now. He took after his father in that respect, whereas the other two children were taller and leaner, more like the woman in the photograph. Bernard moved the pictures around casually as he searched for a pen.

He had no luck, so, murmuring to himself, went to the cabinet again and began rifling through its lower drawers. I continued to survey the pictures from the armchair, sipping the brandy at the same time. There were a couple of shots of Bernard himself, one as a young police cadet receiving his graduation diploma from the head of whatever academy he had happened to study in. The other photograph was much more recent, could indeed have been taken yesterday as the backdrop was one of snow-covered mountains. It showed the Police-Chief on a horse, a rifle resting across his arm, as he gazed straight into the camera. The expression was one I had yet to see on his face; absent was the joviality, the general bonhomie that, from the evidence of that day, seemed a distinctive feature of the man. Instead, I detected in the staring eyes and the pursed lips a far more serious note. The man looked hard, proud and dangerous. His squat shape – bulging belly and fat thighs – which had earlier made me consider the man comical, now only served to reinforce the hardness of his expression.

"Here we are," he suddenly said, forcing me to turn my head before I could look in any detail at the other photograph that stood on the mantelpiece; I noticed that it was a head and shoulders portrait of a young woman, attractive but somewhat austere, before I once again faced Bernard who was triumphantly holding up a pen in his left hand.

I signed my name in the appropriate space. "Do I fill this in?" I asked referring to the columns labelled 'DATE' and TIME', "or do you?"

"I do," he replied emphatically, and took the ledger away from me. He looked at his watch before writing in the exact time. He then added the date, and signed the entry in a firm, flowing hand. (My own handwriting was crabbed and thin in comparison, not like an artist's at all.)

He returned the ledger to the drawer; then said, "Well then, now that we've got the official business over with, what would you say to a game of chess?"

"Fine," I agreed, although I wasn't much in the mood. "But I ought to warn you that I haven't played for a long, long time."

Having refilled our brandy glasses and placed the bottle on the table at his side, he sat down and began to arrange the pieces into their positions for the opening of the game. He picked up a white pawn and a black one, shuffled them in his hands behind his back; then held his clenched fists out in front of me. I chose the left hand, noticed the thick fingers, the dark hairs extending over the knuckles. He unfurled his fist to reveal the black pawn.

He began the game conventionally, moving his king's pawn to the fourth rank. I followed suit. The game progressed slowly. It soon became clear to me, even though I was no expert, that Bernard had made a study of the game, or rather a study of various games, and was playing to a set pattern. His moves seemed automatic, a process of memory, not of thought. My game, on the other hand was ad hoc, pragmatic. My father had taught me to play chess when I was a schoolboy; I had played fairly regularly then against him and my school friends, but I had never had any great enthusiasm or acumen for the game. I had never studied it in detail, and I had never had the kind of mathematical mind that could plan several moves in advance. So, against Bernard I made moves that did not conform to the game he had in his mind, and as we entered the middle game, having already exchanged three pawns and a knight each, I saw him frown, saw the perplexity in his eyes. I was playing from move to move, which should have made me vulnerable, but he could not, on that occasion, extrapolate himself from the textbook pattern. My failure to conform confused him and caused him to make mistakes.

Then I had him in check, in check again, and three moves after that – and this I did foresee – it was mate.

The Police Chief looked bewildered, then momentarily depressed before he held up his arms and laughed. "Well, you are a man of surprises," he said. "I see I shall have to be wary of you."

"Luck," I said.

"And a certain amount of cunning," he added. "Yes, I see that you are going to be a worthy adversary."

"It's just a game," I said. "I don't take it that seriously."

The Police Chief stood up and poked the logs smouldering in the grate. Sparks flew off the wood as the fire flamed back into life. I sensed that he wanted me to go. I stood up and put my coat on. "Thanks for the brandy," I said.

"There's no need to go so soon," he said for form's sake.

"I'm tired," I lied.

"I understand. Don't forget, nine o'clock tomorrow morning. I'll be in the police station next door."

"I called in there tonight," I told him. "Your men didn't want to open the door."

Bernard tutted in disapproval. "They are from the city," he said. "They don't understand the countryside. They've listened to too many folk-tales."

"And where are you from?" I asked.

"From the North," he said. "From Lauriane."

He ushered me to the door. "Tomorrow then," he said and quickly closed the door behind me once I had stepped back out into the cold night.

I walked carefully down the main street, thinking of Bernard's birthplace. I knew Lauriane well. It was, or used to be, a place where the well-off sought refuge from the stultifying midsummer heat of the capital. My family had been no exception. My sister and I had spent the school holidays there, swimming off the long sandy beaches that fronted the town, or exploring the small coves in the rocky headlands to the west where the water was a cool emerald green. Away from the sea, the landscape of rolling hills was unbelievably lush compared with the general aridness of the Centre and the South.

In winter, however, the town turned in on itself. The hotels and the casino closed, the seas billowed white and cold, the continual rain turned everything grey. According to the national myth-kitty it was this seasonal change that made people from the north temperamental, liable to unpredictable swings of mood, whereas the more extreme climatic variations of the centre were said to give rise to a fatalistic acceptance of things. I wondered half-heartedly if in Bernard's case there might be an element of truth to this generalisation.

I came to the junction where the hotel, the inn and the church stood in a triangular relationship. I fingered the keys in my pocket, and looked at the rambling facade of the hotel. Isabella had left a light burning in the lobby; its beams shone weakly through the cracks where the windows had not been boarded up correctly, where the door did not fit exactly into its frame. I hesitated. The light emanating from the inn seemed a lot more welcoming. I succumbed to the temptation and went in. It was far less busy than it had been at lunchtime. A group of young men were playing darts at one end of the room. Two elderly men sat at the bar, and a handful of others were playing dominoes at the tables in front of a dwindling fire.

"The poet's out late," Angela said to me half sardonically, half flirtatiously.

I looked at my watch. It wasn't yet nine o'clock. "I had to report to the Police Chief," I said." I was on my way back and desired a drink."

"What would you like, beer or brandy?"

I asked for a brandy. Angela poured a generous helping into a glass for me and then poured one for herself too. "You don't mind if I keep you company, do you?" she said.

"Not at all," I replied.

"So, did you play chess against Bernard?" she asked.

"Yes," I said.

"And?"

"And what?"

"Who won?"

"I did."

She gave a smile of mischievous gratification. "He won't be happy about that," she said.

"Won't he?"

"He prides himself on his chess," she said. "He doesn't often lose, but when he does ..." She raised her eyebrows and made a cutting gesture across her throat with the index finger of her right hand.

I laughed at the exaggeration. "Who does he usually play against?" I asked.

"Henry, the schoolteacher. The priest, occasionally, when he's sober. Then there was the one who was here before you; I don't think Bernard ever won a game against him."

"Who was that?" I asked.

Angela drank some brandy, swirling it around in her mouth to savour the taste before she swallowed it.

"His name was Robert."

"Robert who?"

"Belmont, I think. I can't recall exactly. It was a while ago and nobody referred to him by his last name. Besides, he kept himself to himself. He never came in here, apart from towards the end."

"He went back?"

"No. He killed himself," she said as a simple matter of fact, as if the act were inconsequential.

I finished my drink and asked for another.

"How much for the drink?" one of the old men at the bar called out brusquely before she could serve me. Angela went over to deal with him. I looked at the man's grizzled face, watched him carefully count his change before he slouched out of the inn.

"Cheerful soul!" I remarked to Angela, as she poured a drink for me.

"He's harmless enough," she responded; then said thoughtfully, "But you'll find this isn't a particularly cheerful place. The village I mean," she added quickly, as if to disassociate herself and the inn from the criticism she had just made.

"You're not from here, are you?" I asked.

"No. I'm from the south."

"That's what I thought. So what brought you to the mountains?"

She took a cigarette out of a packet she had picked up from behind the counter and lit it. She offered me one only as an afterthought. She looked surprised when I accepted. "You weren't smoking at lunchtime," she said.

"You're very observant," I remarked.

"You notice things if you work behind a bar, especially when it's a stranger. You don't see many new faces in the village any more."

"You didn't answer my question?" I said.

"What question?"

"About why you came to Cagot."

"Oh, there's no mystery there. My parents left the south when I was a child. The province was poor then – poorer even than it is these days – and many people left to find work elsewhere. My father eventually ended up in charge of a small brewery in Rona. My mother was a seamstress. Philip's father owned this inn then; he got to know my father when he came down to Rona on business. Philip and I met and got married and we took over the inn when his father retired."

I had temporarily forgotten about Philip, but her words brought him back to my mind's eye – his thin frame, his pale face, his thin pale fingers around the brandy glass – and I could not associate Angela with him, could not put the two together, so physically inapposite did they appear.

As if thinking had conjured him up, the innkeeper suddenly appeared through a door set back in the wall at the other end of the bar. He wiped his hands on his apron and stepped over to us, looking disparagingly at the cigarette in his wife's hand. For me he managed a smile. "I hope … you're … settling in … well," he stammered politely.

"I'm coping," I said, adding amiably, "The brandy helps."

"Yes, it does," he said. "Would you … like … another?"

"No thanks," I said. "I think I've had enough for one day."

I finished the little that was left in my glass and paid. "By the way," I asked, as I was fastening my coat, "why was that man –Robert, wasn't it? – why was he sent to Cagot?"

I had addressed my question to Angela. She looked to Philip to supply the answer. "We were ... never told," he replied simply. "He never ... came in ... here."

"Except towards the end," I said and smiled.

Philip looked puzzled, like a man having difficulty remembering something of importance. He picked up the brandy bottle that Angela had left on the counter and put it back on the shelf. Then he leaned on the bar and said even more slowly than usual, as if it were a great effort, "We don't talk ... much about ... such things in the village.... We feel it's best to ... to ..."

"To let the past rest," Angela finished his sentence for him.

"I see," I said, and wishing them goodnight, left the inn, carefully closing the door behind me.

I slept well and woke refreshed in the morning. There was, however, no hot water in the bathroom, so I walked along the corridor in my thin dressing gown to speak to Isabella. I found her in the kitchen; she had only just arrived and was still wearing a black hat and a thick black coat, which matched her black skirt, black stockings and black shoes. There was soil on her shoes and hands, all of which gave the impression that she had not only been to a funeral, but helped to dig the grave as well. When I entered she was taking various foodstuffs out of a shopping bag and putting them on the kitchen table.

"There's no hot water," I told her.

"No, there wouldn't be," she answered bluntly.

"Why not?" I asked, irritated by her unsympathetic attitude.

"Because the boiler has to be heated. Because I have only just arrived and have not had time to light the wood that heats the boiler. Because there is no wood yet anyway. Because I have instructions to only heat the boiler in the evenings."

"So I am expected to bathe in cold water?" I retaliated, but not as forcefully as I would have liked. Her attack had taken me by surprise.

"You are expected not to bathe at all – except in the evenings."

"And did the man who was here before me – Robert – did he do the same?" I asked, wanting to see how she would react when I mentioned his name.

"He was a working man; you had only to look at his hands to see that he knew what work was. He was satisfied with a bath twice a week, like the rest of us here in the village. Now if you'll excuse me, I have to prepare your breakfast."

She turned her back on me, dismissively.

Suitably chastened, I went back along the corridor to the bathroom. I washed quickly in water which seemed as cold as the snow outside; then, because the hotel was unheated, dressed up warmly for breakfast. I looked at the fireplace in my room. There were grey ashes in the grate, with a small pile of wood to the side that would not last long.

Over breakfast Isabella was dour and uncommunicative as she served me, but I did learn that hawkers sold wood in front of the church every morning after ten o'clock. After breakfast I went to the police station to register my presence, like a schoolboy I thought, but there were no schoolchildren to be seen. Then I realised it was Saturday, the weekend – a division of time which had long since ceased to have any meaning for me.

This time the door to the police station opened to my push. Bernard was at his desk; the ledger was ready on its surface beside him. He didn't look up immediately, but continued scanning some official papers through rounded spectacles that made his appearance even more agreeably amusing. However, this morning he was officious, unconcerned with pleasantries. I signed my name. He wrote the time, the date, and signed it himself.

"This evening at seven o'clock," he said brusquely and returned to his paperwork.

Opposite the police station a road led up the hillside through a pine forest. I followed it, in spite of the fact that it was unpleasant underfoot. The weather had changed overnight; the wind had veered, bringing rain and an increase in temperature, so that the village was resonant with the steady dripping of melting ice. The snow on the road was losing its crispness, becoming mushy and slippery. Still, that didn't bother me much. I was grateful to have the forest to myself. I breathed in the resiny smell of the conifers and followed the road as it climbed and wound above the village. Through the trees, I could make out the forested slopes on the other side of the valley. Again, I was struck by the silence of the place, apart from the continual drip, drip, dripping of the melting snow and the thin calls of tits and goldcrests, invisible in the trees.

The road began to descend gradually, past uninhabited, isolated cottages hemmed in by banks of snow. Then, on the right hand side of the road, the forest suddenly ceased; the trees gave way to a long, high wall, which ran parallel to the road for a considerable distance. Halfway along the wall there was a barred metal gate. Here the road dipped away to the left on its way back to the village. Curious, I paused at the gate and peered through the bars. A small security checkpoint just inside the grounds was unoccupied. A tarmacked driveway that had been cleared of snow glistened black between two lines of tall trees; the driveway came to a halt at a house, and, although it was too far away for me to make out much detail, I could see the classical pillars of the porte-cochere, and the large windows set in the grey stone facade looking out onto the snow-covered gardens. It was a building obviously meant to impress, but it was its incongruity – such grandeur in such a remote place – that struck and puzzled me.

I headed on down the road. The smell of wood smoke indicated that I was approaching the village well before the trees thinned out and the roofs of the buildings came into view. Just before the first of the buildings, a track led off to the right. Boot marks were printed in the churned up snow and mud of the track, which curved out of sight between patches of head high scrub. From behind the scrub, came the regular sound of metal chipping against stone. I didn't follow the track, but kept on down the road to the village.

As I passed the inn, I noticed the idiots sitting together outside on the wall; this time they ignored me. The inn-door was open and Angela was sweeping the previous night's dust and cigarette ends out into the street. She smiled at me as I went by. Women were just arriving at the church with the firewood. They came down the main street with a springy gait, the wood tied together in bundles and balanced on their heads. They were thickset; their faces were tanned and leathery, their skin delved with wrinkles so that it was difficult to assess their ages with any degree of exactitude.

Other villagers, women for the most part, waited until the bundles of wood had been lain down against the wall of the church before they inspected them. They lifted the bundles to test their weight, fingered the individual sticks carefully to check that they weren't rotten. I did the same, but inexpertly.

"That's no good; it's weevil-ridden," a voice said as I was about to pay for the wood I had chosen.

It was Isabella. She took the wood and placed it back against the wall. "This one is fine," she said, choosing another bundle and putting it down at my feet. She then chose six more bundles and told me the price without consulting the hawker at all. I paid for them. The hawker accepted the money I gave her without question.

A girl in her late teens helped us to carry the wood back to the hotel. She was dressed in black like Isabella, and had the same kind of ascetic moroseness about her, so I wasn't surprised when Isabella announced by way of succinct explanation, "My daughter – Rose. " Rose didn't catch my eye, and she made no attempt to speak to me.

Isabella kept two bundles for the boiler. I took the rest to my room. There, I cleared out the ashes from the previous day, and lit a new fire to take the chill off the room. While the wood took, I stepped outside onto the balcony and scanned the peaks through my field glasses. They seemed silent, lifeless, but I did observe a party of choughs drifting above the sheer crags before they tumbled down out of view.

I went back inside. The sitting room was large and adequately equipped, even if the furniture was ancient. There was a heavy writing desk, which I managed, with some exertion, to move slightly nearer to the fire. From the suitcase I took out two notebooks; one was for natural history notes, the other for the final versions of any poems I might write. I opened one of the books, and wrote my name on the inside cover; then a third of the way down the next page, I wrote in block letters POEMS OF LOVE AND DEATH.

The thin man had kept my notebook back from me, but I held the poems in my memory. It was still necessary, however, to give them the tangibility of the written form; poems have a life of their own outside their creator, and as their creator I could not deny them that life. So I began to write the poems down, just as I had written them down in the cottage near the sea.

The poems were mainly, at least in the beginning, about Maria. They had been my way of working through the grief; then the sense of nullity that had embraced me. The poems had come slowly, painfully – reluctant, so it seemed, to be dragged out of consciousness into the light of day. There had been days when the words had refused to come at all. I had found relief then by turning to my nature journal, focussing on the external world in the cooler medium of prose. Eventually the poems came back to me, and I realised that, in time, there would be enough for a new book. It hadn't occurred to me on the coast that I might not, because of the change in the intellectual climate brought about by the Colonel, find a publisher for the work. Now, exiled in the mountains, I considered that possibility and came to the conclusion that I probably wouldn't be allowed to submit the manuscript. Still, I would persist.

I turned the page, wrote the title 'Absence', and began to write the poem that I had created several years before on that Sunday night on the English coast:

Days begin to taste of winter

> Now, bitter to the palate's edge,
> And the wind parodies laughter.

And as I continued I remembered the sense of loneliness that had inspired me:

> ... But night is worse.
> Then nothing fills the empty space
> Save wind and curlews' hollow cries,
> While inside the lamp-lit glass reflects
> My image....

I hadn't really known that that empty space existed until Maria, by her absence, made me aware of it. In another poem I had written:

> ... Habit
> Dulls the senses,
> Conditions us to
> Accept what is.

Maria, by her presence, had stripped away that skin of habit, and reawakened my senses.

'Absence' had remained a private poem, something personal to Maria and myself; it had never been published. Now it seemed apposite that it should be the first poem in the collection, the first expression of love. There were other poems inspired by Maria that had never entered the public sphere, many of them unabashed expressions of the happiness and fulfilment that I experienced with her. 'Epithalamium' was the one I now copied into the journal, followed by the semi-erotic pieces that she had encouraged me to write. These poems made up the first section of the book; they were celebratory. The second section was much darker. The poems were short, intense, oblique; the events that inspired them had to be inferred, as they were not directly stated in the verse. I could not, at that time, have stated them directly. Those poems, such as 'The Knife' and 'The Street', were written in despair, and that despair was evident in them, so much so that I had once thought of relegating them to the rubbish bin. I hadn't done so because I came to realise they were valid reflections of what I had experienced, and I believed that other people would be able to identify with my expression of loss. We all have death in common.

Writing those poems had helped me to cauterise the emotional wound. After the despair came a feeling of hollowness, a sense of not being fully alive. It was as if I had taken a drug, so that my mind and reality were out of joint; I was distanced, muffled from the world. It was in this state that I had left the capital and drifted aimlessly through the country, finally stopping in the fishing village on the south-east coast. There I had written nothing for twelve months.

Outwardly, my life on the coast had been calm, well-regulated, but my deeper needs remained unassuaged. So, a year to the day that Maria had been killed, it all came flooding back to me. I had gotten drunk in Alfred's bar, deliberately, savagely, breaking away from the rhythm that had sustained me since my arrival. Back in the cottage I confronted my image in the dressing table mirror; or my image confronted me. I couldn't stand what I saw – the degradation, the self-pity – so I picked up a paperweight and struck it repeatedly against the glass, cutting my fingers, watching my reflection fragment and fragment further still.

Then I sat down and wrote the four-line poem, Fragments':
> A mirror broken into a thousand strands;
> Myriad reflections between my hands.
> Which one the I? Which one the real?
> What truth can fragments, if at all, reveal?

The drunkenness, the violent action, the writing of the poem acted as a catharsis. 'Fragments' began the third part of my book. I thought of this as the healing section, where I began to view my loss with a certain detachment, to look out at the world again and recognise its otherness. The poems slowly moved away from the personal, so that they were no longer just about Maria, but more abstract, more general. The last poem I had written was 'Shearwaters', in which the birds were
> the birds themselves

117

> Stiff-winged, volatile
> Above the swollen sea

but something more, because they appeared to me as
> In motion, suspended,
> Still on the air.

The poem offered a moment of peace, however brief, amidst the flux of things. I was, in a way, back to writing about the act of creativity in itself, as I had done in 'Another Country'. I intended to continue in the same vein, looking more analytically at the relationship between art, love and death, in order to have enough poems to make the volume complete.

I was halfway through copying 'Shearwaters' into the notebook when there was a knock on the door. It was Isabella's daughter, Rose, come to inform me that lunch was ready. I looked at my watch. It was one o'clock exactly. My life suddenly seemed to be dominated by the clock, with fixed times for eating, and fixed times for reporting to Bernard. I completed the poem and placed the notebook in the drawer of the writing desk. I locked the drawer and put the key in my trouser pocket.

All of the tables in the hotel restaurant still had white tablecloths on them; only one place was laid, and that was for me. The general whiteness contrasted with the sombre hue of Isabella's dress as she entered from the kitchen with my food, a stew similar to the offering of the day before. On this occasion, she brought me a bottle of beer and a pewter mug without my having to ask, a gesture which pleased me. Rose stood at the kitchen door watching the proceedings.

"How old is your daughter?" I enquired amiably, making conversation.

Isabella eyed me with suspicion. "Sixteen," she answered.

"But not at school?"

"Here in the village the school only takes children up to the age of eleven. After that they have to go to Rona. Rose didn't want to leave her mother."

"And her father?"

"He died eight years ago."

"Yet you mourn him like it was yesterday," I said, not without sympathy.

"He was a good man. I owe it to his memory."

I didn't pursue the matter, but drank my beer as the widow looked on.

After lunch I returned to my room to fetch my field glasses, and a small shoulder bag in which I placed my bird-guide, a small notebook, pens and pencils. I left the hotel and followed the main road east up the valley. The river was on my left; on my right there was a string of buildings, mainly houses, although a sign over the double doors of one single storey building read GOVERNMENT RESTHOUSE. The doors were closed, the windows barred.

Several hundred metres from here, a denuded spur of land split the river and road into two. I now had two valleys to choose from. In both cases, I noted, the sealed roads abruptly terminated, becoming muddy tracks. I took the track to my right, and went over a bridge.

The river flowed beneath me, and continued to the right of the track I was now on. Across the river, the valley slope was steep and heavily forested; it faced north, and so was in shadow. The hilly land immediately adjacent to the track was treeless and more gently undulating. Several houses had been built on its slopes, but most of them looked derelict, abandoned. There was a string of buildings – basic wooden shacks – at the base of the hill alongside the track. One of them served as a general provisions store and here the doors had been flung wide open to reveal three men squatting on the wooden floor around a fire glowing in a circular metal container. They were drinking tea from small, enamel cups. Two of the men were elderly, and were smoking pipes; the third was much younger. His neatly cropped hair, his smooth, clean-shaven skin made it difficult to discern his age exactly. I took him to be in his early twenties; I later discovered that he was, in fact, closer to thirty.

It was this man who beckoned me to join them, so I took my muddy boots off and left them outside; then sat down in front of the burning logs with my back to the forested slopes. The interior of the shop was spartan. There was a counter, bare except for an antiquated till, and a few shelves containing old tins, matches, rope, dull coloured pans and two jars of sweets.

I was given a cup of tea, a hot, over-brewed concoction that tasted bitter on my tongue.

"Are you the engineer?" the old man to my immediate left asked me. He had a straggly white beard. His teeth were tobacco stained.

"The engineer?" I asked.

"From the capital," the old man offered in explanation.

"It's too early yet," the young man intervened. "He won't be here until the summer, when the snow's gone. This is the poet I told you about."

I forced a smile. The man sitting opposite me on the other side of the fire gave a grunt of disapproval. I studied his features while he spoke. Rough stubble sprouted from his chin, and his face was dark and gnarled, like a weathered oak.

"We need a doctor or another teacher," the man complained. "And the Government sends us a poet!"

"I didn't choose to come here," I said.

"We know," the young man said placatingly. "Luis wasn't being personal. It's the Government's priorities that irritate him."

"And do you need an engineer?" I asked.

The choleric Luis spat into the fire. "They should leave the dead alone," he said. "It's a sacrilege to even ..."

"Nothing will come of it," the man with the beard interrupted. "You'll see. It's just not practical."

"They should still leave us alone," Luis persisted." They left us alone for over a hundred years, and we managed well enough then."

The young man sighed in the manner of someone who had heard all of this before. "Would you mind if I had a look through your glasses?" he asked me politely.

We stood together in the doorway as I explained how to focus the binoculars. He scanned the trees across the river, looked up and down the valley. "What do you use them for?" he asked.

"Bird watching," I told him.

"You should try further up the valley," he advised. It's not so disturbed up there."

I thanked the men for the drink, put my boots back on and continued my walk. The thaw showed no sign of abating. The snow on the slopes was melting quickly, turning into rivulets that flowed and joined and washed across the track, making it uncomfortably slushy and muddy. Then, when the sun dipped below the peaks long before setting, and the air turned colder, I decided that I had had enough and retraced my steps.

I had seen little going up the valley; I was luckier going back down. A dipper, white-breasted, black-bellied, bobbed comically on the rocks in the middle of the river. Further on, a lammergeier glided over the forest, then flew directly over my head before disappearing over the highest ridge of the denuded hill. I took out my sketchbook and, in spite of my cold hands, managed to draw the bird: the long, tapering wings and the diamond-shaped tail, the dark colour of these contrasting with the yellowish head and under parts. It was the first time I had ever seen the species in the wild.

Back in the hotel I lit a new fire and started my nature journal, making notes about the grey wagtail I had observed the day before, and the birds I had seen or heard in the forest earlier that morning. Then I made a number of fair drawings from my rough sketches of the lammergeier. This concentrated activity put me in a good mood.

Over dinner I asked Isabella about Robert Belmont. At first, she seemed reluctant to reply but, unexpectedly, she warmed up in the telling. "He was sent here almost as soon as the Colonel took over," she told me. "He was a trade unionist, active in Esmée at the time. Some people said he was a communist."

"And he stayed here in the hotel?"

"Yes, in the room you're in now."

"So it seems there's only room for one visitor at a time."

Isabella made no response to that.

"What kind of man was he, this Robert?" I asked.

"Quiet, withdrawn," she said slowly, painting an image at odds with my idea of a trade union agitator. "He hated the village."

"Why?"

"He didn't know what to do with his time. He was used to the ways of the city. He spent hours doing nothing. Just brooding."

"I thought he used to play chess with Bernard?"

"Who?"

"The Police Chief."

"Oh, of course. Well, he was like you – he had to register at the police station twice a day; sometimes he stayed in the evenings. The Police Chief is always playing the game, and I suppose Robert had little choice, but he didn't play regularly. The Chief wouldn't let him, I think. I don't really know much about it."

"Apparently, Belmont was a good player," I explained, "and Bernard is a sore loser. I imagine Bernard didn't like losing too often."

Isabella went out to the kitchen to get me a second beer. When she returned, and I had refilled my glass, I asked her how Belmont had committed suicide.

"So you know about that too?" she asked.

"Yes."

"A terrible sin," she said, shaking her head.

"But you know what happened?"

"Of course. Everyone does."

"So how did he do it?" I asked quietly.

"With a shotgun. The Police Chief's hunting gun, in fact. Robert was at the police-station one evening to report as he always did."

"Was that in the police-station itself, or in Bernard's quarters?" I asked.

"In his quarters," she replied, and continued her story, "The Police Chief had to go to the police-station for something, and he left Robert alone in the room. He was in the police-station when he heard a shot. My house is at that end of the village, and I heard it clearly too. I went out to see what was happening. This is a quiet place; you know when something is wrong. The policemen tried to keep us back, of course, but I managed to see Robert's body on the floor. There was blood everywhere."

"And where was the gun?"

"On the floor beside him."

"It's a grisly story," I commented. "I wonder why he did it."

"I told you, he brooded too much. He was lonely. He made no effort. God gives us strength if we are willing to accept Him, but Robert wasn't a believer. He was a sad man in many respects."

"And what about you?" I asked needlessly.

"I have faith," she said.

Which I didn't doubt, yet it seemed to me that her belief was dark and brooding, much as she had described Robert's non-belief as being. Joy was not concomitant with her faith and that seemed to be generally true of religion in our country as a whole. The Church had always been, at least from a liberal perspective, powerful and repressive. It was associated with right wing governments, and had tacitly supported the Military during the establishment of the Old Régime. Very few priests had spoken out against the deaths that followed; the few that did had swiftly met the same fate. I had no love for the Church, no belief in God. Neither would Robert have had. But I still didn't find Isabella's explanation totally adequate.

After dinner I returned to my room, and put on my coat, scarf and boots. I heard Isabella washing up in the kitchen as I passed on my way to the lobby and the entrance door. The shrouded furniture loomed forlornly in the dimly lit foyer. I checked that I had my keys and locked the door behind me. Isabella entered and left the building through the door that led directly from the housekeeper's room into a side street.

Outside, the stars were veiled by the clouds. The temperature had remained above freezing, so the street was wet but not slippery. I walked briskly to the police headquarters, this time ignoring the police station, and went directly to the Police Chief's residence.

He wasn't alone. The man who sat opposite him, carefully studying the chessboard, was the young man who had invited me into the store for tea on my walk that afternoon.

He stood up when Bernard introduced us. "... And this is Henry. Henry is the schoolteacher."

Henry shook my hand, and told Bernard that we had met earlier that day. "Did you see any birds?" he asked me.

"Not many," I answered," but I did see a lammergeier – not far from the shop, in fact."

"A lammergeier?" Bernard asked.

"A bearded vulture," Henry explained knowledgeably to him. Then he turned to me. "That's what they're known as in these parts."

"They're impressive birds," I said.

"Some of the farmers don't think so," Henry informed me. "They believe that they take their sheep. The species is pretty scarce in these parts. You occasionally see them at this time of year, but the shepherds will be moving their sheep back up to pasture soon, and they'll be taking their guns with them. They regard any large bird or prey as a pest and will shoot if they get the opportunity."

At the mention of guns I looked around the room. Bernard's shotgun leaned carelessly up against the wall in one corner.

"Enough of this sentimental talk," Bernard began.

"I wouldn't say it was sentimental," I interrupted.

Bernard dismissed my comment with a wave of his hand. "Henry and I have a game to finish."

We went through the usual business of registration. Bernard showed me to the door. "Come at nine-thirty tomorrow morning," he told me, adding in explanation, "Because it's Sunday."

I said goodnight to Henry and walked back up the main street to the inn. "You've become a regular already," Angela said as I sat down at the bar. "Brandy?"

"I think I'll have a beer."

I looked around the room as she filled the tankard. It was busier than the night before. More of the tables were occupied by people playing dominoes or cards. Amongst them was the bearded old man from the shop; he acknowledged me with a nod of the head. The same young people were at the dartboard, joking raucously with one another.

I lit a cigarette, my first of the day. Angela gave me the beer. "You're earlier this evening," she said. "Was Bernard frightened of losing again?"

"No, he's playing against Henry."

"Of course, it's Saturday," she said. "I forgot. One day is much like any other around here. Henry usually plays chess on Saturday; then he comes in here for a drink on his way home. It's a regular ritual."

"Doesn't Henry come in on any other day?" I asked.

"Rarely. Henry is a man of moderation," she replied, a little sarcastically I thought.

There was a sudden burst of laughter from the young men at the dartboard. Angela looked in their direction. "Soldiers!" she said, and arched her eyebrows. "They spend more time in here than at the barracks. Saturday is always the worst night; that's when they deliberately set out to get drunk."

"Not much else for them to do," I suggested.

"Not in this village – no," she said. "It's not the most popular posting."

"Why is there an army post here anyway?" I asked.

"Because if you carry on up the valley and go over the tops you eventually come to the border. That's the reason the soldiers give, anyway."

"I didn't realise we were so close."

"We're not that close," she said. "This just happens to be the nearest village."

"Do people ever do it – cross the border, I mean?"

She looked at me. "It's a hard slog," she said. "The passes are blocked until midsummer. The shepherds wander around up there, and it doesn't seem to bother them which country they're in. Other than them – no, not really. No-one's got any reason to go over the border; there are only rocks and trees, the same as on this side."

"No smuggling?" I asked.

Angela grinned, the same mischievous grin that I had noticed when she learned that I had beaten Bernard at chess. "What is there to smuggle?" she said, and left it at that.

"Good evening," Philip said in his slow, deliberate way as he appeared behind the bar from the alcove leading into the private living area.

"Evening," I replied. "How's business?"

"Good," he said.

"It's been better," Angela put in.

"We make a living," Philip insisted; then thought for a while before saying, "We might ... make a better ... one if you spent more ... time working and less ... time chatting." It was difficult to tell whether this admonition was meant to be good-humoured or damning, as it took such a concentrated effort on Philip's part to string the words together. It wasn't exactly that he stuttered, more that he paused sporadically, splitting up phrases which should logically have hung together.

Angela responded gaily: "I'm just keeping the customers happy, Philip. That's part of my job."

I assumed from the manner of her reaction that they were indulging in friendly banter. Still, Angela moved away to wash some glasses. Philip went over to the tables with a jug of wine in his hand to see if anyone wanted their glasses refilling.

Henry came in later on, as Angela had predicted. I ordered a beer for him and another for myself.

"How did the game go?" I asked him.

"A draw," he said, "which is usually the case. Bernard and I have been playing against each other for too long. Do you play?"

"Yes. Didn't Bernard tell you?"

"No, he didn't. We'll have to arrange a game some time," he said noncommittally.

I agreed, and we left it at that. We drank our beer. "Are you from Cagot?" I asked him, making conversation.

"No, I'm from Rona. I was sent here when I'd finished my training. That's the usual policy, to send newly qualified teachers out to the more remote areas."

"And experienced teachers?" I asked.

He shrugged. "I've put in for a transfer every year for the past three years. As you can see, I'm still here."

"An exile like me," I suggested lightly.

"But I'm free to come and go as I please," he said.

"But you are not free to teach where you please," I answered back calmly.

"There is freedom and there is freedom. We all have limitations placed on us. I could leave the valley tomorrow if I wanted, but I choose to stay in my job. You see, I do have a choice."

"And I don't?"

"That seems to be the case."

"That's not strictly true," I argued. "Take the case of Robert Belmont, for example. He couldn't leave the valley, but he made a choice."

"So you know about Robert, do you?" he said, a little nervously, I thought. "He was an unhappy fellow. But is suicide really the result of a choice?"

"The fundamental one – between life and death.

"I would have thought that it was the opposite – the realisation that choice was exhausted. The suicide feels that he has no option but to kill himself. The genuine suicide, that is; I'm not talking about attempted suicide, which is a different matter."

Angela had come to our end of the bar, and had been listening to our conversation. "What's the difference?" she asked.

Henry answered her question: "The suicide wants to kill himself – full stop. The attempted suicide is taking a gamble, or making a gesture; a cry for help, if you like. "

"It sounds morbid to me. You can think about such things too much," she said to both of us; then to me, "Like your Isabella."

"My Isabella?"

"The Perpetual Widow we call her. It's been eight years now, but she carries on like it was only yesterday. It's unnatural."

"She's religious," I said.

"Well, there's too much religion in this country if you ask me," she retorted.

"You're being very radical tonight, Angela," Henry said. "Better mind out that Bernard doesn't hear you – you might end up in one of his reports."

"Bernard knows my opinions," she replied tartly, " and I don't give a fig for his reports."

"Angela! We're dying of thirst over here," one of the soldiers shouted from the vicinity of the dartboard.

"I've only got one pair of hands," she shouted in reply. She turned back to us. "And if he writes about me, what are they going to do?" She indicated me. "They can't send me here – I already live here; and if they sent me somewhere else that could only be a blessing."

"There are worse places," Henry said.

"Where?" she demanded, and went off to serve the soldiers without waiting for an answer.

"She doesn't mean it," Henry said to me.

"She's a little drunk," I said.

"Yes, she is, although it isn't always easy to tell. She's often ..." He dug for the appropriate word.

"Lively?" I suggested.

"Provocative," was the word he decided on. "She likes to shock just for the sake of it."

Having said that, he finished his drink and stood up to go. "Thanks for the beer," he said. "My turn next time!"

"Going already?" Angela said, as she was pouring beer for the soldiers.

"I have some work to do," he said.

"All work and no play ..."

Henry lowered his eyes at this, and blushed a little.

"And what about you?" she asked, pointing to my empty glass after Henry had left.

"You could tempt me," I said.

"I know," she said, "but I was asking if you'd like another drink."

"Yes, when you're ready," I answered, and wondered about the possibility.

Then I saw Philip, tall and pallid, drinking brandy at the end of the bar and put the idea out of my mind.

The following morning Rose served my breakfast in shy silence. "Where's your mother?" I asked directly, forcing her to speak.

She kept her eyes fixed on the plate that lay in front of me. "At Mass," she said.

After I had finished breakfast I stepped outside without bothering to fetch my coat from my room, and strode across the road to the church. The exterior doors were open. I went through them into a small porch, which had various yellowing notices pinned to its walls. Another closed set of doors led into the main body of the church. I turned the handle quietly, and slipped into a pew right at the back. The interior of the church belied the starkness of its external appearance. The fixtures were gaudily baroque. The walls were lined with statues of the Saints that were poorly executed, sentimental in style. At the altar the Priest was preparing the wafers and wine for the Eucharist. He was in his fifties. His face was florid, baggy, heavily jowled. His belly swelled beneath his cassock. I was surprised at how few people there were in the congregation. I counted nine women and five men. Isabella was the only woman I recognised. Bernard was amongst the men. He sat in the front pew next to a man who was unfamiliar to me. Henry was also there. He sat by himself, two pews behind the Police Chief. He turned around not long after I had entered the church and, having caught my eye, nodded in greeting, before turning round to face the altar again.

I stayed in the church for a few minutes only; then slipped out and returned to my room. I killed time before reporting to the police station by making rough sketches of the view from my balcony. I noticed that a lot more snow had melted overnight. I looked at my watch, and was about to make a move, when someone shouted, "Hello there!" I looked down from the balcony. It was Henry.

"I was hoping I'd catch you," he said. "I wanted to invite you for tea this afternoon – nothing fancy, I'm afraid: just sandwiches, cake, that kind of thing."

"That sounds fine to me," I replied. "Yes, I would like to."

"Five o'clock?"

"Yes."

"Good. I'll see you then."

He made to move away. "But I don't know where you live," I called to him.

He raised his boyish face and laughed. "Strange, I assumed you did. I live behind the school – the second building."

"I'll find it," I assured him. Then he went on his way.

I registered at the police station; then returned to my room. I made up and lit the fire; then settled down at the desk with a blank piece of paper before me. It was my intention to write. I needed more poems to complete my 'Love and Death' volume. My idea was to write about the pilgrims I had seen on the station platform in the middle of the night, to somehow relate them to the metaphysical notions I had been exploring in 'Shearwaters' – the notions of movement and calm, how the two can be co-occurrent, not necessarily contradictory. However, the words wouldn't come; the paper stayed blank, inert, and I grew increasingly restless (this because I was forcing an idea onto a particular situation, and not allowing the idea to grow naturally out of that situation. In the end I had to concede that the two couldn't accommodate each other).

My restlessness manifested itself physically; my throat became dry, my teeth were on edge, so eventually I gave in and decided to go to the inn for a drink. I met Isabella outside the hotel. "You are coming for lunch, aren't you?" she asked doubtfully, seemingly aware of where I was going.

"At one o'clock on the dot," I assured her.

The inn was the busiest I had seen it, full of men, and there were no women at all. I managed to find a standing space at the bar and had to wait a while before Angela was free to serve me.

"They all come here while their wives prepare Sunday lunch," she explained when I mentioned that business was particularly good that morning.

I scanned the room and saw Bernard sitting at a table next to the man I had seen him with in the church.

"Who's that with Bernard?" I asked Angela when the opportunity arose.

"That's Hubert Duval. He owns the quarry," she told me.

"Quarry?"

"Just up the road from here. They use the stone to make religious statues, and sell them throughout the country. He's the richest man in the village."

"He wouldn't own that mansion in the forest, would he?" I asked.

"Yes, that's the one."

"I passed it yesterday," I told her.

"You couldn't very well miss it, could you?" she joked, before being called away to serve another thirsty customer.

On his way out, Bernard came over to me with Duval, and introduced him to me by his Christian name. We shook hands and exchanged pleasantries. He was, I reckoned, in his mid-forties. His dark hair and dark, military moustache gave him a distinguished air, which was matched by his polite, if slightly superior manner.

"I do quite a lot of reading, myself," he said in a neutral accent. "You must come and have dinner with me one evening."

"Thank you," I replied, assuming that he didn't mean it.

My impression was of a rather cold man, and remarked as such to Angela after Bernard and he had gone.

"Oh, he has his needs just like any other man," she said. Then she added, "Well, most men anyway."

I pressed her to expand on her enigmatic remark, but she pulled a face at me and refused to pursue the topic.

I finished my drink and returned to the hotel, only a little late for lunch, but I was still subjected to Isabella's disapproving glances. Her air of moral righteousness compounded the irritation I was feeling – going to the inn hadn't much helped my mood – so, ungraciously, I asked her, "Did your husband never drink?"

"Not in that inn. Not with that woman there. He had his self-respect."

The vehemence of her response took me aback. "Most of the men don't seem to mind," I said.

"This is a godless place," she said, her eyes piercing mine like some dark, avenging angel. "And they are godless people."

I thought of the near-empty church and the dissipated priest. "You don't believe either, do you?" she asked, interrupting my speculations.

"No," I admitted.

"You will fit in well, then," she said, before making her exit to the kitchen.

I found her in the kitchen, reading a leather-bound copy of the Bible, a few minutes later. I told her that I wouldn't be needing dinner as Henry had invited me for tea.

"Good," she said simply, and turned back to the Book.

In my room I made another attempt to conjure up a poem, but again I failed. Beer and lunch had made me tired, so I went into the bedroom, crept beneath the eiderdown and slept for a while.

I dreamed I was in a darkened room with a woman. The woman was naked, but I couldn't see her face as she had her back to me, was running away from me. I chased her, moved to desire by the suppleness of skin, the curve of the spine, the rounded buttocks, but she ran as fast as I did, so we were like the lovers in Keats's poem about the Grecian urn. That is until the woman fell, and turned her face towards me; it was Isabella's face, so I froze, and she opened her mouth wide, wide like some hideous wolf, and howled with laughter. It was the laughter that woke me up. I was sweating.

I went out to the bathroom and swilled cold water over my neck and face. I decided to go to Henry's then, even though I knew I would be early.

He lived in one of two identical cabins behind the school. The school caretaker lived in the other. The cabin was small and basic. Henry showed me around. The kitchen and bathroom were tiny, the bedroom contained a bed and a wardrobe, leaving no room for anything else, not even a bedside table. The remaining room, which had to serve as a sitting room and a dining room, was a little more spacious. The spartan nature of the furniture also made it feel less cramped. There was a wooden table, with two chairs made of the same kind of wood pushed under it, and there were two easy chairs, the worse for wear and age, placed in front of the fireplace. Apart from a small cupboard and a few shelves, that was it. The starkness of the surroundings had, however, been softened by the addition of various items. There was a tablecloth on the table, and curtains, of the same colour and pattern as the tablecloth, at the windows. The shelves had books on them. There were reproductions of the English Pre-Raphaelite painters on the walls. The mantelpiece above the blazing fire was covered with small ornaments and knickknacks. There seemed something vaguely feminine about the way the room had been made more habitable, and I wondered if Henry had furnished it with a woman's help.

Henry had put out cakes and sandwiches on the table before my arrival. Now he went to the kitchen to make a pot of tea. I stood in the kitchen doorway, as he poured water from the tap into the kettle, and put the kettle on the gas to boil. He took a tin containing tea leaves out of a small cupboard under the sink. As he did this I noticed for the first time how fastidious his movements were. He did everything very carefully, very precisely, as if he were handling delicate china rather than old, battered metal.

"I was surprised to see you in church," he said as he prepared the tea, "although I noticed that you didn't take Mass."

"I was surprised to see you as well," I responded. "I didn't think of you as religious."

"Why ever not?"

"I suppose most of the teachers I've known have been radicals of one sort or another."

"Can't you be radical and a Christian?" he asked.

"In our country the two don't seem to go together."

The kettle whistled as it came to the boil. Henry poured some hot water into the teapot, swirled it around and then poured it out into the sink. After that he added the tea – the leaves were green, pungent – to the pot, and filled it from the kettle. He carried the pot out into the sitting room. I carried a milk jug he had given me, and placed it on the table beside the teapot. We sat down on the wooden chairs.

"It was a promise I made to my mother," he explained, as we waited for the tea to brew. "She's a religious woman. She always insisted on taking me to Mass with her when I was a boy. When I was posted here she made me swear to continue the practice." He pointed to a photograph hung in an oval frame on the wall.   "That's my mother," he said.

I looked at the portrait; its sepia tints suggested it had not been taken recently. The face, proud and determined, was framed by a black shawl.

"It was done when I was a young boy. She is a lot older now, of course."

"And your father?" I asked.

"Retired," he replied. "What about your parents?"

"My mother died three years ago. My father is alive, but very unwell. I'd be surprised if he sees the year out."

"I'm sorry."

"We're not close," I told him.

We drank the tea. I took a ham sandwich. The bread was cut neatly into triangular shapes. The meat was fresh and delicious, but it made me think of the slaughterhouse, of the crimson stream.

"There weren't many people in church this morning," I commented.

"And what do you conclude from that?" he asked with a certain amused sparkle in his eye."

"Isabella told me that Cagot is a godless place, that the villagers are godless too."

"That's a bit of an exaggeration – Isabella has a jaundiced view of things. At Easter and at Christmas the church is full enough. But it's true that there are some in the village who feel that God has forsaken them."

"Forsaken? Why?"

"You mean you don't know?"

"Know what?"

"About the cave. About what happened eight years ago."

"No," I replied. "All I do know is that Isabella's husband died eight years ago and that there is a huge, crumbling hotel that houses only one guest – me."

"There was a time when the hotel was full," he said quietly, "a time when the village couldn't even really cope with the number of visitors. They were pilgrims. You see, a day's ride from here, up in the mountains near the border, there is a cave – or rather, there was a cave; you can't get into it now.

"The cave was in a remote place and the entrance was only visible from close by. That's why it wasn't discovered until nine years ago. A shepherd found it. There are plenty of other caves up there, and he would probably have passed it by without giving it a second thought, but a storm blew up, so he took shelter. The storm was violent. It rained and thundered and there were sporadic lightning flashes. The lightning lit up the inside of the cave and the shepherd saw that there were paintings on the walls.

"The shepherd returned the next day with an oil lamp to take a closer look. The paintings were done in black and red, and were mainly of animals – buffalo, deer, bears – the typical stuff you associate with prehistoric caves. The cave cut a long way into the mountain, but the shepherd was nervous, and didn't explore much beyond the entrance.

"We learned about the discovery when he came through the village on his way to lower pastures. No one was particularly interested – the villagers are an insular lot – except for Hubert Duval."

"Bernard introduced me to him in the inn at lunch time," I told him. "He seems to be an influential man."

"He is. He has no official title, because official titles don't exist in this part of the country anymore, but his grandfather was known as the Count, and he is still regarded as being of the aristocracy. He is the most powerful man in the village.

"Anyway, Hubert was interested in what the shepherd had seen, and decided to investigate further. He managed to get a party of men together, and paid the shepherd to take them back up to the cave.

"It was a bad time to go up the mountain. Many of the villagers baulked at the idea because the weather was beginning to turn. But Duval had the bit between his teeth. He had no intention of waiting until the following summer, and he made the men follow him, by force of will mainly. Money too, of course.

"The weather held. They made a thorough exploration of the cave. They found several more paintings. There were also a lot of stones on the cave floor that had been painted in red – miniature pictures of eyes and snakes and abstract symbols. I have one on the mantelpiece."

He stood up to show me. The pebble was rounded, cool and smooth to the touch. I turned it between my fingers, studying the red lines that spiralled around its grey surface. I handed it back to Henry. He returned it to the mantelpiece.

"They followed the cave deep into the mountain, as far as they could go," he continued. "The tunnel narrowed, so Duval told the others to wait for him and he went forward by himself. He was forced to crawl on his hands and knees until the passage opened out into a kind of alcove. There, at the cave's end, he discovered a natural hollow in the wall. The surprising thing was that this had been made into a shrine. There was a stone ledge, and on the ledge was a statue carved in black stone. It was a statue of the Virgin.

"There was room in the alcove for three people only. Duval went back and told the other members of the party what he had found. He then returned to the alcove, and stood there holding a light over the statue, while the men took it in turns, two at a time, to crawl along the passage and inspect the discovery. They all agreed that, in spite of its rather abstract nature, it was a representation of the Madonna, and not a prehistoric artefact. They all agreed that it was beautiful. They also said that it moved them spiritually, as if they were in the presence of something miraculous. They were rather vague about this because they didn't really seem to have the words to express themselves adequately."

"Not even Hubert?" I interrupted.

"He was the only one who didn't experience it. There were other things on his mind. He must have realised the potential the moment he set eyes on the carving. The others wanted to take the statue back with them, but Hubert objected, saying it would be sacrilegious to handle it. However, that wasn't his main concern. I think he must have dreamed up the idea of the pilgrimage the moment he saw the statue – that's the way his mind works. First of all, though, he needed official verification. So they rode back to the village – it's a full day's journey – and the day after that they went back up yet again, this time with the Priest in tow."

"The same Priest as now?" I asked.

"Yes, but remember this was eight years ago. The Priest was a younger, fitter man then. They made it to the cave, but this time the weather turned against them. They were trapped there for three days. Hubert had made sure that they had enough food for such a contingency, but the men could not overcome their anxiety. These are superstitious people; they don't always view nature rationally. The Priest saw the statue, and verified that it was indeed an image of the Virgin, although quite unlike any he had come across before. However, he came to feel, in those three days when they were cold and trapped inside the cave, that the statue should be left undisturbed. He had an uneasy feeling in his bones about it, as did some of the other men in the party. Hubert, as you might expect, was undeterred; later, in private, he was very dismissive of these "wimps and whingers" as he called them.

"On the fourth day the day the snow stopped, and they set off. It was a hazardous journey. They lost three of their horses, and one of the men broke his leg. That wasn't all; the people in the village had set up a rescue party; one of them lost his life when he slipped and fell down a crevasse.

"There were murmurings in the village. A meeting was convened in the Village Hall. Ironically, the meeting had been called to censure Duval, but, as Head of the Council, he took complete command. He apologised for the accidents and promised immediate compensation from his own purse – to me, the apology was perfunctory, the money given more as a bribe for their silence than out of remorseful generosity. It was something he needed to get out of the way before he outlined his scheme for making the village prosperous. He told them about the cave and the statue of the Virgin. He went on to outline how the cave could become an important pilgrimage centre. Then he described the economic benefits that this would bring to the village. He talked of a hotel, new shops, scores of new jobs. The man believed in his vision. He was very persuasive.

"There were a few dissenting voices. The Priest tried to explain how he had felt in the cave. Unfortunately, he has never been a very eloquent man; it was difficult for him to express his sense of foreboding. He was no match for Duval, who said the Priest and some of the other men had been frightened that they might not get out of the cave alive. Their reactions had been the result of over-active imaginations, a matter of emotional transference. 'How could the Madonna not be benign?' he asked.

"Someone else suggested that the influx of a large number of strangers would cause the character of the village to change for the worse. Duval disposed of that idea with contempt. 'What character?' he asked. 'Do you call this dullness, this poverty, character?'

"I had only just arrived in the village at the time and wasn't one of those who went up to the cave, but to me, after listening to Duval, the result was a foregone conclusion. There was a show of hands. The vote was virtually unanimous. I think everyone except for the Priest raised their hands in favour of the project.

"Hubert needed the Bishop of Rona to approve the project. The Bishop did more than that. When he was shown the photographs that Duval had had taken, he could hardly contain his enthusiasm. The Bishop is something of a scholar, an historian, and the Black Virgin, apparently, had a history behind it, going back to well before the Islamic invasions twelve centuries ago. Its origins are vague, but it's clear from 'The Chronicles' that it was a highly revered object, and was associated with a number of miracles. Scholars believed it had been destroyed by the Moslems, although this was never proved; there was always the possibility that it had been hidden in a safe place."

"And the Bishop believed that Hubert had rediscovered the original statue?"

"Sufficiently so, for him to take a very active role in promoting the pilgrimage."

"What about the Priest?" I asked. "Didn't he express his opposition to the Bishop?"

"As far as I know, he remained silent."

"And took to drink?"

"No, that came later. It has been said that Duval put pressure on him – of what kind, I don't know. Maybe the Priest had his own reasons for not creating controversy. Anyway, the news of the discovery spread; the photographs were circulated throughout the Province, and a central agency was set up to organise the first pilgrimages. The hotel was built that winter. People said that it couldn't be done, given the bad weather, the short days, the lack of skilled labour. Duval paid no heed. He brought the people he needed up from Rona, even from Esmée. The snow was cleared as quickly as it fell. He had floodlights rigged up, powered by a generator he paid for himself, so that the men could work through the night. The villagers themselves were unskilled; they did the hard labouring jobs, but he saw that they were well paid for it.

"In April, when the snow had gone from the valley – the cave was still inaccessible at that time, of course – all of the necessary furniture was brought up by road. I've never seen anything like it. It was like a strange pilgrimage in itself –

lorries laden with wardrobes, cupboards, chairs, tables, beds, snaking slowly in convoy up to the village.

"Duval went off to the capital, and returned with the managerial staff for the hotel. He poached them from some of the best hotels in the country. Again he ensured that the manual work should be done as far as possible by the villagers. They welcomed this; they hoped it would stop the flow of young people away to the towns and cities. And it probably would have done."

"Who owned the hotel?" I asked.

"Duval, of course! There were other backers, but we were never told who."

Henry continued the story. "The villagers also acted as guides and porters. Duval even set up a tent-making industry. The pilgrims had to spend at least one night on the mountain, and, as it turned out, there were often too many people to fit in the hotel, so they had to camp out in the fields and woods around the village. The women cut and sewed the fabric; the men made the support poles. A week before the pilgrimage was due to start, Duval sent men up to the cave to prepare the area.

"Duval thought of everything. The pilgrimage was a success. There were visions, healings, and the news spread. Then in August, when the pilgrimage was at its peak, tragedy struck. Remember, to get to the shrine you had to crawl along a narrow tunnel, and there was only space for three people at a time to look at the statue. Consequently, there was a large queue of people along the length of the cave, and outside the cave as well.

"No one is really sure what happened. Those outside the cave speak of hearing a rumbling noise and voices screaming in panic, but there are contradictory reports about which of these occurred first. Whatever, it seems that the mountain fractured internally. The cave simply ceased to exist. That was discovered when they rolled away the loose rocks blocking the entrance. There was no hollow beyond the rubble; it was just solid rock.

"Over four hundred people were killed, including several guides from the village. Isabella's husband was one of them. The village was dumb with disbelief. You see, they had always been a backward, fatalistic lot. Duval had galvanised them into action, made them feel proud, richer – and I don't mean that in just the materialistic sense. Many of them had blessed the Madonna for their good fortune, only adding to the myths that had accreted around the statue.

"Their belief in the Virgin and in themselves was destroyed in one blow. And there was worse; for a start, there was no way of getting to the bodies. As I said, rescue-workers were confronted by solid rock. No one had ever seen anything like it before.

"The Sunday after the disaster the church was packed with locals and with pilgrims. Pilgrims were still arriving, of course. Some didn't know what had happened, but others came to satisfy their morbid curiosity. Prayers were said for the dead. In the address that followed, the Priest found the eloquence that he had never been able to muster before, and has been incapable of since. Unfortunately, it wasn't what the people wanted to hear. He attacked the villagers, called them sinners everyone, called the incident an act of divine retribution because they'd abandoned themselves to Mammon.

"Then he attacked himself. He said that he had been opposed to the scheme. He reminded us how he had spoken out against it at the meeting, but after that he had remained silent in spite of his misgivings. He too had been open to corruption, he said, without being specific – and it's that that makes me think Duval had found some weakness to exploit in him.

"He said that the village would not revert to its former self, but to its original status – a place for the outcast that no one with any sense would want to visit – and every inhabitant would bear the guilt until his or her dying day.

"It was impressive rhetoric, and he spoke the truth in some respects. Ever since that time there has been an air of stagnation, of oppression about the valley."

"Symbolised by the hotel," I suggested.

"There were calls for it to be razed, but neither Duval nor the Priest would agree to it."

"Why not? Hubert, I can understand, but the Priest?"

"Who knows? Perhaps he wanted the building to stand as a perpetual reminder to the villagers. A symbol, as you said."

We had finished our tea. It was almost dark outside, even darker in the room. Henry got up and lit the lamps – he, too, was not connected to a generator. There was a rush of black smoke from the wicks as he applied the match.

"See," he said. "If it weren't for the statue of the Madonna, we would have had electricity by now."

"You believe in the Madonna's power, then?" I asked.

"No, but the Government has begun damming rivers for hydroelectric schemes, and other villages in the valleys parallel to this one have power. We haven't. The Government has turned its back on us, like the Priest said it would."

"What was that about the village's original status?" I asked. "I didn't understand."

"Cagot isn't a natural village," Henry explained. "It was founded in the middle of the eighteenth century as a leper colony. The powers-that-were chose it for its remoteness. They rounded up the lepers from all over Rona Province, transported them here and more or less left them to fend for themselves."

"Perhaps the place is cursed, after all," I commented.

"Perhaps," Henry responded quietly.

It was time for me to go. I stood up and thanked Henry for the tea. "It's been a very interesting afternoon," I said.

"Perhaps we can do it again some time," Henry suggested.

"But next time I will be the host," I insisted.

"I'll look forward to it," he replied.

Dusk was quickly eating up the light when I left the cottage and walked past the school. I had some time to kill before I had to register with Bernard, so I paused on the bridge across the river, resting my elbows on its wooden frame. The water rushed white below me, but most objects now were shapes of indistinct colour. On a boulder in the middle of the river, a grey wagtail – presumably the same bird as I had seen before – wagged its tail rhythmically up and down. I watched it hawk an insect before it flew off undulating downstream. Then I looked across to the hotel; it loomed up through the encroaching darkness, a shape only – no lights shone within – reminiscent, I thought, of a set for a cheap, American horror movie.

I walked to the road and headed towards the police station. As I passed the front of the hotel, I noticed that Isabella had again left a light shining in the lobby, the final ritual act of her day's work. I welcomed it; the prospect of returning to that large, empty building and stumbling blindly along its dark corridors to my room was not a pleasant one.

I went on through the village; it was cold, silent, deserted. The windows of the buildings were shuttered, so that little light extruded; there was no music; I heard no voices. It did seem a desultory, forsaken place.

I was glad when I reached Bernard's quarters. He was alone and this time greeted me affably. We went through the registration process. He invited me to sit down and have a brandy.

"Settling in okay?" he asked, as he poured a large measure into my glass.

"Fine," I answered. "I've just had tea with Henry. He told me a lot about the village."

"Good," Bernard said, and began arranging the chess pieces for the start of a game. "I suggested to him this morning that he might try to make you feel at home. Henry's intelligent and well-informed. And he's fond of telling stories. From the first, you struck me as someone who would want to know about things, so I thought to myself, 'Henry! Henry's the one to fill him in.' It stops you from pestering me, you see."

I laughed. "Does Henry always do as you suggest?"

The Police Chief looked up from the chessboard. The black and white pieces were now neatly arranged in their battle positions. "Henry is always glad to have someone interesting to talk to. He is an intelligent man. Sometimes, I wonder how he stands it here; he must find it even duller than I do," he said, not answering my question.

I drew black again, and Bernard began the game.

"I don't know," I said, as I matched his opening move of pawn to king four. "You seem happy enough to me."

"Do I?" he said, and laughed, moving his knight forward to king bishop three. "You should be wary of confusing appearance and reality."

I moved my queen knight to protect my pawn. "I don't," I said. "As a writer, I'm interested in the truth behind appearances. I imagine it's the same for a policeman."

"I prefer to think of it in terms of controlling reality," he said forcefully, before mellowing his tone. "In my job it's important to know how people will behave, how they will react under different circumstances."

"A bit like chess, you mean?"

"If you like."

He moved his bishop out to bishop four, and I did the same with my piece. He sipped his brandy.

"I'll give you an example. I used to work in Catronia – this was before the days of the Old Régime. It was a rough place for a policeman because the separatists were particularly active at the time and no Government official was safe from a terrorist attack. I saw friends shot before my eyes. I had to examine the maimed bodies of people blown up in their cars – it has an effect on you, you know, constantly looking death in the eye. It makes you harder, colder."

He paused to let his words sink in. I drank my brandy, saying nothing.

"There was a man there named Malvia."

"The name is familiar," I interrupted, remembering. "He was a turncoat."

"That's right, he was. But the interesting question is: how did we turn him? How did we manage to control a man like Malvia? Look at his record. He was a scourge of the Establishment when we were a democracy. He was an avowed socialist, a formidable speaker who occupied the moral high ground, so that when he denounced the bosses for their profiteering at the expense of the workers, people listened to him. When he attacked the Government for their corruption, people listened to him. And although he condemned the separatists for their violence, he attacked the Police and the Army just as aggressively.

"When the Military coup occurred, he made a forceful speech; he said the people of Catronia would never bow down to a dictatorship, that they would defend their towns and cities to the end. 'The last drop of blood.... Men, not insects.... Life without freedom is no life at all.' Those were the words he used. You know the rhetoric?"

"Of course," I said.

"Then the Military moved in. They were fully prepared for the resistance, and they made no compromises. The barricades set up by the workers were razed. Demonstrators were killed in their hundreds. One group shut themselves up in a factory, taking the manager with them as an hostage. The Military destroyed the factory. No one came out of the building alive."

"I know all of this," I said.

"And do you remember that Malvia suddenly capitulated? Initially he had urged attack; then he clamoured for restraint. He spoke on the radio, stating baldly that resistance was futile, that too much blood would be wasted. But of course you remember, don't you? You wrote a poem about it – what was it called?"

He waited for me to supply the title. I didn't. I simply said, "I can't remember."

"'Betrayal'. That was it," he said, correctly naming the title. "We all make propaganda, whichever side we are on. Malvia's change of heart was good propaganda for us. But it nearly didn't come about. The Military were unsubtle in those days, as you know. They had as much finesse as a lorry load of butchers. They wanted to kill Malvia along with the rest.

"I had a different idea. I persuaded the Catronian Head of Police to talk to the Military Commander – they were both from the capital; they had social and family ties – to let me try to bring Malvia over to our side. The Head of Police knew my capabilities. I was given the chance.

"I was ambitious. I cultivated people in those days. Malvia and I were on different sides of the fence, but we had had dealings; we respected each other. That's the first thing you need, respect – or fear. Then you need to know a man's weaknesses, to find his Achilles' heel. Every man is vulnerable somewhere. Once you know that, then you are in control.

"Malvia appeared strong, but he was easy. He was married, he had children – and I don't think that threatening them would have made much difference. Neither would have torturing him. Your poem makes him out to be a coward, but he wasn't a coward in the way you thought he was. However, he did have a moral flaw; you see, he had a passion for girls – fourteen and fifteen year old girls, sometimes even younger. In the Catronian capital, there was a place that catered for men with such needs. We allowed it to exist. It proved very useful.

"I personally showed Malvia the photographs. Malvia didn't want the world to know about his indiscretions, as is natural. He was a very vain man really, very ambitious – but weak in his soul. We came to an arrangement. He would announce his conversion, and the negatives would be destroyed. He was a lucky man. He went on to study Economics at the local university – after it had been purged, of course. Eventually he became a professor there, a man of mild, approved views. More brandy?"

I accepted. "Not every man would have behaved in the same way," I said, as Bernard refilled our glasses.

"No, but I knew Malvia would, and moulded the situation accordingly. I had a man in the union. It was he who introduced Malvia to that particular brothel in the first place."

Bernard reached down to the chessboard, and moved his pawn to queen knight four, which seemed to me to be a whimsical move. I couldn't see what he was up to. However, I accepted the gambit and took the pawn with my bishop.

He went on to easily defeat me. This time he knew all the permutations of the game he had chosen to play. When it came to his turn, he moved his pieces without hesitation, whereas I floundered, was indecisive.

I couldn't concentrate. From time to time I would glance at the photographs on the mantelpiece, scrutinising in particular the recent portrait of the Police Chief on his horse. The way he had spoken of Malvia confirmed the impression I had received from that photograph when I had first seen it. Bernard was a man fond of psychological games. Obviously he had talked as he had for a reason. I took it as a challenge and a warning, without really understanding what was intended. It was, I surmised, part of Bernard's opening game.

The thaw continued. Winter melted perceptibly into spring and for a few days the village was filled with the tinkling of sheep, as the shepherds paused to buy provisions on their journey up into the mountains. Migratory birds arrived from the continent to the south: chiffchaffs sang monotonously in the forests; wheatears flitted from stone to stone in the grassy area along the river, flashing their opulent white rumps; swallows and martins pursued insects over the fields, and, as the season advanced, swifts scythed across the evening sky.

Through my field glasses I watched men and women till and plant the terraced fields on the lower slopes of the valley. It was Henry who told me that the main crop was corn, that potatoes and tobacco were also grown.

Henry was a useful source of knowledge. I had learnt most of what there was to know about the village from him during my first few days of internal exile. I discovered for myself that there were no radios, no telephones, no newspapers.

"That's the way it is," Henry had responded, when I mentioned it to him. "It suits the Government and the villagers to keep it like that." He didn't explain why that was the case, and I didn't press him. At the time it suited me as well.

My life fell into a regular rhythm. At first I had intended to go on as I had begun – breakfast, the police station, the morning writing, lunch, afternoon exploration of the valleys to the east, dinner, the Police Chief's, the inn but it didn't work out like that. I suffered from writer's block. No new poems came to me; the blank pages stayed blank. After two weeks of frustration I gave in, and accepted that the Muse would come back of her own accord and not as a response to my conscious desire.

My sense of frustration was exacerbated by Isabella. We were at odds; her morbid religiosity, the way her daughter meekly succumbed to her will, oppressed me. I needed to be away from her, so I arranged for her to make me a packed lunch every day. After I had registered at the police station in the morning, I would head straight up one of the valleys with my sandwiches and a flask in a haversack on my back, my notebook in my jacket pocket, and my field glasses around my neck. I didn't return until late in the afternoon, in time for a bath before dinner.

I enjoyed my walks, my simple lunches in the open air. Often, after I had eaten, and if there were few birds to be seen, I would stretch out on some south-facing slope and doze in the sunshine. That time of day, however, when the sun was at its zenith, was good for birds of prey taking advantage of the rising thermals. I found one particular spot that looked out across the valley onto an area of vertical cliffs. Here, in spite of what Henry had said, there were usually vultures, eagles and kites soaring or hovering on the sultry air. This became my favourite place, and I spent hours in pleasant solitude sketching the raptors from my viewpoint across the valley.

I saw Henry regularly. We had tea together every Sunday, alternating between his cabin and my room (Isabella, it must be said, was very accommodating. She did all the preparation for me; for some reason, probably because he was a regular church-goer, she approved of Henry). Henry talked freely about the village and its inhabitants, and he also told me about himself.

He had been born in Rona, where his father had managed to scrape together a living by running a bookshop. The father was now retired and the bookshop was managed by Henry's younger brother. The shop had provided Henry with his own personal library, and his father made no fuss about his taking away the books to read as long as he returned them in good condition. His father, as Henry described him, was mild, unpretentious, self-effacing. His mother, as was evident from the photograph I had seen, was the dominant partner in the marriage. Encouraged, in their different ways, by his parents

Henry had done well at school; given his background it was not surprising he had become a Government-employed teacher.

He had been a schoolboy when the Military takeover occurred and the Old Régime was established. The coup had made little difference in this part of the country. Rona had always been a conservative provincial centre and the people took the political changes as a matter of course. Henry had spent the last nine years in Cagot, invariably returning to his family house in Rona during the school holidays.

It seemed to me a trammelled existence, because I believed that Henry had the potential to achieve so much more. I told him as much at one of our tea time tête-à-têtes after he had just returned from a fortnight's vacation in Rona. I remember it because it was a particularly beautiful day: the mountains were clear, now totally devoid of snow; the sky was a deep, pellucid blue. We were having tea on the balcony of my room to take full advantage of the late spring sunshine.

I forget quite how I gave expression to my sense that Henry was unnecessarily placing limitations upon himself, but he remonstrated with me immediately. "I'm happy doing what I'm doing," he said. "Isn't that enough?"

"But you told me you keep putting in for a transfer and you are always turned down," I argued, but only half-heartedly. The sun was warming my face, and that afternoon we had broken with habit by drinking a bottle of wine between us.

"It's a kind of annual ritual," he said. "It's true that I would prefer to be permanently based in Rona because both of my parents are getting older."

I momentarily gave a thought to how different my relationship with my parents had been.

"But I'm not too far away here," he continued. "Anyway, I think there's a good chance that I will be moved this year."

"Why?"

"Just a feeling," he replied vaguely.

"And you?" he said, turning the questions onto me, "Are you content here?"

"At the moment, yes, I suppose I am," I replied.

"And in general?"

"In general? Yes, as much I can be. But sometimes it does feel rather unreal, like being on a long holiday."

"That implies that you've got a life elsewhere to go back to. Have you? I mean, given the option. There's a sister, isn't there?"

"My sister married into a 'good' family," I said. "She will have nothing to do with me. So in the sense that you've got a life in Rona to go back to, then no I haven't.

"So you accept your position here?"

"I haven't got sufficient energy to resist."

"To be honest," Henry said, "I've never really understood why you were sent here in the first place."

"I'm a writer, a subversive."

"That's not strictly true, is it?"

"What? That I'm a writer – or a subversive?"

"The latter. When I was back in Rona, I found one of your books – 'Another Country' – in the bookshop. From what I understood of it, it seemed more like a renunciation, hardly a threat to the Government."

"That's what I told the Colonel. I told him that all I wanted was to be left alone, but that was unacceptable to him."

"He didn't believe you?"

"I'm not sure, but it's a moot point anyway. The thing is, the Colonel sees things differently. My being sent here has more to do with the past than with the present."

We were silent for a while; then Henry said casually, "Are you writing now?"

"No," I admitted. "I'm suffering from writer's block. Nothing will come to me. Perhaps that's why I'm starting to feel unsettled."

"But you're trying?"

"No, I've given up for the time being. Why all of these questions about my writing, Henry?" I asked. It was unusual for him to be quite so probing.

"Interest," he replied. "We are friends, after all, aren't we?" There was a hint of special pleading in this question, which put me slightly on my guard.

"Yes, we are," I answered, and smiled. Placated, he smiled in return.

I assumed that it was as a result of this profession of mutual friendship, which caused Henry to say, as he was on the point of leaving, "By the way, I know it's none of my business, but I think I ought to tell you that people in the village are beginning to gossip."

I didn't need to ask what the villagers were gossiping about.

"Let them gossip," I retorted, a little irritated.

He frowned at this, but didn't pursue the matter. He climbed over the balcony and dropped to the ground, looking more like a teenager than a man in his thirties. I liked Henry – he was good company – but as I watched him walk away across the grass and go over the bridge, I considered that, for all of his intelligence, there was something slightly naive, something disingenuous about him.

He said that he liked his work, yet, from what I had seen, he was ineffectual as a teacher. It was true that the situation militated against him. There was only one class in the school and Henry was the only teacher. There were over forty pupils in his class; the youngest student was five years old, the oldest student was eleven. How anyone could teach such a class successfully, I don't know, but I do know that discipline is an essential element. This, Henry didn't have; he was too mild with the children, so they did as they pleased. This had been evident on the occasions that I had walked by the school, and heard the unholy racket going on inside. I found it embarrassing, but Henry seemed to accept it as part of the natural course of things. And no one complained about the way their children were being educated. That was what it was like in the village.

The gossip that Henry had attempted to warn me about concerned Angela and myself. I had gone to the inn almost every evening on my way back to the hotel from Bernard's. The bar was usually quiet, and Angela and I spent a lot of time talking together. She was my other main source of information about the village and its residents. I had told her what Henry had told me about the cave. "He was surprised that I hadn't heard about it before," I said.

"I don't see why," she responded with exaggerated indignation. "The whole thing was hushed up."

"Surely you can't keep a thing like that quiet," I said.

"Not entirely," she agreed, "but there could have been a national scandal, and there wasn't – nowhere near it. The newspapers in Rona made little mention of it. In the capital, there was nothing. The relatives of the victims were compensated – blood money, I call it – then the village was cut off. That's when they set up the army post here. They wanted to pretend that the cave had never existed."

"What about the bodies?" I asked.

"Left there, in the mountain. Some kind of service was held up there for the dead, and that was that. Now no one talks about it. They feel it better to let the past rest," she said, mockingly echoing her husband's sentiments.

"It's funny though," she went on. "It was the Dark Virgin that brought me to the village. I told you that Philip's father and my father were business friends. Well, they decided between themselves that Philip and I would get married. Philip's father wanted to please Philip – you see, the boy doted on me; he couldn't help himself – but he also knew that his son hadn't got enough sense to manage the inn by himself once that he was dead or retired. And it's true, Philip isn't over-intelligent. He has absolutely no business sense. He's a good barman though, and the customers feel comfortable with him because he's a villager – one of them."

"And you?" I asked.

"I'm tolerated, but I'm an outsider. Anyone not born here is an outsider."

She continued her story. "It made business sense for my father as well, and he reckoned that I couldn't get up to much mischief in a village like Cagot."

The way she raised her eyebrows seemed to indicate that her father had been mistaken about the latter point.

"I wasn't interested and refused to commit myself, but then Hubert Duval came to visit my father. He brought Philip with him. I was called into the sitting room. I remember standing by my father's chair, looking at Philip. He was so embarrassed that he couldn't look at me. Not like Hubert, who stared at me so hard that I had to turn my eyes away. He explained that he had come on Philip's father's behalf – the man was sick; he wasn't well enough to make the journey because of the weather – to ask that I accept Philip as my husband. I blushed, and was about to open my mouth, but Hubert went on speaking. He said that he personally approved of the match. It would make the inn more youthful, more appealing, he said, and that was necessary because the village was going to change. He told us about the statue, and said he had spoken to the Bishop and the Governor, who had given approval for his plans. He said that the village, and the inn with it, would become prosperous."

"Did you know Hubert before this?" I asked.

"Yes," she said, and quickly continued her story." As a brewer, my father saw that the marriage would be to his own advantage, especially when Hubert mentioned that Philip's father wished to retire and intended to turn the management of the inn over to Philip once he was securely married. So I told Hubert I would think about it.

"He would have none of that. He said that they were returning to Cagot after the interview; he wanted an immediate answer.

"It was then that Philip turned his head and looked at me a bit like a lost sheep. It made me want to laugh, but I didn't. Instead, I decided to reject the proposal. I opened my mouth to say no, looked straight at Hubert – and said, 'Yes.' I couldn't help myself. A month later Philip and I were husband and wife, and I was manageress of this inn.

"It was winter by then. It was really bleak and cold, and I would have regretted my decision, but the village – can you imagine it? – was a lot more lively than Rona. In fact, there were quite a few people I knew from Rona up here working on the hotel.

"Hubert was in command – like a General overseeing an army. He took an interest in Philip and me. He was good to us.

He gave us money so that we could repaint the inn and buy some new tables and chairs.

"The inn was busy. I was busy – which made me happy, and as I said, it was me who ran the place. I still do, of course, not as though there's much to run these days. In May the pilgrims began arriving. The village could hardly cope. We even had people sleeping overnight on the floor of the inn. Then you know what happened; it all came to an end. And here we are now – a few soldiers playing darts, a few old men, me, you and Philip."

"Why didn't you leave?" I asked her.

"I don't know," she said; then added as if in explanation, "The villagers here have a saying: 'Once live in Cagot, never leave Cagot'. Maybe it's true."

"Maybe," I said.

That conversation took place in the early days, when Angela and I were friends only. As the weeks passed, and the sun warmed the land, the attraction grew stronger. She was interested in what I did during the day, but couldn't really take me seriously when I talked about my bird watching. I told her about my special place on the hillside where I sat quietly observing the vultures circling above the cliff-face on the opposite side of the valley, or simply dozed in the sun.

"I don't believe you," she remonstrated good-humouredly. "I believe you have a lover. I will have to come with you one day just to make sure."

I thought nothing more about this until one evening she announced, "Philip has agreed to let me have the afternoon off tomorrow, so that I can go hiking with you – to your secret place. You can show me the vultures and eagles you talk about so much."

"You're teasing me," I said.

"No," she replied and looked me straight in the eye.

"And Philip?"

"Oh, he can't do too much damage in a day."

"No. I mean I wouldn't want to ..."

"Philip!" she shouted, bringing him across to us from the vicinity of the till, brandy glass in hand. "Our poet friend here doesn't believe you've given me permission to go walking with him."

"Well, he's ... wrong then isn't ... he?" he said, in his habitual disjointed way, and then, addressing me in a rush of words, "I think it will do her good." He stopped, seemingly surprised at his sudden fluency.

So the following morning found me walking up the north-eastern valley with Angela. I was self-conscious with her beside me, aware that the greetings of the farmers we passed had a different intonation from usual – they had a knowing, suggestive ring to them. Angela feigned not to notice and greeted everyone with cheerful familiarity. She wore a red and white check shirt, a loose red skirt that fell to just below her knees, short socks and stout walking shoes. The small rucksack on her back that I had advised her to bring was also red. The colour suited her, went with her olive skin and her brazen personality. Her usual golden ear rings dangled from her lobes. The gypsy element again, I thought.

The track we were on was wide enough for the two of us. We walked side by side, and climbed steadily up above the river; then followed a ridge through the interior of a pine forest. It was dark, enclosed, and the smell of resin was powerful. There were few birds.

"This is eerie," Angela said, as if she had never been in such a forest before, and she turned to me in fright when a bird as big as a turkey suddenly burst into flight and clattered low above the undergrowth.

"A capercaillie," I told her. "It's a kind of game bird."

We descended the ridge and the forest opened out. The track met the river again. I pointed out a dipper that was feeding midstream.

"You really are interested in birds, aren't you?" Angela said in a manner that suggested she had actually doubted me.

The side of the valley we were on gradually became rockier. There were loose boulders scattered around the grassy slopes; then the slope itself became craggy, precipitous. The other side of the valley, however, was less eroded, and was forested half way up.

"We have to cross the river," I said.

At this point the river widened and was fairly shallow. There was one particular spot where the stones that lay on the bed protruded above the water's surface and were close enough together for a person to step from one to the other. I went across first. Angela followed, but lost her footing on a wet stone; both of her feet slid into the cold, mountain water. She held onto the rocks, and managed to haul herself back up again.

"The water's icy," she said, a little breathlessly, once she had gained the bank.

"It's not far from here," I said, pointing up the hill. "You can take your socks and boots off when we get there and they'll dry in the sun."

"My skirt got wet as well," she said.

It was a scramble up the hill to where the forest started. We followed the edge of the conifers along the hillside to the vantage point – a slab of rock with a flat, even surface that was embedded securely into the grassy incline. This platform gave an uninterrupted perspective of the cliff face, now ochre-coloured in the midday sun, that took up the whole of the valley side opposite.

"The Poet's throne," Angela said jokingly.

I went off amongst the trees to relieve myself. When I came back, Angela was lying down with her head and back on the grass, her legs stretched out on the warm slab. Her boots and socks were drying beside her on the rock. She had pulled her skirt up to her thighs to expose the whole length of her legs to the sun. Her eyes were closed.

"It's good here," she said, sensing me standing over her, without opening her eyes.

I placed my haversack and field glasses on the grass; then sat down next to her on the rock. I ran my hand down her right leg from the thigh to the knee, gently stroking the smooth, warm flesh; then ran my hand back up again. I felt her tremble slightly, as she moved her legs apart. I continued to stroke her, and felt her moisten through the fabric of her underwear.

We undressed and moved away from the rock onto a level area of grass just above it. The grass was coarse; it grazed our skin as we made love to each other. Afterwards we lay together, scarcely touching, exposed to the naked blue sky. A griffon vulture gliding across the valley flew directly overhead, briefly darkening our bodies with its shadow.

"I told you there were vultures," I said.

"I hope it doesn't think we're dead," she commented.

"There's no chance of that," I replied.

Our affair went on from there, so that it too took on a ritualistic quality: the long walk, the lovemaking above the Poet's Throne, as Angela called it, every Thursday. Philip didn't seem to mind; indeed he welcomed Angela's weekly excursion. "It's unhealthy ... being cooped ... up behind a bar from ... morning to night," was how he rationalised it to himself. He seemed happy in his ignorance. My own feelings were ambivalent. Angela had a wild, reckless side to her nature. She was the kind of woman that fascinated men – but from a distance. Close to, they saw her potential for domination. It was she who was the driving force in our relationship. She decided that Thursdays would suit her for our walk; if she couldn't make it – and there were times when she couldn't – she would only let me know at the last moment, leaving me feeling a little like the boy who knocks on his friend's door, only to be told that his friend can't come out to play because ...

She was also unpredictable. Once I was awakened at two o'clock in the morning by a rattling at the French windows. There was a full moon, so I had no need to light the lamps; the night seemed strangely luminous; the furniture was sharply outlined under the lunar glow. When I opened the windows – knowing who it was – the first thing I noticed wasn't Angela in particular, but the shadowy peaks of the mountains etched against a slightly paler sky.

"I had to come," she said." I know it's stupid and dangerous, but ..."

"Woman wailing for her demon lover," I quoted in English, aware, in my sleepy state, of the romantic absurdity of the situation.

"What?" she murmured, not understanding.

"It doesn't matter," I said. In truth, she was the demonic one. She looked wild, like someone compelled by forces beyond her control. She had draped a dark coat around her, but it had fallen open to reveal a long, white nightdress that made her appear virginal. She was barefoot and she was breathing quickly, audibly. I could smell the brandy on her breath.

She entered the sitting room, saw, in the moonlight, the open bedroom door and the bedraggled sheets on the bed inside, and went through without hesitation. By the time I had locked the windows behind her and followed her, she was lying naked on top of the sheets, her legs unashamedly raised and splayed.

"It's all right," she said, slurring her words a little. "Philip is asleep. He sleeps like an ox. But I couldn't sleep."

No other woman in my life had aroused me like Angela could arouse me. She was a sensualist, who abandoned herself totally to the pleasures of the moment. That night I didn't know who I was, I didn't know who she was, and I didn't care. But after she had gone, before dawn light had begun to creep into the room, as I smelled her lingering scent on my fingers, tasted it in my mouth, I felt strangely unfulfilled, not quite human somehow, and I longed for the reality of the sunrise.

It was not long after this night that Henry had told me about the gossipmongers. I had heard nothing directly myself, which I suppose was to be expected, but the fact that Isabella had become even surlier of late – she rarely spoke to me now – gave me some indication of what was going on. One evening, I mentioned it to Angela.

"Let them talk," she retorted vehemently. "People here have nothing better to do. I spit on them."

And she literally spat on the ground.

She only came to my room on one more occasion, however, and that was to look at my poems, not to make love to me.

"I want to see if you have written about me," was the reason she gave, when she made her request in the inn one evening.

"I'm sorry to disappoint you, but I haven't," I said in response. "I haven't written anything new since I arrived in Cagot."

"I am disappointed," she joked flirtatiously. "Don't I inspire you?"

"Not to words," I said.

"But I would still like to see some of your poems. Can I?"

I agreed, but still found her desire unusual, for, whatever else Angela may have been, she certainly wasn't a reader of literature.

"Bring them to the inn tomorrow evening," she said.

"No," I replied. "If you want to see them, you'll have to come to the hotel."

She laughed. "So I have to pay for the privilege?" she said.

"Not at all. The poems are private – at the moment, anyway – and I prefer to keep it like that."

"I'll come tonight then – as soon as I can get away."

She knocked on the French windows just after one o'clock. She was fully clothed. She kissed me briefly, making it obvious that on this occasion she was fully in control of her faculties.

"The poems?" she asked.

I pointed to the notebook on the desk that was illuminated by an oil lamp.

"I can't stay long," she said. "Philip is restless tonight, and he might wake up and miss me."

"I thought he slept like an ox," I said.

"He normally does, but every now and then he suffers from migraine. He has taken something to help him sleep, but it isn't always effective. He sometimes wakes up with the pain."

She said this as she leafed through 'Poems of Love and Death', from 'Absence' onwards, scarcely glancing at the words. When she came to 'Shearwaters', and saw that it was the final poem, she paused and examined the verse more carefully. "What are shearwaters?" she asked.

"Seabirds," I told her, and reached my field-guide down from the shelf. I turned to the second plate. There in black and white were the birds of the ocean – gannet, fulmar, petrels, and the four species of shearwater that occurred in Europe. I pointed to the illustration of the Balearic shearwater.

She read the poem, although with what degree of understanding I can't say. She then flicked back through the notebook, and dipped into poems at random. Some she read quickly; others, especially the early love poems and the erotic poems, she studied more deeply.

"Do you have a picture of your wife?" she asked.

Like the poems, the photograph I had of Maria – the one that the thin man had allowed me to keep – was personal to me. I kept it in the drawer of the desk. I told Angela where it was. She opened the drawer and took out the picture, holding it close to the light so that she could see Maria's face more clearly.

"She is very pretty," she said.

"Yes, she was," I agreed simply.

Angela put the photograph back in the drawer. "I must go back now," she said, and gave me a chaste kiss before leaving.

So that night, only the second time she had come to my room, we didn't make love. The fact that she was unusually subdued made me wonder, after she had gone, if it presaged the end of our affair. It didn't. Our Thursday walks continued as before. We made love as usual on the grass that now bore the imprint of our bodies above the Poet's Throne.

However, there was a change. Angela began to show more interest in me, particularly where my past was concerned, and during that summer I told her a great deal about myself, especially about my relationship with Maria.

"Where did you live when you got married," she asked me after I had told her how Maria and I had met.

We were walking back to Cagot, and were in the forest where she had been frightened by the capercaillie on our first walk. Now she thought nothing of the silent trees that excluded the light, made no mention of their 'eerie' nature. They had become familiar to her.

"Did you stay by the sea?"

"No," I said. "Maria would have liked to, but I needed a job. We lived in London. Maria had a flat there. It was small, but adequate. Fortunately Maria knew people who knew people, and I got a job on a magazine, writing about this and that – pedestrian stuff really, but it helped to pay the bills."

"What about your poetry? You said you'd finished the book."

"That was published – but poetry's an act of love; you can't live off of it."

We walked on in silence, and I remembered those early days in London. They had not been easy, for Maria's reticence to get involved with me had stemmed from the fact that she already had a lover, a man who had been part of her life for two years. As it happened, the relationship had turned sour, was nearly at an end; my involvement only hastened the inevitable. The man, however, had refused to quit gracefully. There had been scenes, recriminations, embarrassing appeals for Maria to change her mind and return to him. Only when we were married in the December of that year did he accept the situation and disappear from our lives for good.

On another occasion, after we had emerged from the forest, and were following the river back down the valley, Angela asked me why I had come back. "You'd been away so long," she said. "You had another life." Implicit in her remark was the notion that she herself would never have returned.

"I didn't choose to live abroad," I explained. "I couldn't have come back earlier, because I would have been imprisoned – or killed. There were a lot of us exiles, and it looked as though we'd got on, established ourselves abroad, settled down – but for most of us that was appearance only. It was superficial. Our country is in our blood. Most of us always wanted to return; we were just waiting for the opportunity.

"So when the amnesty was declared, we took full advantage of it. We wanted to be part of the reforms and help to reshape the country. Surprising, really, how we still had ideals – and how naive we were, in spite of everything."

"We saw no reforms in the village," Angela said. "Nothing changed at all in those two years."

"I don't understand you," I said. "If you're so discontented, why don't you go? It still puzzles me why you didn't leave after the cave collapsed."

"There was no one to take me away," she said, and laughed at herself. "No, it's true my marriage to Philip was a business arrangement. I was greedy. Hubert persuaded me I would be rich; I believed him. Who knows, perhaps I would have been if God hadn't played that trick on us."

"So?"

"So here I am my own mistress. I control the inn. I come here with you because I choose to do so. I might not have that freedom in another place."

"Suppose Philip suddenly said that you couldn't come with me any more?"

"He wouldn't do that," she replied decisively. "You see, Philip is – not quite like a child, but a little – strange, a little simple. There are a few people like that in the village – not totally daft like the three parrots. But still ..."

"The what?" I interrupted.

"The three boys who sit together on the wall outside the inn. That's what they're known as. Philip's not like them, but he isn't totally normal either."

I was curious. "Do you and he ...?"

"He's my husband. I like to keep him happy, and I do."

"I'm sure you do," I said. "But doesn't he get jealous? Doesn't he suspect that we're lovers?"

"Philip is an innocent," she said, and added," It's a pity that all the villagers aren't like that."

Philip's innocence suited Angela, but in itself innocence was not a virtue that Angela greatly admired. I had noticed since my arrival in the village that there was a certain tension in the way that Angela and Henry related to one another. She often teased him about his sexuality, or rather lack of it. At first I had paid little attention to this, thinking that Angela was being merely playful, but throughout the summer the tone of the innuendos had gradually changed. She began to call him 'The Innocent', twisting her mouth mockingly around the syllables whenever she pronounced the words. It was the brandy that reduced her to momentary ugliness.

Henry continued to come into the inn on Saturday nights, and as with the soldiers at the dartboard, it was on Saturday that Angela chose to get deliberately drunk. I suppose it was her way of achieving a kind of catharsis, and at times her provocative speeches were amusing enough, but too often they turned bitter. It was Henry who bore the brunt of that bitterness.

I had reproached her about this in private, but she laughed and said Henry could take care of himself, couldn't he? Henry didn't seem unduly perturbed by Angela's behaviour. Occasionally, he showed signs of embarrassment, but it seemed to me that, for the most part, he allowed her words to wash over him.

I was wrong about the depth of Henry's response. I discovered his true feelings late one Saturday night at the beginning of July. I was sitting at the bar next to Henry. Angela was serving two soldiers who were drunk and chafing at the bit.

"You're enjoying yourselves tonight, aren't you boys?" Angela said. She too, as usual, had had too many brandies.

"It's no fun without a woman," one of them complained.

"Oh, I don't know," she said. "Take Henry here; he's lived in the village for nine years now, and I've never once heard of him having a woman. But he's happy enough. He never gets drunk."

Henry replied dryly, "I'm discreet," stressing the subject pronoun to imply that she wasn't.

"Very!" she replied tartly.

Angela had never taunted him so savagely before, like that in front of others; normally she confined her remarks to Henry and myself. The soldiers were embarrassed and moved away towards the dartboard. Henry finished his drink in silence and left. I went with him. I was annoyed with Angela, but I was also annoyed with Henry because he hadn't retaliated, merely sulked.

"She gets worse," Henry said when we were outside, walking away from the inn. In the summer twilight I could see that he was seething with frustration and, I thought, on the verge of tears. He began to speak, "She tried to seduce me once, you know – but she's not the sort of woman I ..."

"Quite," I interrupted him sharply.

We stopped outside the hotel.

"I think I should tell you," he began, "for your own good. Angela has a reputation."

"I don't doubt it," I replied.

"They say she has been with Duval, with Bernard ..."

"With the Priest," I suggested sarcastically.

"No," he replied in all seriousness. "But your name has been added to the list."

"Goodnight, Henry," I said firmly. I didn't want to hear any more.

"Look, I'm so..."

"Forget it Henry," I said. "Go home. Please."

I turned my back on him, and entered the hotel. In my room I smoked a cigarette and drank some brandy. I recognised the anger in myself, knew that it was directed mainly at Henry, although he was the one who had been wronged. His revelations – his means of achieving some sort of revenge rather than through concern for me – had been spiteful and immature. He was a man with limited defences. I also had to admit to myself that the idea of Angela being the village whore had stung me. Well, not quite the village whore, my thoughts mocked me; it appeared that she only did it with the people who mattered – if I were to believe Henry.

I asked Angela about it on the following Thursday, after we had made love above the 'Poet's Throne'. She was lying on her back with her eyes closed. I was leaning on my elbow, casually teasing her with a blade of grass. I ran it round the convex curve of her left breast; then gently stroked the dark areola and nipple.

"Henry told me that you tried to seduce him once, but he refused. I don't know how he could," I said.

She opened her eyes. I saw myself reflected in her emerald irides. "Henry isn't a man. He doesn't have a man's feelings," she said.

"You mean he's a homosexual?" I asked.

"I mean he is nothing, a neuter. What else did he tell you?"

"That you've slept with Hubert and Bernard."

"Henry talks a lot," she said.

"Yes, he does. But it was you who caused him to tell me all of this."

"Henry asks to be treated badly, don't you think?" she said unapologetically.

"No, I don't," I replied, considering, as I spoke, that perhaps she had a point.

She stood up and began putting on her clothes. "Well?" she said, buttoning up her shirt. "Aren't you going to ask me?"

"Ask you what?"

"If it's true what Henry said?"

"Would you answer if I did?"

"No," she said, and gave a brief laugh.

"Then there's no point in my asking, is there?" I said.

I stood up and dressed. We gathered our belongings and set off back to the village. And I thought that I had no need to ask the question anyway, as I already knew the answer, and Angela knew that I knew. It was a simple matter; if I wanted the woman I had to take her as I found her. And, for the time being at least, I wanted her.

THE BORDER

As spring blossomed into summer, Bernard coerced me into playing chess with him far more regularly. He had taken my measure and usually defeated me; occasionally he allowed me to win. His moods during this period were variable; sometimes he was ebullient, other times he could be silent and dismissive.

More than this, however, was his watchfulness. As the weeks passed, I grew more conscious of the fact that he was observing me, looking for signs of any change in my psychological make-up.

Fortunately Bernard was away for the best part of June and July. The trip was part vacation, part official business, he had told me, before he had left without supplying any further details. He didn't, however, look renewed after his absence. The creases on his forehead were more prominent, and he seemed less prone to spontaneous laughter. He was a preoccupied man.

He had not returned to the village alone. Duval, who had been absent since April, reappeared at the same time. The engineer came with him. I had learnt of the imminent arrival of the engineer a week beforehand, when Isabella and her melancholic daughter suddenly became erratic in their punctuality. Breakfast might be early or late, dinner likewise. At first I thought they were punishing me for my relationship with Angela, but Isabella was apologetic when I complained.

It materialised that not only was she in charge of the hotel, she was also the keeper of the Government Rest house across the road.

"It hasn't been used for two years," she explained, "and I've got a week to get it ready. The engineer's coming!"

"Why can't he stay in the hotel?" I asked.

"Oh, that wouldn't do," she said simply, and left it at that, as if it was sufficient explanation. "I'm so busy," she continued. "It's so damp for a start. And we can't get the generator to work."

"The building has its own generator?" I exclaimed. "And here we ..."

Isabella shrugged. There was nothing she could do about it. Everyone knew that the engineer was coming to the village – they had known since the winter – but no one officially knew why. The visit had apparently been arranged by Hubert Duval. Because of this it was rumoured that they were going to see if they could get inside the cave of the Dark Virgin. The rumour quickly took on the status of truth.

It was a controversial issue. Firstly, it wasn't known what Hubert's motives were for the putative excavation. Some said that Duval wanted to make amends by providing the dead victims with a proper Christian burial. Others were more suspicious; they whispered that it was the statue he wanted, and he didn't give a fig about the crushed bodies. Secondly, there were those who believed that it didn't matter what Duval's motives were – it would be a sacrilege to disturb the dead after so many years. Some who expressed this view were afraid that further trespass might bring even more disaster. They were afraid of the Madonna's power. Finally, there was a small group who doubted that the cave was the reason for the engineers visit in the first place. They argued that the man was a Government servant, and the Government had no reason to be interested in the cave; they suspected that, as in parallel valleys, the Government might, at last, have ideas of implementing a hydro-electric scheme.

I learned of these opinions from Henry – our friendship had persisted, albeit tenuously – and from conversations overheard or shared in the inn; the latter tended to increase in frequency in the week before the man's arrival.

Bernard and the engineer arrived at lunchtime on the feast day of St Mary Magdalene. They went straight to the inn. "It's always the same," Angela told me later that evening – I had been up the valley as usual at the time – "Whenever anyone new arrives, Bernard takes them straight to the inn and makes them drink brandy with Philip and himself. It's a kind of test."

"And did the man pass or fail?" I asked.

"He isn't a drinker," she said and smiled. "He wouldn't even accept the brandy. A small glass of white wine was his limit."

"So he didn't get anywhere near drunk enough for you to ask him why he was here?" I teased her.

"No, but I asked him anyway. Bernard wouldn't let him answer – you know how he is, jolly when it suits him." Then she mocked him, copying his hand gestures, mimicking the inflexions of his voice: "Don't pester the man, Angela. Let him enjoy himself. Show him how hospitable you can be." – Here she gave a lascivious wink. – "Make him feel at home."

I laughed. The voice was wrong, but she had successfully captured Bernard's s mannerisms.

I didn't actually see Bernard on the day of his return. Before visiting the inn, I had registered with his Second-in-Command as I had done for the preceding seven weeks. Bernard was there the following morning though, having resumed control and relegated his subordinate back to his usual seat in an adjoining annexe.

He shook my hand, asked me how I was. I asked about his holiday. Our conversation was polite, but mechanical. Bernard's thoughts seemed to be elsewhere. We filled in the details in the register as usual.

"I have something to give you," he said; then handed me an envelope with my name written in a flowing hand on the front. "It's all right, you can open it. Hubert Duval is having a small dinner party this evening – nothing very formal – and he asked me to pass the invitation on to you. I assume you'll accept."

"Yes," I said, trying to contain my surprise.

"It will give you a chance to meet our engineer," he said. "An eccentric fellow – he doesn't drink – but an expert in his field. Now if you'll excuse me, I've a lot of work to catch up with. It's always the same when I go away; nothing gets done around here, so I have three times as much work to do when I get back."

I left him alone, and set off up the valley with my rucksack and field glasses. It was a Thursday, but Angela had said she couldn't come – she didn't say why. She hadn't missed one of our excursions for a month, and her presence had become important to me. I admit that this was mainly for sexual reasons; I loved the malleability of her body, the complete lack of self-consciousness in the way she undressed and made love to me under the blue sky. I had come to need that weekly release.

So I spent the day alone and frustrated. I took the first track where the river divided instead of the second, not wishing to remind myself of what I was missing. This valley was not as varied as the other. There were no exposed cliffs, no places where the path took the walker away from the river. There was the river, the track and the forested hillsides, the same for kilometres and kilometres. True, the forests along this valley were good for birds, better, for some reason, than the forests in the other valley. There were lots of woodpeckers here, including the large black woodpecker with its crown the colour of blood; there were eagle owls as well. But this Thursday at the end of July the woods were quiet, and I was dissatisfied when I returned to the hotel to get ready for the evening at Hubert's.

The invitation was for seven o'clock, the time I normally registered. "Don't worry. I'll bring the logbook to Hubert's," Bernard had said. "We can do it as soon as you arrive."

I put on a jacket and tie. As I was leaving the hotel I met Henry who was also dressed more formally than usual. "Are you going where I'm going?" he asked while we were crossing the street.

"It looks like it," I said; then, as we were outside the inn, asked, "Why don't we have a drink first?"

"We'll be late if we do," Henry said as a statement of fact.

"I know," I said, and stopped.

Henry hesitated; then sighed before giving an ironic smile. "You haven't got much respect for authority, have you?"

"Is Hubert Duval authority, then?" I said quickly before adding, "No, I haven't. I don't trust authority."

"Why not?" Henry asked.

"It's just the way I am," I replied. "Are we having that drink or not?"

"Okay," he agreed. "A quick one!"

Philip was behind the bar. "You ... both look ... smart tonight," he said, his speech more dislocated than usual. "Going ... to ... Duval's house?"

"Yes," Henry replied, and ordered two beers.

"Isn't it possible to do anything in this village, without everyone knowing about it?" I said to Henry, a shade impatiently while Philip pulled on the handle of the cask.

"No," he answered flatly.

The beer came cool and strong. "I wonder where Angela is tonight?" I said, once Philip had moved away to serve another customer.

"Duval's," Henry said.

"What? As a guest?" I expressed my surprise.

"No. Duval likes to have beautiful women to wait upon the table for him. He doesn't entertain very often, but when he does Angela usually helps out."

"I didn't know," I said.

We drank our beer and left the inn, heading uphill, into the forest. Although it had been a hot day, there was now a chill in the air. The smell of the pines was heavy, potent.

There was a guard at the entrance to the grounds of Hubert's house. He was unfamiliar to me, to Henry as well. I had forgotten to carry my invitation. Henry had his and was permitted to enter. I was only allowed through once the guard had radioed the house from his security booth and confirmed that I was expected.

"Does he get many gatecrashers?" I asked sarcastically, as we walked up the long drive towards the mansion.

Henry gave a subdued laugh. "I wouldn't know. I think I've been to this house three times in nine years. Of course, Duval is very rarely here; he spends most of his time abroad."

"I haven't seen him since the first week I arrived here." I said. "What does he do?"

"He's a businessman, although what business is anybody's guess. He also has a reputation as being a gambler, a bit of a playboy."

We arrived at the house, which was less imposing close to than from a distance. It was a matter of detail. The flower beds that fronted the building were ill-kept, strangled by weeds. The stone walls were cracked and weathered. The wooden window frames appeared warped, discoloured by damp; the windows themselves were smudged with dirt. We walked under the porte-cochere with its grand, mock-Corinthian columns, themselves worn yellow with age, and entered the house proper.

There was no one to greet us, so we followed the sound of voices to a large drawing room. Various portraits in oil hung on three of the walls. I assumed they were Duval's ancestors. A skinned and gutted bear, its face downwards, its legs sprawled, took up most of the fourth wall.

"Ah here you are," Duval said, and stepped over to us. He shook hands with Henry. "Bernard was beginning to think that you weren't coming."

"We're sorry," Henry said, over-apologetically. "We got delayed."

I said, "Good evening," as Duval took my hand in his. His palm and fingers were moist from the glass of wine he had been holding.

"Come along," he said. "Let me introduce you to the others."

We walked over to where Bernard was standing with two other men. They were introduced to us as Professor Hermann, the engineer, and his assistant, Sebastian. Henry was introduced as the schoolteacher; I was the poet.

"If you will excuse us for a moment, gentlemen," Bernard said, indicating with a gesture of his head that the pronoun included me, "we have a little private business to get out of the way before we carry on."

"Do we?" I asked.

"Of course," he said, with a smile. "I left the book on the table in the hallway."

As I was following him out of the room, I heard Hubert begin to explain to the newcomers: "Our poet friend is a guest of the Government, if you under..."

"I don't believe this," I hissed at Bernard, as he opened the book and took a pen out of his pocket.

"Don't believe what?" Bernard said innocently as he handed me the pen.

"You are treating me like a child," I rebuked him angrily, but quietly.

Bernard assumed a look of offended puzzlement. "You're over-reacting," he said. "I have to do this. It's a necessary part of my job."

"What is?" I asked meaningfully, and stared him straight in the face.

"To see the book is signed every day," he replied. "What else?"

"To ..." Then I stopped myself. I realised that I was being deliberately manipulated, and I was responding in the way he had intended.

I decided to change tack. "I'm sorry," I said. "I'm a little tired this evening. Let me sign the book."

We returned to the drawing room where Hubert asked me what I would like to drink. I asked for a large Scotch with ice, which was what the assistant, Sebastian, was drinking. The engineer himself was holding a glass of white wine, but rarely drinking from it. When he did so, he raised it to his lips and took the slightest sip. Bernard had called the man eccentric, and he certainly looked the part. He was short and very thin; his rounded spectacles and his wispy beard gave him the appearance of an intellectual goat. He wore baggy tweed trousers and a baggy tweed jacket. A tweed waistcoat added to his anachronistic appearance.

Once I had received my whisky, and taken a much needed swig, the engineer spoke to me. His voice was quiet, refined. "What kind of poems do you write?" he asked.

"I suppose you could say I'm a romantic," I said, a little tongue in cheek. "I write about the grand themes – love and death."

"That hardly seems a good enough reason for sending you here," the engineer said, thinking aloud more than making conversation.

"He also writes political poems," Bernard said by way of an explanation.

"I see," the engineer said.

"That's no longer true," I said. "I used to write political poems, but that was in the days of the Old Régime."

"It's pretty damning stuff, though," Hubert Duval interrupted with his opinion. "I mean the title of your book, 'Blood on Their Hands' is sufficiently ..."

"It was called 'Poems From Exile'," I said.

"In this country, but not abroad," Bernard added, addressing the engineer.

"I didn't want the book to be published here," I explained, "but I had no choice."

"I don't understand," the engineer's assistant said.

"I wrote the poems abroad," I said. "I was an exile. I came back when the Old Régime collapsed. The poems were published then – the volume Hubert referred to, and one I wrote later called 'Another Country'. You have to read the second book."

"It puts the first in perspective," Henry interjected unnecessarily.

"In what way?" the assistant asked.

"It disowns the sentiments of the first," Henry, my self-appointed defender, answered the question.

"That's just the point," Hubert argued. "I don't think it does." Then he turned to me directly. I finished my whisky in one gulp. The ice tinkled in the glass. "You say you no longer like the poems in 'Blood On Their Hands' – what did you call them in 'Another Country'? – 'fictions in the dark', wasn't it? – because they were written in bad faith. You imply you wrote them to become famous, which may be true, but nowhere do you disown the politics behind them. The poems are subversive; they are anti-Church and anti-State, and as such seem to be a fair representation of your views."

To give Hubert his due, this attack on my art and my politics was done in a rational, disinterested manner. "I'm flattered that you've taken the time to consider my work in such detail," I said in response, trying to conceal my puzzlement at what this conversation meant, trying to recall how it had started. "But I would question that you know what my present views are. After all, I have been silent for the last two and a half years."

"Did you choose silence, or did your wife's death make you silent?" Bernard suddenly asked. "There is a difference, after all."

"I'm afraid I'm being a bad host," Hubert suddenly intervened. "I see your glass is empty. Would you care for another?"

I said that I would.

"And how about you Sebastian?" he asked.

All our drinks were replenished, apart from the engineer's, who still had two-thirds of his wine left. I was grateful for the respite, even more grateful when the conversation drifted onto other topics: Bernard's vacation, about which he made vague reference to Lauriane and the capital; the engineer's journey to the mountains.

It was over dinner that the reason for the engineer's visit to Cagot was touched upon. We sat at a polished table, and were served, as Henry had predicted, by Angela and a blonde, Germanic looking woman who I had never seen before. Angela performed her role with detachment; she didn't personally acknowledge anyone in our small group. She might not have known us, and Hubert made no attempt to explain her presence there. It was taken for granted.

It was Henry who asked the engineer directly, "Is it true that you're here to try to get into the cave?"

The engineer looked at Hubert, who gave an approving nod of his head. "Yes," he said.

"Professor Hermann is an expert in the field of mining," Hubert began to explain, laying his knife and fork down on his plate. "Up until now we've assumed that the cave was totally destroyed. Professor Hermann thinks that we might be wrong."

"It's possible," the engineer continued, "that some parts of the tunnel remain intact. My job is to discover if that is the case."

"And then?" I asked.

"Then the remains of the dead can perhaps be exhumed and buried in the proper place," Hubert said. "I feel I owe that to the village."

"But it happened nine years ago," I argued. "There are some who think that the dead should be left in peace."

"And there are others who think otherwise," he replied.

Isabella came to mind. She would support Hubert, I thought. "But why now, after all this time?" I asked.

"It wasn't technologically feasible before," Hubert said. "Now it may be."

"When are you going up to the cave?" Henry asked.

"In three or four days," Hubert answered.

The engineer spoke now. "We're waiting for the equipment to arrive, along with the men who manage it. The lorry should arrive tomorrow, the next day at the latest. From here the equipment will have to be manhandled up to the cave. Bernard is in charge of that."

"You're going up to the cave?" I asked Bernard.

"Yes," he said.

"Well, since you're so keen that I sign your ledger, perhaps I ought to go with you," I said.

"I don't think that would be appropriate," he replied, as he looked at me, trying to gauge how serious I was. "My Second-in-Command is perfectly capable ..."

"I don't see any reason why he shouldn't go with us," Hubert intervened, a look of mild amusement on his face. "You can ride a horse, I presume," he asked me.

"Yes," I answered.

"What do you think, Professor Hermann?" Hubert asked.

"I have no objection," he responded. "After all we're only making initial soundings."

"But it goes outside the bounds of what has been laid down by the Colonel," Bernard argued. "His movements are meant to be confined to ..."

"I have seen the documentation, Bernard," Hubert reminded him. "All it says is that he must report to the authorities at the specified times."

"So as to limit his movements," Bernard protested further.

"That is implied, but it isn't directly stated. For the life of me, I don't really see why you're making such a fuss. It's not as if he is going to escape."

Bernard looked at me, at Hubert again. I was bemused by the conversation, the way they talked about me almost as though I wasn't there in the room with them. It was obvious that Bernard was unhappy about my going up to the cave. I doubted that that was because he would be compromising the conditions of my exile in the village; he was too much his own man for that. Perhaps he really did believe that I might try to escape, but I somehow doubted that as well. He was perceptive enough to know that that wasn't my intention. So the reasons for his opposition eluded me.

"I would appreciate the opportunity," I said, addressing the engineer. "You see, I'm interested in ornithology, and I'm building up a journal of my sightings. I've covered the valleys pretty thoroughly, but I haven't been able to go higher, up past the tree line. It would give me a more complete picture."

"There, that seems innocent enough to me," Hubert said to Bernard, still maintaining the slightly mocking tone he had adopted while discussing the issue.

Bernard sighed, but acquiesced. "Very well! On this occasion I suppose we could make an exception. But I would hate for him to get the idea that he is a free man," he said, making the motive for his opposition clearer.

"I have never considered myself not to be a free agent," I said in reply.

"We will see."

The table fell silent for a while. Bernard picked up his glass and drank his wine.

I walked back to the village with Henry. It was a moonless night. The trees were dark, vague shapes that seemed to merge into the consuming blackness of the sky. Fortunately, Henry had had the good sense to bring a small torch with him. Its beam cut a white hole in the darkness.

"A strange evening," he commented as we walked downhill.

"Yes," I agreed noncommittally.

"It's interesting," Henry said. "Bernard has always been a moody fellow – buoyant one day, morose the next – but every year since I've known him, he has had a break in the summer, and he's always come back the better for it. Except this year. It's very noticeable, don't you think. There's something ill-humoured, odd about him."

"And why's that, do you think?"

"I don't know. Perhaps he's come to realise that Cagot is a kind of exile for him, as well as for other people."

"I thought he chose to come here," I said.

"What made you think that?"

"The impression he gives of always being in control."

"He wasn't in control tonight, though, was he? He didn't want you to go up the mountain, but he lost the argument."

"True," I conceded, "although I doubt it's that important to him. If it was, I'm sure he would have found a way of stopping me."

There was a noise in the forest off to our left. Henry swept the torchlight in a wide arc, slicing into the sombre pines. We saw nothing.

"There used to be bears here," Henry told me. "You saw the skin on the wall in Duval's drawing room. Bernard shot that one three years ago, not far from where we are now. It was a particularly hard winter. The bear must have been forced down from higher up the mountain to look for food. A boy – one of my students in fact – was badly mauled. Bernard put some bait down to attract the bear; then shot it."

"What's the connection between Bernard and Duval?" I asked, wondering how the bear had ended up on Duval's wall.

"It's difficult to say. Cagot is like many villages in this chain of mountains. Its history, its isolation, kept it apart from the rest of the country for many years. It developed independently of what was happening in the centre. Two generations ago, the valley was virtually a feudal kingdom and the Duval's were the Lords of the manor. Then the Government put a stop to that. The Duvals' privileges were rescinded, and their titles taken away from them. They hadn't been conferred by the Government in the first place, of course; the Duvals had taken them upon themselves."

"With the acceptance of the villagers," I said.

"As far as I can gather there was no opposition. The villagers in Cagot have always been an apathetic lot, not surprising when you consider. Anyway, it was a paper decree only. The Government made little attempt to enforce the new rules, so the Duvals carried on much as they had done before. And it's still there. Duval is a powerful man. He has the weight of tradition behind him. In recent years the Government has made more effort to bring the village into the fold ..."

"But I remember you telling me that after the cave collapsed, the Government turned its back on the village," I said.

"They did, but I meant economically. In the last four or five years, they have become more concerned with what is going on here in the mountains. Nothing is going on, of course, but the Government wants to ensure they are in complete command, at the fringes as well as the centre. That's why they sent the army here. That's why Bernard was posted here as Chief of Police."

"He doesn't seem to have made much difference in terms of Duval's influence," I said.

"I'm not sure you're right there," Henry answered. "The engineer isn't Duval's man. He's a Government official – that's why he's staying at the Government Rest house, and not at Duval's house. And Bernard's been assigned a major role in the business. He has to go up to the cave with them. You see, it's my impression that it's Bernard's job to court Duval, to make him amenable to Government influence."

"So you're saying that this is essentially a Government scheme?" I asked, trying to understand Henry's argument.

"It makes sense. If they can get to the bodies and give them a proper burial, the Government will take credit; a gold star to the Governor of Rona, and a gold star, ultimately, to the Colonel."

"But it was hushed up previously," I argued. "Why open old wounds?"

"People in Rona have long memories," Henry said. "What happened may not have appeared in the media, but everyone in the province knows about it. The Governor and the Bishop actively promoted the pilgrimage, and they are still blamed for what occurred. They would like to redeem themselves as much as Duval, probably more so. Duval has presented them with a possible means of accomplishing that."

"Couldn't the Government do it without him?" I asked.

"But this is Duval's idea."

"As it was in the first place."

"He was unlucky. He could have put the province on the map, and made the people who mattered even more influential. They know that; they respect him because he is a man, not only of ideas, but also of action. It seems to me that they need Duval on their side, and he needs them to carry the idea through."

By now we had left the forest behind us, and entered the village proper. Yellow lights, suggestive of warmth and security, shone from the windows of the inn. Neither of us mentioned going inside for a drink. It was late, and I was tired and I knew that Angela was still at Duval's. I said goodnight to Henry and went to my room, where I went straight to bed.

The plans were put into effect for the journey to the cave. The lorry arrived the day after the dinner at Duval's. It contained several large packing cases. Five men who knew how to assemble and operate the equipment inside arrived with it. The lorry was unloaded, and the cases stored at the army headquarters just outside the village. The various pieces of equipment were then unpacked and put together in smaller parcels for transportation up the mountain. The parcels had to be carried, so they were laid out on makeshift stretchers – sturdy, leather sheets attached to wooden poles at either side. It would take four men, balancing the end of the poles on their shoulders, to carry one load, and there were twelve loads altogether. Most of the men were soldiers commanded to do the task, but Bernard also recruited a handful of villagers to make up the numbers.

It would take these men two days to reach the cave on foot, providing there were no mishaps along the way. The plan was to split the expedition into two parties. The first party, led by Duval, would go ahead of the second in order to set up camp. The engineer insisted on staying with his equipment all the way up to the cave. Bernard felt obliged to stay with him, so I had to ride with the second party as well. We began our journey three days after Hubert had left with the advance party.

There were sixty-five of us altogether. Bernard and I rode at the front of the column, followed by soldiers leading packhorses laden with tents and supplies for our overnight stop halfway along the route. The engineer and his assistant rode at the rear of the party to keep a watchful eye on the men carrying the equipment ahead of them. We took the second valley, following the river, which Bernard told me was called the Vilaro.

"I know," I said. "I've often walked this way."

"I know," he said in return.

We progressed slowly, climbing above the river, which was shallow and slow-flowing at this season. Although it was early, the sun was white in the sky. The heat was intense. I felt the beads of sweat form on my forehead and drip down into my eyes, in spite of the wide-brimmed hat I was wearing. It was a relief when we came to the forest and the slender pines cut out the sun.

Bernard reined in his horse, took off his peaked cap, and ran his arm across his brow. He blew air out through his mouth to express how hot he felt; then reached down for his water bottle that hung from his saddle. He took a swig; then offered the bottle to me. I accepted and drank the water, which had already become tepid in its leather container.

"We would have to choose the hottest day of the year," he said.

We continued through the forest and descended the ridge, halting where the forest came to the river's edge, in order for the party to coalesce. Everyone was relieved to pause for a while, resting in the shade of the trees while the horses drank from the river.

The engineer's assistant, Sebastian, came up to me. He was tall and fair, with the kind of youthful good looks that reminded me of Henry. He had been riding without a hat; the sun had already reddened the skin on his face and neck.

"Are you glad you came now?" he asked. "It's so hot, and I don't think I've seen or heard a single bird."

"It's a quiet time of year," I answered. "But I did hear a couple of woodpeckers in the forest." He sat down beside me in the shade. "You should wear something to protect your neck," I told him. "From now on it's rocky, open country. You'll be totally exposed to the sun."

"Oh, I'll be all right," he said with the overconfidence of youth. "You're familiar with the mountains then?"

"I've only been so far," I said. "It will be interesting to go right up."

"I must admit I'm a city lad," he said. "I don't get much enjoyment out of this. It makes me feel uncomfortable."

"But in your job you must often find yourself in remote areas," I said.

"Yes, it's paradoxical, isn't it?" he replied and smiled.

"Maybe you do it for the challenge," I said. "Testing your own moral and physical stamina. Or for the money?"

He laughed at the last idea. "I work for the Government. That's hardly going to make me a rich man."

"But it's enough to live on back in the city, isn't it?"

"I suppose so," he said. "Looks like it's time to press on."

Bernard had mounted his horse, and was beckoning the rest of us to stand up. I got back on my horse and joined him at the head of the party again. We rode on, out into the exposed, rocky landscape. The sun beat down from a monotone sky, glared off the water and the rocks. When I looked into the distance through my field glasses, details were lost in the sultry haze. Bernard grunted with discomfort at my side.

We came to where the mountainside dropped sheer to the valley floor. The crags and precipices appeared a dull ochre under the mid-day sky. I scanned the rocky wall through my binoculars, saw a loose group of eight griffon vultures soaring lazily on the thermals. I pointed them out to Bernard and handed him my field glasses. He held them to his eyes.

"Horrible creatures," he said, and meant it. He handed the glasses back to me. "In Catronia, I once received a phone call from a group of terrorists. They told me where I could find the corpse of one of my men. He'd been working undercover, and had penetrated one of their cells. They'd found him out, killed him and dumped his body in the countryside. We went to recover the body. It had taken them three days to make the call. When we arrived at the spot – it was a barren, isolated part of the province – the body was being picked at by the vultures. It was sickening. I can still see it now – the entrails, the birds' heads plunged deep into the man's stomach." He continued his description with poetic vividness, and seemed to find some kind of perverse enjoyment in doing so.

I only half listened. I glanced across the valley to where the dark green forest ran along the hillside, and picked out the

183

rocky platform that held such pleasurable memories for me. So, as Bernard imagined vultures picking at decaying flesh, I visualised Angel's skin and wondered when I would taste it again. I hadn't seen her since the dinner party at Duval's, for he had entertained every night since then also, and Angela had been absent from the inn.

Bernard was silent now. He too was looking across the valley. "Anything interesting?" he asked.

"Nothing," I replied.

We left the rock face behind. The valley opened out a little to our right, the slopes becoming gentler, more undulating, bare apart from a thin scattering of trees. In contrast, the other side of the valley was steep, and the forest fell to the valley floor, straggling along the river bank. Once, a party of citril finches flew over our heads towards the conifers on the other side.

We rested again in the middle of the afternoon at a spot where the track rejoined the river. Some members of the group sheltered in the shade of the boulders that dotted the riverbank, but most of us waded across the river and sat in the forest, our backs propped up against the wrinkled trunks of the trees. Sebastian, however, sprawled flat out on the ground with a white handkerchief, discoloured by sweat, spread over his face. He was suffering for his earlier negligence.

Bernard allowed us twenty minutes to rest and take some refreshment. Then he spoke to us all. "We have about two hours more to do today. It's a hard, uphill stretch – the steepest we encounter on the trip. I should warn you that there are lots of loose stones on the slopes, so tread carefully. Once we're past that, we'll set up camp for the night."

Bernard was impressive in command. He clearly knew the route and everybody seemed confident in his ability. I looked anxiously at Sebastian, as we stood up to go. The brief respite from the journey appeared to have done him good. He had regained some of his normal colour, and mounted his horse with no problem, after dipping his handkerchief into the river, and knotting it over his head.

"The intrepid adventurer," he said self-mockingly to me when he saw I was observing him.

Bernard had been correct about the next stage of the journey. Steep, scree-covered slopes squeezed the river in. The track wound and climbed upwards, constantly doubling back itself. Looking down from our leading position, I saw the column snaking below us. The soldiers and volunteers from the village struggled to maintain their balance as the poles weighed down on their shoulders, and the parcels containing the machine-pieces sloped at dangerous angles because of the gradient of the track.

I have never seen such a desolate-looking hillside. It consisted entirely of weathered shards of grey rock. There were no trees, no patches of green vegetation; only the vertical face that stretched along the top of the hill broke the monotony, as the rock there was solid, substantial. It was this we were heading for, moving slowly, carefully, along the track, yet from where we were, I could see no gap that breached its walls.

The track itself was now very narrow; it could scarcely accommodate two people side by side, let alone two men separated by stretchers. It meant that some of the men were forced to walk on the scree, making it sharp and slippery underfoot. The engineer was anxious. The air was still here, and there were no objects to muffle or divert sounds. His voice rose clearly from the back of the column, chastening men, urging caution, admonishing them when they nearly slipped, which happened too frequently for comfort. The men swore under their breath, but maintained their calm. The task in hand demanded all their concentration. Amazingly there were no accidents. Everyone made it to the top of the hillside without mishap. Here, the track curved behind a protruding layer of rock – the rock had concealed the passageway until we were upon it – and cut through a very narrow canyon. We found ourselves in complete shadow. The sides of this vertical valley were so close to each other, that there was scarcely room for the men to get through.

"I've always thought of this as the perfect place for an ambush," Bernard said to me.

"Who is there to ambush us?" I asked.

"No one," he replied. "Just an indulgence of mine."

I didn't like that valley. It made me understand how Angela had felt that first time in the forest when the capercaillie had burst into flight at her feet – trapped – hemmed in; the fear was almost physical.

"Claustrophobic?" Bernard said, sensing my fear.

"A little," I said.

We emerged from that roofless tunnel into a wide valley, more like a plateau than a valley; the mountain peaks had receded into the distance, leaving us in a world of meadows and of space. Sheep dotted the landscape, nibbling at the grass.

We waited for the rest of the men to arrive. Bernard checked that no mishaps had occurred; then pointed to some low peaks, purple shades to the north-east. "That's where we're going tomorrow," he informed us. "For now though we'll pitch camp."

He led us to an area of raised ground not far from the river. It was flat and dry. The soldiers methodically set about putting up the tents and laying out the small gas stoves and pots and pans for the meal later on. I put up the small tent that I had borrowed from Henry, and rolled out my sleeping bag inside. When everything was ready, and had been inspected by Bernard and the young army officer who had been in charge of the supplies, the men were allowed their freedom.

Most of the soldiers made their way to the river, where they stripped naked and bathed in the cold water. The engineer inspected his equipment to see that it was all in order. Sebastian had succumbed to sunstroke. He retired to the tent he was sharing with the engineer, and lay there with his eyes closed, nursing a splitting headache. His body radiated heat. I went in for a while and ran a cold cloth gently over his forehead. I could smell the perspiration, acrid on his skin.

"If it's a test, I guess I've failed," he murmured as I tried to soothe him.

"You'll be all right in the morning," I reassured him. "The point is that you learn from your mistakes. The air is thinner up here; the sun penetrates more easily. You should always make sure your skin is protected."

"Professor Hermann will be annoyed with me," he said. "He's a man of little patience."

"So I gathered," I said, referring implicitly to the way he had harangued the men on the scree-slope.

"He loves those machines more than his children," the assistant said. "They're the latest technology, of course. He had a hand in their development and their trials."

"He's married?" I asked.

"You sound surprised," Sebastian said, and opened his eyes. The pain in his head made him close them again immediately.

"I didn't picture him as a family man."

"And what about me?"

"You? I imagine you as the young bachelor," I said confidently.

"I'm married as well," he told me.

"Which goes to show how much value you should attach to artistic insight," I joked.

"And you?" he asked. "Are you married?"

"I was. My wife died." I told him what had happened.

"That's terribly sad," he said. "So meaningless."

I left him with the damp cloth plastered across his forehead. I took my field glasses and walked to the river. The soldiers were still splashing around in the shallow water totally unselfconscious of their nakedness; several of them were sunbathing on the grass. None of the villagers had joined them, I noticed; they had stayed together in the camp.

I walked upriver in the direction of the cave. The river ran sluggishly; gravel islands rose above the level of the water. The meadow was boggy in places and I had to tread carefully. Water pipits were the common bird species here. They rose up from under my feet, dull brown apart from their white outer-tail feathers, calling 'see-ip' and flying weakly away. Insipid birds, their commonness soon made them monotonous to me.

The only other birds I saw were a single wheatear, and a distant raven.

I turned back for the camp just as the clouds came rolling in over the peaks to the south, quickly obscuring the sun. The air temperature cooled perceptibly, and by the time I had reached the camp the cloud had completely enveloped the plateau, reducing visibility to a few metres.

The men sat around the tents in distinct groups, huddled now in their coats. The calor gas had been lit on the cookers and meals were being prepared. I went and sat with Bernard and the engineer on a tarpaulin laid over the grass.

"I was beginning to think you'd got lost," Bernard said. "You have to be careful up here; the weather can change so quickly."

"I didn't stray from the river," I said. "That was my guideline."

A soldier brought us some food; a simple meal of bread, cold meat and beans. The engineer eyed it with disgust. "Don't worry," Bernard said on seeing the man's reaction. "There will be better food at the cave. Hubert has seen to that. I think we need something to wash it down."

He went to his tent and returned with a large bottle of brandy and a bag containing metal cups. He poured some brandy into one of the cups and handed it to me. I thanked him.

"Professor Hermann?" he asked.

"No thank you," the engineer replied.

Bernard shrugged his hefty shoulders, and poured himself some. He drank it in one go and emitted a sigh of satisfaction before pouring some more into his cup.

I ate my food. The heat of the day had affected the bread and meat, making them hard and dry. It was only the brandy that made the meal palatable.

"How is Sebastian now?" I asked the engineer who had been toying with the food on his plate. He put it down on the tarpaulin sheet beside him.

"He's sleeping. He should be all right in the morning."

"A foolish fellow," Bernard commented mildly – he was in a good mood. "Hasn't he been out in the sun before?"

"We have worked together on two other jobs," the engineer explained. "On both of those we travelled by jeep. This is the first time that either of us has had to travel on horseback."

"Does it bother you?" Bernard asked.

"I don't mind it," the engineer responded. "It's just good to get away from the capital for a while."

"You have a family, don't you?" I asked.

The engineer frowned, as if he found the subject uncongenial. "Yes, but I am a busy man – I have to be – I don't have as much time for family life as I would like."

Night was drawing in, so lamps were lit. They cast shadows of tents and men onto the curtain of the mist. Bernard had not only brought his brandy with him, but his chess set as well; he and the engineer crouched over one of the lamps and played together. I went to my tent to get an early night.

We set off again in the middle of the morning, once the cloud had dispersed. Bernard had been unwilling to continue until he could see the peaks to the northeast. "There's no real track across the plateau," he told the men. "We could go around in circles for hours."

We didn't head directly towards the peaks, but approached them by a semi-circular route, which took us away from the river. This meant that we avoided the marshier areas of the meadow. I chose to ride at the rear of the party with Sebastian and the engineer. Sebastian was fit enough to ride, although was rather subdued at first. That may have been because of the engineer's presence. He talked more openly once Professor Hermann, fearful again for his machinery, left us to ride in the middle of the column.

"At least it's cooler today," he began, looking up at the sky which was covered by a layer of white cloud. "I was burning up yesterday. Thanks for helping me out. I appreciate it."

"It was nothing," I said.

"You asked about my wife. Would you like to see her photograph?" he asked.

"Yes, I would," I replied.

We stopped for a while. He took out a small wallet from his saddlebag, opened it and handed me the picture of his wife. She was young, had straight dark hair and smooth, unblemished skin. It was a face I would have liked to touch.

"She is very attractive," I said.

I gave the photograph back to him, and we coaxed our horses into a saunter again.

"Any children?" I asked, as we rode together side by side.

"Not yet. We're waiting," he said; then paused. "You asked me yesterday why I was doing this?"

I looked at him, waiting for him to continue.

"Well, I wasn't quite honest with you. I'm doing it to gain experience. Then I hope to get away, to get a job in America."

"Why America?"

"Because there are more opportunities there."

"More money," I suggested.

"Is there anything wrong with wanting to earn more money?" he asked defensively.

"No," I replied uneasily. "And what about this country?"

He shrugged. "This country is old. I want to be free, and I don't feel that I can be free here."

I envied Sebastian his youth and his ambition, but I did not envy his desire for escape. "I love this country," I said.

"I don't understand what that means," he said. He spoke more confidently now. "A country is an abstraction. Or you could say a collection of individual people. Surely, you can't love an abstraction; and how many individual people do you love?"

"It's not as simple as that," I replied. "It's something in the blood."

"Ah, that's the problem," he argued. "That's typical of our race. When pushed to offer a rational explanation, we revert to mysticism. I want to live in the modern world."

"I'm a poet," I offered weakly.

"I don't want to sound offensive," he said, "but you seem a strangely old-fashioned one."

"How can you say that without having read any?"

"But I have. Hubert lent me 'Poems From Exile' and 'Another Country' after the night we had dinner."

"So Hubert actually has the books?" I said.

"Yes."

"Well, you're entitled to your opinion," I said.

"Look, I didn't mean to ..."

"No," I stopped him. "It's fine."

"You see, what I can't stand," he continued, " is the fact that you spent all those years abroad because you would have been killed if you'd come back. Then when you come back your wife is murdered. Then you are made a virtual prisoner in these Godforsaken mountains. Just knowing that this is happening in this country – and has been happening for as long as I can remember – makes me want to get out. I don't understand how you can talk of love, unless you have aspirations to be some kind of saint." He spoke passionately, with a poignant edge to his words that made me listen. More than that though, there was something familiar in the way he spoke that reminded me of others I had known.

"I think there are enough saints in the country already, don't you?" I responded calmly.

He didn't answer.

"So what's your story?" I pressed him.

"My story?"

"Yes. Who did they take away from you?"

"How did you know?"

"I've had lots of experience," I said. "I'm sorry, that sounds arrogant. I mean I've met many people – too many – whose families were victims of the Military. You get to recognise the signs."

"With me, it was my father," he confessed. "At the time when the Military first seized power, he was a factory-worker, a skilled mechanic. He wasn't political in any real sense of the word, but that didn't stop them. One night they came for him and took him away. We never saw him or heard from him again. I was ten years old at the time."

"I'm sorry," I said, recognising the ineffectuality of my words.

"I've put it behind me. As you said, he was just one of many. My mother was strong. She slaved to support my brother and I. Somehow she managed to see us both through college. And I worked like a slave as well to be successful. And I was. Professor Hermann doesn't just take any old geologist on these projects."

"I'm sure he doesn't," I said.

"And what kept me going was the ambition, the single-minded desire, to get out of here as soon as I can. And I will; next year or the year after I'll go, and I'll never come back. And I can tell you that there are many others like me. Can you honestly blame us for wanting to get out after what happened to our parents?"

"But then who is going to change things?" I asked. "Who is going to clean up the mess that our country has got itself into?"

"I'm just facing facts," he replied. "Things won't change while the Colonel is in power. They probably won't change much after- wards either. The important thing, as far as I'm concerned, is to look after myself and my family."

"It's the country's loss," I said.

"I can't see that I'm any different from you," he said. "After all, haven't you given in? You say you are no longer politically minded. You accept your exile, almost as if you desired it. Where has your fight gone?"

"I am older than you," I said.

"Then you should have less to lose," he rebuked me.

"I've lost too much already," I replied. "I no longer have the energy."

We rode on and gradually drew closer to the peaks. As we did so, the meadow became wetter; numerous streams dissected the green sward. We had no option but to wade across them, which was fine for us on horseback, but cold and uncomfortable for those carrying the machinery. This went on for a kilometre or more – stream, boggy grass, stream, boggy grass – until we reached the lower slopes of the north-eastern chain of mountains. Here the streams had cut deeper into the rock, so the ground we trod was well above the flowing water, and therefore drier. We rested for a while where some rough, stone huts were clustered together. These were the shepherds' quarters during their summer sojourn in the high valley. Two of them emerged when we arrived. They were coarse looking individuals: their matted hair fell to their shoulders; their beards were as thick and knotted as their hair. They spoke in a dialect that I could hardly understand, although Bernard seemed to have little difficulty in comprehending them.

"They said that a party of soldiers passed through three days ago – and Hubert, of course," Bernard explained later, when the two men had disappeared up a nearby valley in search of their sheep.

"They know Hubert?" I asked.

"Oh yes. It was one of those men who discovered the cave."

"And he's been doing this ever since?"

"It's his life," Bernard said.

"No wonder they look half-crazed," I commented.

I stood up and walked over to my horse, which was some way off. I took out my cigarettes from the saddlebag and lit one. It was the first one I had had that day, and it tasted good. I gazed up the slope of the mountain. Its gradient was relatively gentle until two-thirds of the way up when it became steeper and rockier. The highest point was a peak with an almost perfect inverted V shape. Through my field glasses I followed a track – the one I assumed we would be taking – as far as the sudden change in the angle of the slope; then lost it as it dipped behind a ridge.

I was correct about the track. We took it up the mountain when we started on the final leg of our journey. I rode at the front with Bernard again.

"It isn't far now," he told me. We have to go round Devil's Peak – that's what it's called – then the cave is in the valley beyond."

"It's a rather ironic name," I said.

"It's always been known as that," he responded humourlessly. "There's no connection."

We climbed upwards, up to the spot where I had no longer been able to see the track through my field glasses. We found ourselves on the outer lip of a huge cirque, looking down into the waters of a black lake that reflected the bare crests of the mountains behind it.

"And that's called Devil's Lake," Bernard said.

We entered the crater and descended to the water's edge. We made our way round the northern end of the lake and up the other side of the cirque. The track then levelled out, and curved around the lower slopes of the mountain crowned by Devil's Peak. Once we had lost sight of the lake, we gradually descended to the floor of a narrow, boulder-strewn valley. On the descent I made out the tents and campfires of Hubert's party further up the valley. Bernard and I waited for the men in our party to pass us, pointing out the distant smoke as we did so.

"There they are," Bernard said encouragingly as each group of men passed. "Not far to go now."

We regained the head of the column when all the men were safely down in the valley. Hubert, having seen us descend, rode out to meet us. "Any problems on the journey?" he asked Bernard, who responded in the negative.

We rode ahead with Hubert to the encampment. The advance party had been busy: latrines had been dug and covered; a system of pipes diverted water from the adjacent hillside to a large tank; other pipes led off from the tank to a series of makeshift showers; a large marquee had been erected to serve as cookhouse and mess.

"This is what it was like nine years ago," Hubert explained, "although it was on a much larger scale then, of course. The tank and pipes were still in place. We had to patch up the tank, and clean the rust away as best we could, and we had to replace most of the pipes, but the system's still usable."

"Where was the cave?" I asked.

"That slope over there," Hubert replied, pointing to a rocky section of the hillside two hundred metres away. "The entrance is – or was – around the other side, invisible from this valley, which is why it went undetected for so long."

The rest of our party soon arrived, weary after the day's slog. The engineer insisted, however, that the machinery be carefully unloaded and set down under the large canopy that the advance party had set up for the purpose, before the men could relax. By the time they had put up their own tents and showered, the cloud had descended, dampening and chilling the air. Night was drawing in rapidly. We went to the marquee to eat. Inside, two large pots were bubbling on calor-gas stoves, watched over by the army cook. There was a single trestle table containing plates and cutlery. There were no tables for the men to eat at, but folding canvas chairs had been provided, and the men were sitting around on these in small groups, waiting for their meal to be served.

The engineer and his assistant were the last to arrive, to a chorus of mumbled comment from those soldiers who had carried the equipment up the mountain. It was clear that the engineer was not a popular person, but I doubt that he noticed; if he did, he paid no heed.

Duval nodded to the army officer in charge, and the latter gave the order for the men to line up to be served. The soldiers were given food from one of the pots – the cook ladled it onto their plates; the rest of us served ourselves from the other pot.

"Why this demarcation?" I asked Bernard, as we waited for Hubert, ahead of us in the line, to fill his plate.

"The soldiers requested it," he said.

"Why?"

"It's a military tradition that soldiers and civilians don't eat out of the same pot. It's of no great importance."

We served ourselves to the stew; the predominant ingredient was a rich, dark meat. "It's chamois," Hubert said. "Two of the soldiers went hunting this morning. They said they saw several of them up towards the border."

"Good," Bernard said. "I was hoping to get some shooting in."

"Well you should have plenty of time," Hubert said. "We'll get the equipment set up tomorrow; then it's up to Professor Hermann and his men."

"How long should it take?" I asked the engineer, who, as usual, was picking desultorily over his food.

"Three days. Four days. No longer than a week. It depends how much of the cave interior remains," he answered.

The machinery was constructed and put into place on the following day. As far as I could understand it, a generator powered a series of drills. The drills penetrated a little way into the rock, enough to allow for the insertion of a sounding device. It was this device that the engineer had been working on, and it had only recently been tried out in field conditions. Apparently, the device was able to pick up and record differences in the levels of stress in the rock. Where rock was absent, as it would be in the case of underground caverns and tunnels, this would show up clearly in the readings, and the engineer said that it would be possible to estimate the depth and dimensions of the hollow space inside the mountain.

"All we have to do," the engineer explained once the equipment had been put into place, "is to keep on drilling and taking readings until we find the tunnel, or until we are convinced that it no longer exists."

So from then on, there was little for the majority of the party to do. The engineer and his assistants busied themselves with the machines, making copious notes which were incomprehensible to all but the initiated. Occasionally, throughout the day, the engineer would call upon the soldiers to move the equipment to a different place on the hillside, but Bernard, Hubert and I were left to our own devices.

I had thought, given the circumstances, that Bernard might have shown some flexibility over my registering with him. He didn't; he still insisted that I write my signature in the logbook at nine in the morning and seven at night.

"It is my job," he reiterated, when I made some comment about his obsession with regularity. But it wasn't that simple. I surmised that he just liked to keep me dangling on the hook.

Apart from those times, however, and during meals, I saw little of him. He spent most of the day hunting away from the camp alone. He was a skilled hunter. On the first day he returned with a chamois – to show he was as good as the soldiers, so I thought. On the second day he brought back three mountain hares for the pot.

I spent the first two days exploring the rocky slopes, sketching the birds I found there. Their names echoed their environment. There were snowfinches, conspicuous against the brown rocks when they flew because of their black and white wings. Other birds, like the Alpine accentors and the rock buntings I saw, tended to blend inconspicuously into the background. It was only through field glasses that their delicate feather-patterning could be discerned. There were birds of prey this high up as well. I saw griffon vultures on both those days, and a single lammergeier on the second. Once a peregrine plummeted from the sky; sleek and streamlined with its wings closed, it looked as though it was going to fly straight into the ground, but it sheered upwards at the last possible moment. Through my glasses I made out a young hare crouching under the overhang of a rock; there was something wrong with one of its back legs; it scurried away weakly as the falcon manoeuvred for a second strike. This time the bird was successful. Its talons dug into the hare's fur, drawing blood. The hare squealed twice; then was silent. The falcon pecked at its neck until it was dead. I moved away to let the bird feast undisturbed on its prey.

By the morning of the third day, the engineer had come up with nothing, and was becoming increasingly pessimistic. "It was a big tunnel," he said. "There were hundreds of people in there. We should have found it by now."

"Have you tested every possibility?" Duval asked.

"No, and there is still a slight chance we will find something. But I would prepare myself for a disappointment, if I were you."

It was after this conversation that Duval proposed I ride with him up the valley towards the border. "I could do with a change," he said. This was probably true. As far as I knew, he hadn't left the vicinity of the camp since my arrival. He had simply been waiting impatiently for the cavern to be discovered.

So we headed up the valley towards a gap visible in the range to the east. "What will you do if they don't find anything?" I asked as we rode side by side.

"There's nothing I can do," he said resignedly. "But at least we made the attempt; there will be people who will be grateful for that."

"And that's important to you?"

"Yes. What happened was very unfortunate."

"An act of God?"

"There are some who say so, but I'm a rationalist. I don't subscribe to that theory. The Earth is unstable here. Ask Sebastian. He will tell you about it. There was a weakness in the rock, and it seems likely that the noise made by so many people caused a vibration."

"That does seem the logical explanation," I agreed.

"Nevertheless, it was my idea. I hoped to profit by it, and I wanted the village to profit by it as well." Here he spoke more emotionally. "You only have to look at the village to realise how dismal it is. It's so inward-looking, so sterile. And that would have changed. Anyway, I was responsible for the pilgrimage, so I feel that, to a certain extent, I have a responsibility to the relatives of the people who died. When I learnt of Professor Hermann's machine, I felt that at last I had a chance to make good that responsibility."

Ragged white cumulus clouds drifted across the blue sky. We spurred our horses on along the steep, rocky track – it was narrow now, so we had to ride in single file; I rode behind Duval – up towards that hollow gap between the peaks.

Near the top the track petered out, merging into the loose scree that now made up the surface. We dismounted, leaving the horses to feed where the vegetation came to an end, and scrambled up to what I took to be the rim of the pass. That was illusory. Beyond that ridge was a further ridge. We made our way cautiously over the shards of rock towards it. There was no further ridge after that. There was nothing. The ground just dropped away at my feet. I saw as a vulture would have seen: a vista of clouds and sky, of valleys and hills, of peaks receding into the distance, turning from green to blue to grey.

We were immediately above a huge cirque. "Where we're standing now is the dividing line between the two countries," Duval said; then pointed. "You follow the rim that way; then pick up the track that winds down to the bottom."

I could see the thin path snaking down the scree-covered slope.

"Then you head straight down that valley. That's your way to freedom," he continued, urging me, I felt, to take that track.

"I told you," I said. "I've no desire to leave my country."

Duval smiled. "Be it on your own head. At least you won't be able to say that you never had the opportunity."

"Why should you be so eager to see me go?" I asked.

"Oh, I'm not all that eager," he replied. "I'm just interested."

"There is another thing," I said. "I don't think Bernard would let me."

"What's Bernard got ...?"

"He's here," I interrupted him.

Duval turned around as Bernard emerged over the first ridge, holding his shotgun under his arm. He hurried over the scree, moving awkwardly in his haste. He was out of breath when he reached us. Sweat dribbled down his forehead.

"What kind of trick is this?" he addressed Duval sternly.

Duval remained calm. "What do you mean, Bernard? We decided to take a ride together, that's all."

"To the border? You were leading the man into temptation."

"A temptation he refused."

Bernard looked at me. "You knew I was following you, didn't you?"

"Only when I saw you come over the rise," I answered.

I was lying. I had noticed him half an hour or so before we had reached the pass, skulking behind us in the distance.

"You have a suspicious nature, Bernard," Duval said.

"I'm a policeman. It's ..."

"Yes, I know. It's your job," Duval said with sardonic weariness.

Bernard reddened. It was the only time I had seen him genuinely angry. He opened his mouth to speak, but must have thought the better of it in my presence. "Should he escape, I shall hold you responsible," he said to Duval.

Duval merely smiled, but I sensed that the menace implicit in the Police Chief's words was real enough, and Duval must have sensed it too. Again I remembered the photograph I had seen in Bernard's quarters. I was witnessing that side of the man now, in the flesh.

"Very well! I trust I will see you both in the camp this evening," he said and, turning his back on us, he walked away.

We remained standing on the edge of the cirque, peering down on the mountain landscape. I lit a cigarette and offered Duval one. He accepted. His hands, I noticed, as I held a match out for him, were steady.

"Bernard is a dangerous man," he said after a while. "You mustn't underestimate him."

"I know," I said.

"Do you?" he asked doubtfully. "Sometimes I think he is not quite sane."

"He's always struck me as being totally in control," I said.

"I'm not so sure." He drew on his cigarette, blowing the smoke out through his mouth. It drifted over the border; then dissipated above the cirque. "He did crack up once, you know. It was long before he came here, long before I knew him."

"Then how do you ...?"

"I make it my business to find out such things."

"Like reading my poetry?"

"Yes," he admitted. "This is my territory; I like to know who I'm dealing with."

"So what about Bernard?"

"Have you noticed the photograph in his quarters – the picture of the woman?"

"The solemn looking one?" I asked.

"Yes. That's Bernard's sister, or rather that was his sister. She's been dead a long time. Apparently, Bernard and she were very close, so close that when I was checking up on him I heard the odd murmured rumour."

Far below us sheep speckled the meadows, and an eagle soared effortlessly across a grey peak. I smoked my cigarette and listened intently to Duval's story.

"Total nonsense, of course! It was true that Bernard loved his sister, but only in the platonic sense. To him she was the embodiment of spiritual purity. He would never have violated her. He would never have thought of her in sexual terms in the slightest. He had his own needs, of course; like many soldiers, he went to brothels to relieve them. Unfortunately, her sister had her needs as well. She was not the angel that Bernard made her out to be."

"This is hard to believe," I remonstrated. "Bernard as a romantic idealist!"

"Yes, but even the most cynical of us were young once. Did you never love anyone in a totally abstract way, with a totally asexual passion?"

"I suppose so," I said.

"So did I! So did most other boys that I knew. It's part and parcel of our Catholic culture – part of the myth fostered by mothers. Unfortunately, reality has a way of intruding. Bernard's sister became pregnant. She had no one to turn to, so she turned to him. Remember, Bernard didn't just worship his sister from afar. They were friends, confidantes, like lovers without the physical complications.

"She should never have told him, of course. It was the verbal equivalent of sticking a knife in his ribs. The problem was that they didn't really understand one another. From what I've gathered she was a little coarse, a little stupid. Whereas he felt his sister's violation physically; to him, it was black, disgusting, revolting. He wouldn't let her forget it. He preyed on her. He tormented her mentally, so that she came to see her pregnancy the same way as he saw it. In the end, she committed suicide."

"Like killing part of himself," I said. My cigarette was finished. I lit another one.

"Ultimately," Duval agreed.

"How did she do it?"

"She threw herself off a sea-cliff. Her neck and back were broken. It was only after, at the inquest, that her parents learned that she had been pregnant. To them her death was a relief; it saved them from the scandal and the disgrace."

"And Bernard?"

"He went to pieces. His parents believed he was simply grieving over his sister's death – they had no idea that he had been the catalyst, the driving force that caused her death. It may not have mattered much anyway. They sent him to a sanatorium. He recovered – fairly swiftly, in fact – but as far as I am aware, he has never been able to love anyone since."

"Merely hate?" I suggested.

"No, I don't think so," he said. "He has moved beyond love and hate. The problem now is that he likes playing God."

We walked cautiously back down to our horses. They were where we had left them, nibbling contentedly at the grass. Bernard was nowhere in sight.

"We won't see him again until we get back to the camp," Duval said. "He wanted to reassure himself, that's all."

He was correct. We didn't see Bernard, although we did hear the occasional shot in the distance. He arrived back at the camp after us, this time with a solitary hare and two dead lammergeiers dangling from his saddle. The hare was for the pot. The vultures he ostentatiously threw down at my feet before backing his horse away, saying nothing.

At the end of the fourth day, the engineer conceded defeat. "There is no tunnel," he said. "It was completely destroyed."

So we packed up the equipment and went back to Cagot.

On the evening of our return I was invited to the inn for a non-celebratory drink before the departure of Professor Hermann and his team on the following day. It was a Saturday and Henry was already at the bar when I arrived. As none of the expedition members were there yet I joined him for a drink. He bought me a beer. I noticed that he seemed tipsy when he gave Angela the order. Angela herself was uncharacteristically solemn. Her disappointment at our failure to penetrate the mountain was quickly made apparent. Henry and I were talking about the expedition when she gave us our beer.

She said, "It means that Hubert won't stay much longer in the village. He'll soon be off abroad again."

"You seem to manage perfectly well without him," I commented, trying to tone down the envy in my voice.

She shrugged at this, seemingly paying no attention to my feelings. But then she said, "Perhaps you won't be here much longer either. Who knows?"

"What a strange thing to say," I responded. "What is this? Some kind of gypsy premonition?"

She raised her eyebrows. Her nostrils flared slightly. "It seems to be a time for leaving," she said. "Bernard has hinted that he might be retiring soon, and Henry here has just received his transfer papers."

"Is that true?" I asked Henry.

Henry lowered his head in his shy, adolescent way – or perhaps, in retrospect, it was mere affectation. "Yes," he admitted as he raised his eyes to meet mine. They were the eyes of a satisfied man. "I received the letter two days ago. So tonight I am celebrating."

"Congratulations," I said, and meant it. "Is it to Rona?" I asked.

"Yes. They have given me what I wanted – at last."

"I'm glad," I said, and cajoled him into accepting a glass of decent brandy to go with the beer. Angela served us, but refused one herself. She left us alone, and I toasted Henry and his success.

He then returned to the topic of the journey. "Was the expedition a complete waste of time, then?" he asked.

"Duval doesn't think so. He believes the attempt in itself is enough to exonerate him."

"But he must be disappointed?" Henry said.

"If he is, he didn't show it on the way back. He seemed very tranquil."

I wonder," Henry said.

"What?"

"If his motives for the expedition were so altruistic?"

I shrugged my shoulders. "I doubt it," I said. "I tend to agree with those villagers who thought that his real motive was to get his hands on the statue."

"So do I," Henry concurred.

Our conversation was interrupted by the arrival of Bernard with the engineer and his assistants, including Sebastian. Some of the soldiers and villagers who had accompanied us to the cave were also with them.

The engineer ordered wine, and after everyone had been served, felt compelled to make a little speech. "I am sorry that we found nothing up the mountain," he said, "and I know that Hubert Duval, who has been so generous to us during our stay in the village, is terribly disappointed. He had hoped to – but I am stepping onto personal ground here. What I would like to say is that we tried our best, and I thank you all for supporting me in the effort, even if I was at times an irritating taskmaster."

"Hear! Hear!" some of the soldiers shouted at this last comment, but the engineer took it in good humour. We raised our glasses to his safe journey back to the capital.

Then it was Bernard's turn. "It was Hubert Duval who made the expedition possible. Unfortunately, he has a prior commitment and is unable to be with us tonight, but he has asked me, on his behalf, to publicly thank the engineer and his assistants for their efforts. He has also asked me to thank the rest of you for your hard work and cooperation. So, gentlemen, a toast to you all!"

He raised his brandy glass; we raised our glasses in return, and drank to one another's health.

"And Hubert told me to tell you that the rest of the drinks for this evening are on him. So please, enjoy yourselves."

That was the end of the formal business. The engineer drank a little of his wine; then made his excuses. "An early start in the morning. I still have some equipment to pack up properly." He shook my hand before he left.

The soldiers drifted towards the dartboard, and were soon their usual rowdy Saturday night selves. The villagers sat at their customary tables. Bernard drank his brandy and left. He was a puzzle in that respect; most lunch-times he would be at the inn, drinking and talking freely with the villagers, yet he rarely drank there in the evenings.

Sebastian joined Henry and me at the bar. "So what now?" Henry asked him.

"Back to the capital! There will be reports to write up. Then it depends where the Government wants to send me for my next assignment. Somewhere less primitive, I hope."

Henry laughed. "You think the village is primitive?"

"Not the village particularly – although those three boys make my hair bristle, you know, the retarded ones."

"They're harmless enough," Henry said.

"No, it was the area around the cave I was referring to. It felt so far from civilisation."

"I thought the soldiers did a good job," I said, "providing the facilities that they did."

"I guess I like my creature comforts too much," Sebastian said. "But it was more than that. I don't know how to explain. I spent hours up on that hill, drilling and taking readings. And all of the time I was there I felt uneasy. The hill itself seemed like a primitive force ..."

Henry made a sceptical face, and Sebastian noticed, but persisted with his explanation. "It's difficult enough to describe, so I know what it must to be like to try and understand – but to me, that hill was like a living creature, and, come the end, I felt that we had in some way violated its sanctity."

"So is there still a tunnel there or not?" I asked.

"The instruments said not, and the instruments are currently the best available."

"But?"

"This sounds nonsensical, but my impression is that we weren't meant to find a tunnel."

"I don't understand," Henry said.

Sebastian looked at me appealingly. I encouraged him to continue with his explication.

"There may or may not be an extant cavern in the hill," he said. "Professor Hermann says there isn't because we didn't find any evidence of one. And we went over that hillside as thoroughly as anyone could, with the most modern equipment available."

"So that means there isn't," Henry said.

"Rationally, logically – yes," Sebastian agreed. "But I feel that there was some force preventing us from discovering the truth. We were not meant to find the cave or the dead bodies. I for one would not swear that the tunnel no longer exists."

"That the statue of the Dark Virgin no longer exists," I suggested.

"Yes," he said.

"Are you religious?" Henry asked tersely.

"No," Sebastian answered. "Not at all!"

Henry continued, "I understand what you are trying to express – or at least I think I do – but what are you talking about here when you use the word 'force'? Are you talking about Good or Evil?"

The assistant engineer sighed, and finished the beer he had chosen to drink. "I would like a cognac," he said. "Would you like to join me?"

We both agreed. Sebastian called to Philip – Angela was no longer in the room – and ordered three special brandies. Henry brought us clean glasses, and poured generous measures of the cognac into them. He poured himself one as well.

"Your health!" he said, raising his glass to us. We raised our glasses in return, and drank the smooth tasting alcohol.

"This is a good drink," I said.

"Yes," Henry turned to Sebastian. "You haven't answered my question."

Sebastian smiled. "This is new to me," he said. "I am a scientist, and I like to consider myself a humanist and a rationalist. I think the words good and evil are, in general terms, meaningless. The force, as I experienced it, was neither benevolent nor malevolent."

"But as a humanist, as a rationalist, how do you explain it?" Henry said, pressing the geologist for an answer.

"I can't," he replied. "I can't."

We were silent for a while. I broke that silence. "Why didn't you mention this before?" I asked; then added another question before Sebastian could respond to the first one. "Did anyone else have a similar experience?"

"As far as I know I was the only one, which perhaps answers your first question," he said in response. "But that doesn't mean that no one else felt it. It's the kind of thing you would keep to yourself."

Sebastian gulped down his brandy. Henry offered to buy him another, but he refused, saying he had to stay sober enough to pack. He shook hands with both of us, and left the inn, but not before ordering a round of drinks for the young soldiers at the dartboard. I felt sad to see him go.

"And what do you think?" Henry asked me after he had gone.

"I think we should order two more of these," I said.

Philip poured us two more drinks; then held the bottle up against the light, hesitating. "What ... the hell!" he finally said, filled our glasses to the rim; then poured what remained into his own glass. "On ... the ... house," he managed to say, and we clinked our three glasses together before we drank.

When he had gone to throw the empty bottle out, Henry asked me for my opinion once more. "Did you experience anything?" His voice was now rife with the scepticism he had subdued in Sebastian's presence.

"No," I had to admit. "I didn't pay much attention to the hill; I was busy doing other things. But I believe he experienced what he said he experienced; I can't see that he has any reason to fabricate a story like that."

"Then what does it mean?" he asked.

"It means it's best that the mountain is left alone," I replied. "It seems to me that enough damage has been done already. Hubert would only have created more."

There was a flicker of revelation in Henry's eyes. "You mean that Sebastian fixed the ..."

"I doubt it," I interrupted, more peremptorily than I had intended. "It's of no concern to him what happens here in the mountains. All he wants to do is head off to America."

"America?"

"Yes. The brave new world. He intends to do good by himself."

"Can't he do that here?"

"He says not."

Henry picked up his glass, and I was aware again of the delicacy of his movements, more feminine than a woman's, which I only noticed at occasional moments, as if for most of the time he had that aspect of himself on a tight leash.

"I would have no desire to go to America," he said after he had sipped at his brandy. It struck me in the way that he said those words, how much Henry was limited by his lack of ambition. In that, he was the antithesis of Sebastian.

"I know," I responded. "But what about other people? Sebastian told me that he wasn't the only one. He seemed to be implying that there is a voluntary exodus taking place."

"Well, I suppose it's part of the natural process," Henry said thoughtfully. "Young people from the village leave for Rona. People from Rona look further afield to Esmée. And those in Esmée think of the capital as their Mecca. I suppose if you were born in the capital, the logical extension of this migration is to head abroad. People want to improve themselves, to find excitement; I can see nothing wrong with that."

"What about the drain of talent?" I asked.

"I'm sure the Government will keep close control over who they let go. The new edict ..."

"The new edict?" I repeated questioningly, as the truth began to dawn on me.

"Well, it's not so new. It was issued soon after the Colonel came to power. It encourages applications for emigration, offers incentives for those who wish to leave the country."

"People like Sebastian?" I asked doubtfully.

"I don't think so," Henry said. "I think it was aimed mainly at the unemployed."

"What about radicals? Liberals? Those opposed to the Colonel?"

"Perhaps," he said. "I only know about it because one of my cousins, who was out of work at the time, made enquiries. But I suppose that that would make political sense."

"Like internal exile as opposed to imprisonment. It dilutes reaction," I added.

"Yes," he agreed, "but surely that's better than what happened before. To me, the Colonel is..." Henry struggled for the apt description.

"A benevolent despot?" I suggested.

"That seems appropriate, he said.

"Do you really believe that Henry? Do you really think the Colonel is a good man at heart?"

"Don't you?" he asked.

"I know him personally," I said. "He has no heart."

"You're biased," he said. "It was the Colonel who sent you here, wasn't it?"

"Yes."

"Maybe it was the best he could do under the circumstances. You yourself have said that under the Old Régime you wouldn't have been sent here; you would have been killed."

"Robert Belmont was sent here and the result was the same," I said cynically, although there was no real depth to my comment. Yet Henry paled a little. Unintentionally, I had struck a nerve, as I had done, I recalled, on a previous occasion. His movement suddenly became less controlled, and as he sipped at his brandy, his hands shook momentarily. He quickly calmed himself, however.

"But that was suicide. You aren't suggesting ..."

"Suggesting what?" I asked, since I had been suggesting nothing.

"That Bernard killed him."

"What? Pulled the trigger?"

"Yes, that's what you seem to be implying."

"That never occurred to me," I said. "But, no. That's too crude for Bernard."

"Then what?" he asked with a worried air of expectation.

"Then nothing! The point I'm making is that the New Régime is ultimately no different from the Old Régime. It's just that its methods are more subtle, and its propaganda is far more effective. The result is the same; it doesn't allow the people to be free."

"But you said at Duval's that you were a free agent."

"Freedom is an emotion, like love and hate, not simply a material fact."

"But love and hate are subjective, illusory. If you want to talk of freedom, you have to view it objectively."

I drank my fresh glass of brandy in one go, and suddenly realised that I was drunk. "Enough of this," I said. "I've got a feeling we've been here before. – Circles and circles and circles. – It's time to find a straight line again."

"What?"

"Oh, nothing! I'm rambling. Goodnight Henry," I said as I stood up to leave. I looked around the bar.

"And where is my sweet lady? Gone! So no goodnight there."

I stumbled back to the hotel, and once in my room, poured myself some more brandy from my own private stock. I then sat down at the desk, took out some paper from the drawer and, pen in hand, allowed the words to flow across its unlined whiteness.

Creativity and reality are tangential. By which I mean both touch upon and influence each other, but often not in the most obvious way. After my journey to the cave, to the border, I began to write again, but not about love or death. Instead what came to me was a fictional, narrative poem in rhyming couplets. I called it 'The Village in the Mountains'. The village was Cagot and not Cagot. Why it came to me, I don't know; it wasn't something I particularly wanted to write, and I didn't feel personally involved in it; it gushed out nevertheless:

> Only the poacher with his dripping prey
> Saw the soldiers advancing that way,
> Along the road through the heaving wood.
> Cold, he sweated, felt the rush of blood,
> And knew that it was too late to warn:
> The village would fall well before dawn.
>
> The village fell; events took their course.
> Metallic banging on wooden doors
> Roused sleepers from their usual dreams,
> Confusing 'is' with that of 'seems'....

And so it went on: the foreign army streaming over the border, herding the villagers to the village hall, making an example of a protestor who was summarily shot, advising the villagers that they were now part of the neighbouring country. There followed the acquiescence of a weak central government; the stubborn resistance of the villagers; the ensuing persecution by the foreign invaders.

This was the theme of my new poem, which occupied me for several weeks. Even as I wrote it I felt that it was dishonest, escapist, almost juvenile in its depiction of the villagers' heroism. I didn't believe that the actual inhabitants of Cagot would have behaved in the manner that they did in my poem; I thought that they would have surrendered without a fight. I now believe that the poem was necessary to me at the time precisely because of this escapism. For all my talk of freedom, Cagot had begun to bear down on me, slowly squeezing the life out of me, making me, for the first time, feel caged.

Why this occurred was difficult to define. Partly it was a mental reaction to the shortening of the days as autumn approached; partly it was the awareness, after Angela's talk of people leaving, that the people I had the most contact with – the people who mattered – were all outsiders: Angela, Henry, Bernard – ultimately none of them belonged to the village, and all three reflected, by contrast, the village's limitations.

My affair with Angela fluttered on tentatively. She went with me to the Poet's Throne twice in August, but our lovemaking was unsatisfactory. Her mind, her body were focussed elsewhere – on Hubert Duval.

Interestingly, Angela's annoyance at Duval's failure to rediscover the cave – albeit for purely selfish reasons – was not shared by the rest of the village. Even Isabella muttered to me, "Well, perhaps it's for the best after all," and she had, when I had asked her previously, been wholeheartedly in favour of the enterprise. From conversations I overheard in the inn and in various shops soon after our return I gathered that that was the general consensus. The villagers were relieved that the banal rhythm of their daily lives would continue undisturbed.

Angela had also been wrong about Duval. He didn't leave the village, and she was often absent from the inn in the evenings, being required up at the mansion. As usual, Philip accepted the situation with equanimity, while I crushed the feelings of jealousy that gnawed at me. I had to be realistic.

I asked Henry why Duval hadn't left the village after the failure of his project. He explained that it was because of the forthcoming harvest. From my balcony, I had watched the sun transform the terraced fields across the valley, gradually changing them from brown to green to pale yellow. As the corn ripened, the farmers trod the narrow bunds that bordered the fields, holding long sticks that had polythene bags attached to their ends. These they swished back and forth to scare away the mixed flocks of sparrows, finches and buntings that were attracted to the golden seeds. Once the crop was ready, the farmers along with their wives and children – the school was closed especially for the harvest – cooperated with each other to crop the corn, moving methodically from field to field below the mountain peaks.

The end of the harvest was traditionally a time for celebration. For several seasons the festivities had been muted, but this year Hubert had decided to revive the old spirit of the holiday. The grounds of his house were thrown open to the villagers. A marquee was set up from which free beer and brandy was dispensed – the inn was closed for that afternoon, and Philip was brought in to oversee the proceedings. Some stalls were erected, and there was a simple mechanical roundabout and a small ferris-wheel for the children. Musicians played, and the villagers danced.

It was all vaguely pagan and intoxicating. For once, the villagers let their hair down. I was surprised by the spontaneous laughter, the gaiety of the event. I admired the dancers for their graceful movements, their peasant feet temporarily freed from the pull of the soil.

My admiration didn't prevent me from feeling isolated, however. Even Henry, who had remained to help with the harvest – he admitted he was inept at cutting the corn, but that didn't hinder him – forgot himself in the dancing; his partner was Isabella's daughter, Rose, who for once had shaken off the sombre mask that she habitually wore in her mother's presence.

Still, if I was an onlooker and not a participant in the proceedings, so too was Bernard. I had noticed him for some time, standing alone near the marquee with a glass of brandy in his hand, observing the revelry. He saw that I too was alone, and approached me. "You wouldn't believe it, would you?" he said, indicating with a movement of his arm, the dancing taking place on the lawn.

"I must admit, I am surprised," I said.

"They are simple people, of course."

"And Hubert?" I asked in refutation, for he and Angela were amongst the villagers dancing on the grass.

"They dance well together, don't they?" he said. We both looked at the couple. Angela was sensual, vibrant as ever, raising her skirt as she danced to reveal her tanned legs. Hubert too was unconstrained; he moved in rhythm with his partner, oblivious, like Angela, to the other dancers around him. They seemed to exist for themselves alone.

"Hubert is more complex," Bernard said as we watched. He continued, "It's a pity really. He knows the people here so well. He could have had such an influence."

"But he has, hasn't he? He is making them happy; at least for today."

"Yes, but that's typical of him," he rejoined. "After this, he'll be away. There's no long-term commitment."

"Because of what happened eight years ago?" I ventured.

"I don't think so," Bernard answered. "Oh, I agree that was his pet project. He put a lot of time and money into it, but even if he had been successful, I suspect he would soon have got bored with it, and gone on to something else. That's his way, you see. He is always pursuing the new to make life interesting."

"Do you envy him his freedom?" I asked.

"I think you have more reason to envy him than I do," he replied pointedly.

The music stopped. Henry walked over towards us, hand in hand with Rose until he suddenly became self-conscious and withdrew his palm from hers. "Aren't you dancing?" he asked in his confusion. Rose blushed, and for the first time I warmed to her.

"I must find my mother," she said and left.

"A fine time to be stirring up a young girl's emotions – when you're about to leave," Bernard teased Henry.

"When exactly do you go?" I asked Henry, who had been deliberately vague about the date of his departure.

"The day after tomorrow," he answered abruptly.

"I didn't realise it was so soon," I said.

"It's for the best," Bernard said quietly.

"Yes, I know," Henry conceded, and thrust his hands into his trouser pockets.

I watched as Hubert and Angela moved away from the musicians and walked towards the house together.

"Come," ordered Bernard, suddenly becoming lively. "Let's see how we can do at the fair."

Henry and I followed him to the rough and ready attractions. At the first stall we paid for air-rifles and pellets. The object was to shoot down metallic ducks that were attached to a small conveyor belt at the rear of the stall. The moving ducks were not difficult to hit, as the numerous indentations in the metal showed, but the pellet had to strike the exact centre in order to knock the metal plates flat. Henry and I proved bumbling amateurs compared with Bernard who rarely failed to hit the target successfully. His superior skill put him in a good mood.

"Let's try something else now," he suggested when he became bored with our poor attempts.

We moved on to the next stall, where we paid our money and were given a number of thin wooden hoops. We had to throw the hoops so that they fell over the items – dolls, bottles of brandy, statues made from the stone in Duval's quarry – arranged on a circular table two arm-lengths distant from us. The items stood on wooden blocks; the hoops had to encircle the blocks and lie flat on the table. Bernard was less adept at this activity. Both Henry and I had some success. Henry carried off a doll – "For my niece," he explained – and I managed to win one of the bottles of brandy. Bernard had set his sights on one of the statues, but try as he may, he couldn't make the wooden hoops land over his chosen target. Henry and I watched as the failure etched itself into his face. Eventually he gave up. "Enough of this child's game!" he exclaimed, and stormed off to the marquee for a drink.

"A poor loser," I commented to Henry.

"I've never seen him so much on edge," Henry said.

Bernard had been on edge ever since he had returned to the village from his vacation, and more so since the expedition to the cave. I had, of course, still been seeing him twice a day, a commitment that had become increasingly unpleasant for me. He insisted that we play chess every evening. I felt compelled to accept. He played with a new intensity of concentration, with a total determination to beat me; and he did always defeat me – I had neither strategy nor tactics to stop him – but that didn't satisfy him; he had an insatiable need to repeat his victory, over and over again. The need was visible in his eyes, manifested in a kind of manic glare to his irides.

I had seen such an expression once before in the eyes of a middle-aged man who had written four novels, none of which had found an amenable publisher. Yet he persisted. He was writing his fifth book at the time that I knew him – I was a student then, on the fringe of the literary circle that the man moved in – and during that period his eyes had sparkled with the same manic fixity that I now saw in Bernard's eyes. Funnily enough, the fifth novel was successful. It brought the man a considerable sum of money after years of financial deprivation. Then once he was settled, having apparently achieved his aim, he hanged himself.

I had no fear that Bernard might commit suicide. It was my own well-being I was concerned about. The chess games were meant to intimidate me. They didn't – at least not so that it mattered. Bernard's conversation, however, did. Every now and then he would make a remark that hinted at more than was immediately apparent on the surface. He made comments about Angela's sexuality, about Henry's transfer being a just reward, about my poetry – he knew somehow that I had begun to write 'The Village in the Mountains' – in a way that intimated he had access to facts that I didn't. I felt he was putting pressure on me.

One conversation in particular forewarned me. It occurred one evening soon after our journey to the cave. I had registered with him as usual, and we were in the middle of a game of chess. "By the way," he said, apropos of nothing, which was the way he usually began such conversations, "I met the Colonel during the summer. He asked after you."

I coughed, and took a sip of the brandy that Bernard always generously supplied. "I didn't know you knew him personally," I said.

He made no response to this. He said, "He was surprised you were coping so well here."

"Was he also disappointed?" I asked.

"He is aware of what happened to Robert Belmont," he replied, making me fumble for significances.

But I too could make irrational connections. "I hear that you're planning to retire soon," I said.

"Who told you that?" he asked, but he knew the answer as soon as he had spoken. "Angela, of course," he said quietly to himself. He moderated his tone, "Yes, I hope to retire. I would like to leave the mountains behind me."

"When?" I asked.

"When my work here is finished," he replied immediately, and looked at me.

I averted my eyes, looked at the chess board, and made an impulsive move. Three moves later he had me in checkmate.

Henry left and I missed him more than I had thought I would. August became September and the smell of autumn permeated the mountain air. September turned into an unseasonably mild October, but the shepherds still drove their flocks back down through the village in anticipation of the winter snows. The men paused for two days in order to get drunk at the inn – their way of celebrating their return to civilisation. The villagers avoided them, finding them wild and primitive after their months of isolation. They were relieved when the shepherds continued on their journey.

My affair with Angela was drifting to an end. Hubert was still in the village, which I gathered from Isabella was unprecedented; normally the house would have been boarded up for the winter by early September.

"It's that woman," she said to me with barbed malice. "This time she has managed to get what she wants."

"And what does she want?" I asked.

"You'll see," she said. "You'll see."

On the first Thursday in October Angela had insisted on coming with me along the Vilaro valley, and we had made love on the usual piece of flattened grass. Our love-making had been slow and subdued, hinting at what was to follow.

"I can't come here again," she said in a muted voice as we lay together, side by side, without touching.

"Hubert?" I asked.

"He's leaving soon," she said. "He's taking me with him."

"And Philip?"

"I don't know yet. It's not quite what you think. Hubert has some land on the coast. He's developing a holiday resort there: hotels, apartments, restaurants, that kind of thing. He has asked me to manage part of it. He wants Philip to go as well."

"What does Philip think of the idea?" I asked.

"I haven't spoken to him yet," she admitted.

I could see that she was unwilling to broach the subject with her husband because she knew in advance what the likely response would be. Philip was insular, of the village. He would have little desire for the coast.

"I remember you telling me that Philip belonged in Cagot. Suppose he refuses to go?" I asked.

She bit her lower lip, thinking before she answered my question. "I won't get a second chance," she said. "Do you think I'm wrong?"

"No," I answered. "I'm surprised you've stayed as long as you have." This was only a half truth. I had come to realise that Angela was strong only within the sphere of the village. She had once joked about there being no one to take her away, but she had been more serious than her tone had suggested. Like most people, she didn't have the resolve to break away by herself, to plunge independently into the unknown. She needed someone to give her freedom, and she had finally inveigled Hubert into fulfilling that need.

She stood up and began to dress. I looked at her breasts, the dark pubic triangle, the curve of her buttocks. She fastened her bra, and pulled a t-shirt on over her head, revealing the black growth of hair under her arms. As she dressed, she spoke. "There is some-thing I want to tell you; that I can tell you now I'm sure I'm leaving."

I looked up expectantly.

"It's not very pleasant," she said, and paused.

"Go on," I urged her.

"The reason I came with you in the beginning," she began; then faltered.

"Yes?" I waited for her to continue.

"It was because of Bernard. He asked me to get to know you."

"And?"

"To tell him anything I learnt. What you thought of the village; of him; of Henry."

"The poems?" I said, suddenly remembering that night when she had come to my room for the second time. "You were checking up on me."

"Bernard wanted to know what you were writing. He was annoyed with me when I told him what I had seen. He said it was just old stuff, and you were deceiving me, keeping the new work from me. I told him there were no new poems. There weren't, were there?"

"No," I conceded. "I told you I wasn't able to write then and that was the truth. But I don't understand why Bernard should be so interested."

She picked up on the word 'then'. "You're writing now?" she asked.

"Yes," I said, "but Bernard knows about that already. It appears that you are not his only informant."

"No," she agreed; then, once she was fully dressed, asked, "Shall we go?"

"In a few minutes," I answered.

I liked lying naked on the mountain side, feeling the gentle air, now autumn-cool, on my skin. I reached into my rucksack for a cigarette. Angela took one for herself, and sat down beside me. We smoked our cigarettes together.

"Why?" I asked.

"I have been a whore since I was fourteen," she said bluntly. "I was always attractive. Men noticed me. I learned how to use that for my benefit."

"Hubert?" I asked.

"Yes," she answered. "Long before he came to see my father with Philip in tow. Hubert is a sensual man; he likes his pleasures. But he is also a gentleman. He has always treated me well."

"And Bernard?"

"For him sex is a way of getting rid of his demons. There isn't much pleasure involved. But I haven't been with him for months – since before you came to the village."

"Then why do you do what he asks?"

"I'm rewarded for what I do," she replied hesitantly. "But now I can put it behind me. Do you blame me very much?" she asked.

I doubted my reply would make much difference. Angela had little conscience, had told me as much in the past. "No," I said. "I have enjoyed being with you."

"We were good lovers," she agreed; then stood up once more. She ground her cigarette end under the heel of her boot. "Now can we go?"

She wandered slowly down the hillside while I put on my clothes. I joined her at the river. We crossed over on the stepping stones.

"Tell me about Robert," I said, after we had walked in silence for half an hour or so.

"Robert? Why?" she asked.

"I'm curious. Didn't Bernard want you to seduce him in the same way that he wanted you to seduce me?"

She stopped walking, and gave an ironic laugh.

"You are an innocent, aren't you?" she said.

I frowned, not understanding.

"I would have been no use there. That was man's work."

"I see," I said.

"You must be careful," she said, becoming serious, admonitory. "You're a good man, but a little proud, a little vain. That's what Hubert said anyway. He thinks that you should be more wary of Bernard."

"Yes, he told me," I said.

"Bernard can be dangerous! He likes the feeling of power."

"I know," I said. "But you shouldn't underestimate me either."

I discovered what hold Bernard had over Angela when I got back to the hotel in the late afternoon. A large, plain brown envelope lay on my desk. I opened it. Inside were five 10 X 8 black and white photographs of Angela and a man I vaguely recognised, but couldn't place exactly because his face was partially concealed in the photographs. Both Angela and the man were naked. Their love-making was rendered in explicit detail.

I put the pictures back in the envelope and strode through the village to the police station. Bernard was in his private quarters, eating dinner at the table. I stood while he remained seated, took the photographs out of the envelope and threw them down onto the table. He glanced at them; then looked up at me and held my stare.

"I believe these belong to you," I said, trying to restrain my anger.

Bernard put his knife and fork down neatly onto his plate; then stroked his moustache thoughtfully with the fingers of his left hand. "Where did you find them?" he asked calmly.

"In my room," I replied. "Surely you're not going to deny that you put them there?"

He ignored my comments for the moment. He stood up and, with a frown of puzzlement on his brow, took his plate out to the kitchen. When he returned he asked, "What reason would I have for doing that?"

"Angela told me today how you used her to get at me. She was vague about why she did as you wanted. Now I know why. I imagine you put them in my room to provoke me. Another way of telling me that your will is paramount."

"If that was the case, then I seem to have succeeded," he responded in the same controlled manner."

"Who is the man?" I asked.

"A soldier. Angela had an affair with him. He knew what was going on. Angela didn't."

"And who did you threaten to show them to? Hubert?" I asked.

Bernard laughed at this. "Hubert! They would make no difference to him. No, I told her that they might fall into Philip's hands unless she helped me out when the occasion demanded."

"And she believed you would carry out your threat?"

"Angela has no illusions about me. She knew I wasn't joking. She knew that Philip would be hurt if he saw the photographs and she would hate for that to happen. I told you everybody has a weak spot. For all her lasciviousness, that is hers; she really has a tender streak for Philip. Difficult to believe, I know, but it's a fact. Also, of course, he would probably kick her out. Then where would she go?"

After he had said this, he picked up one of the photographs from the table and looked at it. I saw Angela's splayed legs, the soldier above her, pressing down between her thighs.

"She is an attractive woman," he said. "Very attractive."

He put the photograph back on the table with the others; then faced me again. He crossed his arms, and continued his attack. "I told you I knew human nature," he said coldly.

"And Robert Belmont?" I asked.

"He was easy. He was weak, a furtive homosexual who felt guilty because of it. Would you like to see those photographs as well? They might interest you."

"There's no need," I said.

"Oh, I think you should," he insisted. He walked over to the cupboard where he kept the ledger I had signed twice a day, every day for the last six months. From one of the drawers he took out a number of files, and brought them to the table where I had stood since my entrance. "The camera is one of the great modern inventions," he said as he lay the files down on the table next to the photographs of Angela. "It helps to convince people of the truth so easily."

"Partial truths," I said.

From one of the files he extracted a brown envelope similar to the one I had found in my room. This one had CONFIDENTIAL stamped on it in thick, blue print. "You see," he said, as he handed me the photographs from inside, "more truths."

I looked at the pictures, at Henry and the trade-unionist – the graphic details of tumescence, moisture, flesh.

"You too are so naive," Bernard said sneeringly. "Didn't you know that every word you said to Henry came back to me?"

From another file he took out a sheaf of handwritten notes and gave them to me. I looked down quickly at Henry's fluid script. Set out in diary form, it was, as Bernard had said, an accurate account of the conversations we had had over tea on Sunday afternoons and at the inn on Saturday evenings.

I sat down limply at the table, waited for Bernard to continue.

"And you with your talk of freedom and choice," he went on, in the same contemptuous manner. He reached into another file, and handed me some more papers. "Do you call this freedom?"

They were two typewritten reports with the official government crest at the top. The first had been prepared by a woman, the second by a man. They described in prosaic, but accurate detail what I had done and said on the train journey from the capital to Rona. The woman I had made frantic love to, and the old man I had considered ignorant, had been government agents; the Colonel's insurance policy had I decided to flee the train.

"What was the woman's name?" I asked Bernard, almost in a whisper.

"Annette," he replied, and contented himself with a tight smile.

I sat meekly in my chair, inadequately trying to absorb the facts that Bernard was relentlessly presenting to me. I felt weak, malleable like putty, with no solid core. I was vaguely aware of his tidying up the files, returning all but one to the drawer then coming back to the table with his shotgun in his hand. He leaned it against the table opposite to where I was sitting, so that I could see the barrel protruding above the wooden surface. The remaining file lay unopened on the table between myself and the gun.

"There is one more thing," Bernard began, speaking more slowly. "Your wife, Maria!"

I raised my head to listen.

"You shouldn't have returned to this country. You knew that you had enemies. You knew you were exposing her to danger."

"No," I began to protest.

"There was nothing accidental about her death," he continued, not allowing me to speak. "Inside that file is an order for her elimination."

Although my fingers were numb, I opened the file. Inside was the order as Bernard had said, signed by the Colonel himself before he had secured the ultimate power. It was a bare command; no explanation was given. I then realised that Maria's death had been nothing more than an act of gross personal malice on his part.

"But why?" I asked, my voice a hoarse, almost incoherent whisper. "Why her and not me?"

The Police Chief stooped down and held his face a few inches away from mine. "So that it would come to this," he said, emulating my grating whisper.

He then laid the shotgun across the table in front of me, and walked out of the room.

I don't know whether he had intended that the act should be played through to the end when he had placed the photographs in my room, or whether, after I had gone to his office to protest, he had sensed that the opportunity was there to be seized. Whatever, the scene – the poet, alone in the room with a loaded shotgun – was one that he must have had in mind since my arrival in the village, perhaps even before.

That he had been confident of success was evident from the smug beam of satisfaction on his face when he re-entered the room after I had fired a single shot. The look disappeared instantly when he saw me standing by the chess table, saw the shattered portrait on the mantelpiece.

"What?" he aspirated.

I handed him the gun. He took it; then went over to the fireplace and fingered the fragments of his sister's picture. There was a noise at the door. Two policemen came in, looked to Bernard for his command.

"It's all right," he said, pulling himself together. "A little accident, that's all. No one's hurt."

The soldiers retreated, ushering away the handful of villagers who had gathered outside the building. I heard them repeating Bernard's explanation.

"Why this picture?" Bernard asked.

"Just an indulgence of mine," I said. "Do you want me to sign the ledger now?"

"No," he managed to utter. "I don't think that will be necessary."

I left him standing there at the mantelpiece, clutching broken glass and fragments of his sister's portrait. I went straight to the inn and ordered a large brandy.

"Are you all right?" Angela asked, seeing the distress in my face.

"The brandy!" I repeated harshly.

She poured me the drink, and stood there holding the bottle as I drank the contents of the glass in one go.

"Another!" I demanded.

She replenished my glass. This time I sipped the amber liquid, savouring its warmth on my tongue and in my belly.

"They killed Maria. Did you know that?"

"Who killed Maria?" Angela responded. "I thought you said ..."

I interrupted her. "The Government – or rather the Colonel. He had her murdered."

"How do you know this?" she asked.

"Bernard told me. He told me a lot of other things as well. He also showed me his collection of photographs."

"What do you mean?" she said, and glanced nervously around her to see if anyone else was listening to our conversation.

"What I said," I continued. "To begin with, the photos of you enjoying yourself with your soldier friend."

Angela simply looked at me, for once seemingly speechless. She picked up a glass from behind the bar, and poured herself some brandy. She then refilled my glass to the brim.

"On the house," she said.

We clinked glasses and drank together.

"How much do you know?" I asked.

"I didn't know about your wife," she said earnestly. "And that's the truth."

"What about Robert Belmont? About his death?"

"He killed himself," she said.

I stared at her, attempting to discern if her apparent ignorance was genuine. She stared back at me. "At least you're alive," she said.

"Shouldn't I be?" I asked.

"Hubert and Bernard have a bet," she said.

"You mean ...?"

"It's all right," she said. "It looks as though Hubert's won. I told him you were a survivor. I saw it in your palm."

"Gypsy magic?"

She smiled. "If you like."

I finished my brandy, and reached into my pocket. She held up her hand to stop me.

"No need," she said. "It's on the house, remember."

I thanked her and left the inn.

Back at the hotel I held my head under a cold tap to sober myself up. Then I changed into the clothes I normally wore when I went out walking during the day – jeans, sweater and jacket. I found the flashlight I had bought after that dinner at Hubert's, the time when Henry had had the good sense to bring his. Then I packed a few things into my rucksack: my poems; my nature journal; my field glasses, a packet of biscuits and a water bottle. It was necessary to travel light. I strapped my rucksack over my shoulders and went out through the French windows, closing them gently behind me. I climbed over the balcony rail and jumped down onto the soft grass. There was a full moon, making my flashlight unnecessary for the time being.

I skirted the hotel building, surreal as always in the moonlight, and took the road towards the Vilaro valley. The village was silent; the only noise was the river burbling away, its white foam visible in the darkness.

I kept up a steady pace, needing to put as much distance as I could between myself and the village before morning came. In the pine forest I paused to take a drink of water and to get the torch out of my rucksack, as the tall trees blotted out the light. The yellow beam illuminated the track. I hurried on. The pines seemed watchful, ominous and I was a little afraid, but I kept my fear under control.

I descended the ridge to the river, and looked up at the open sky. The moon, higher now, was partially veiled by cloud. A faint breeze caressed my skin. I kept my torch on, carefully scanning the track for rocks embedded in the ground. Away to my left, invisible, was the Poet's Throne. Looming above me were the vertical crags where vultures soared during the day. A pale glow separated their tops from the indigo sky.

I walked on, and on, fighting the tiredness that had begun to wrap itself around me. Once I made my way carefully down to the river's edge and held my head under the rushing water. Its coldness reinvigorated me. Dripping, I scrambled back to the path and went on. Dawn found me at the place where the track began to snake sharply upwards, traversing the scree-covered mountain sides. I remembered vividly the inhuman landscape, the grey monotony of it all. My memory and my tired legs constrained me. I sat down to rest with my back against a rock and closed my eyes against the burgeoning daylight. When I opened them again the sun momentarily blinded me, and I couldn't at first understand where I was. I heard the deep-throated "pruk" of a raven flying nearby, but I didn't see the bird. Then I looked at my watch. It was the time I should have been having breakfast. I presumed that Isabella would have already raised the alarm. I scrambled to my feet. My calves and thighs felt heavy, leaden; my back ached. I had to force myself to begin the trudge up the slope.

It was a hard, slow slog. Loose rocks were strewn across the narrow path, making walking difficult. The sky was cloudless, and the autumnal, early morning chill soon gave way to a summer-like heat. Sweat formed on my brow. My shirt clung to my back. I tasted salt on my lips. I had to keep stopping to catch my breath. When I did so I focussed on the rock face stretching along the rim of the hill above me, and picked out the spot where I knew the gap through the rock lay. That spot took on the force of an obsession; I willed it to come closer to me, and gradually, as I stumbled and panted along the track, it did so.

I finally made it to the rock that concealed the entrance to the narrow valley. I was exhausted. Stupidly, I had forgotten to bring a hat with me. The sun had burned my neck; it felt red and sore to the touch. I looked below me, at the grey slope, the grey ribbon-like path winding down to the blue strip of river. Two dark shadows suddenly drifted across the grey rock. I raised my eyes to the sky, and watched the vultures glide over my head on outstretched wings, heading towards the marshy plateau beyond the rim.

I entered the sunless canyon, and walked hurriedly between its oppressive walls out into the expansive, green valley. I took my field glasses out of my bag, and scanned the landscape. There was no sign of the vultures, no sign of animal life at all. I went to the river, crossing over the hummock where we had pitched our tents on the journey to the cave, to refill my water bottle. After I had done that, I set off in the direction of the distant peaks, beyond which lay the cave and the border. This time I kept to the river, thinking that the long days of summer sunshine would have dried up the meadows. I was mistaken; the ground was as boggy as before, so I had to retrace my steps; then sweep away from the river onto slightly higher ground, as we had done under Bernard's guidance.

This was the worst part of my escape to the border. The valley seemed to go on without end; the distant peaks held their distance as the hours passed, and my body grew even more fatigued. The grassy sward seemed drained of life; the sheep had gone, of course, driven down the mountain by their human masters, but the birds too had departed, following their instinctual urge. There were no water pipits to be seen, and they had been so common in the summer. Now I missed their reassuring blandness. I walked towards the distant mountain tops like an automaton, driven by a mechanical will. Occasionally, however, I would halt and scan the levels behind me through my field glasses to see if I was being pursued. Through the wavering heat haze I saw nothing; only grass.

It had gone mid-afternoon by the time I came to the streams that radiated across the grassy surface. I had no option but to wade through them, one after the other, so that the water squelched audibly in my boots as I trod the boggy patches between. The water was cold, but more than that, it had a muddy texture to it, making me think of primeval slime.

It was a relief to climb onto higher ground, there where the shepherds' huts now lay deserted until the following summer. I peered inside one of the rough stone buildings. It smelt rank of unwashed flesh and decayed food. The floor was of flattened grass, a straw-green colour, reminding me of the patch below the forest where Angela and I had made love. I moved away; the connection seemed too gross to contemplate.

I forced myself to continue, following the track up towards Devil's Peak. At the edge of the cirque, I surrendered to the reality of my physical condition. I sprawled lengthways on the rocky ground, and gazed blankly at the black lake below. Its surface was smooth, like black glass, and I wondered if waves ever disturbed its flatness; then, in my exhausted state, I remembered it was called Devil's Lake, and I could see how it projected evil.

I imagined how those primitive men, those who had created the images on the cave walls long before the statue of the Dark Virgin had been created, would have looked upon this lake: black, lifeless, devoid of surface vegetation, devoid of birds, devoid of fish. The Void itself.

Momentarily, I perceived it as such myself, and was terrified. The reaction passed, however, or perhaps I willed it to pass. I had chosen a certain path, and it was up to me to follow it through to its completion. I knew that I would not make the border before nightfall, so I decided to rest overnight at the camp near the cave. I dragged myself to my feet and walked down to the lakeshore; then followed the vestigial track that skirted its northern edge. The blackness made the water appear as viscous as tar. I dared myself to touch its surface; it was bitterly cold, but water nonetheless. Ripples radiated outwards from where I had dipped my fingers in, but the lake soon regained its unnatural placidity.

I continued round the lake until the track diverged from the shore, winding up the slope of the cirque. I climbed upwards, spurred on by the knowledge that this would be my final ascent of the day. The lake disappeared from view, and soon I was walking through the narrow valley, making my way to the campsite.

The covered latrines and the refurbished pipes still remained much as they had been left. I took my clothes off and had a shower. The water was warm, as the sun had heated the metal tank during the day. Afterwards I lay naked on a rock, allowing the final rays of the sun, now dipping behind the peaks, to dry me. I dressed; then ate more of my biscuits, considering as I did so where to rest up until dawn.

I decided that to sleep at the campsite itself would be too risky. If anyone was following me it would be an obvious place to look. I therefore walked a little further up the valley, which was now swathed in shadow, in the direction of the border; then headed off up a narrower, connecting valley to my left. There I crawled under an overhanging rock and, using my rucksack as a makeshift pillow, lay flat on the grass. I soon fell asleep.

I woke up shivering with cold, enveloped in a dank mist. I fumbled in my rucksack for the flashlight, and focussed its beam on my watch. It was one o'clock, so I had had a few hours deep sleep, but dawn was a long way off. The hours until then were miserable. I couldn't sleep and I couldn't get warm. I curled into a ball with my knees pulled up towards my chin, like a foetus, but this brought no relief. In the end I crawled out into the open, and did exercises on the spot to keep the cold at bay. This helped a little, but my limbs were stiff and aching from the long walk, so my movements lacked flexibility. Once I thought I heard a horse whinnying in the far distance, but that must just been my imagination playing tricks on me.

Dawn came, but the mist clung to the rocks, clung to the grass, limiting visibility to a few metres. I made my way cautiously back to the main valley; then stopped. I could easily get lost. I had no alternative but to wait.

The mist proved tenacious; it was two hours before the sun became visible, a vague white ball against the moist grey curtain, and a good hour after that before the mist had shifted enough for me to be able to make out the gap between the peaks to the east.

I went on, almost running in order to shake the chill from my bones, along the valley floor; then up the steep, rocky track that led to the border. I didn't stop once until the track disappeared amongst the scree near the col. There, a griffon vulture lay twisted and blood-spattered on the naked rocks. I walked past it, saw that its bare neck was smeared crimson, its one visible eye glazed, unreal, like a bead. I had no idea what had killed the bird.

I scrambled up the scree, past the first ridge, up to top of the second. There I sat down for a while to contemplate the valleys of the country that stretched out beneath me. I wanted my last moments in my native land to be tranquil ones.

I was distracted by a small bird that appeared as if from nowhere and alighted on a nearby rock. It was a chaffinch. It uttered a sharp 'pink, pink' call, before fluttering off low over the scree that I had just climbed. I had at first thought that this was a solitary occurrence, but soon other birds appeared, flying through the col in small parties. I didn't need my field glasses to identify them, as they flew only a few inches above the shards of rock, skimming low over the border, but in the opposite direction to the one I had chosen. Apart from chaffinches, I made out goldfinches and linnets, as well as a few pipits and wagtails.

The migration was a trickle rather than a flood, but it held me entranced. Then the butterflies began to arrive, at first in ones and twos, but soon there were clouds of them fluttering by oblivious to my presence. There were two species involved, which I have now put a name to – red admirals and clouded yellows – but the names are irrelevant; what has stayed with me is the beauty of the occurrence. When I stood up to take the track that Hubert Duval had urged me to follow, the pieces of weathered rock on the col floor were no longer visible. There was no surface, merely a shimmering mass of wings – yellow, red, black and white – streaming at ankle-height over the neck of the pass, down into the country where I had been born, and from which I was now fleeing for good.

Carefully, I waded through the delicate throng, and walked down the cirque into the neighbouring country.

The Village in the Mountains

ABOUT PROVERSE HONG KONG

Proverse Hong Kong is based in Hong Kong with long-term and expanding regional and international connections.

Proverse has published novels, novellas, fictionalized autobiography, non-fiction (including autobiography, biography, history, memoirs, sport, travel narratives), single-author poetry collections, children's, teens / young adult and academic books. Other interests include diaries, and academic works in the humanities, social sciences, cultural studies, linguistics and education. Some Proverse books have accompanying audio texts. Some are translated into Chinese.

Proverse welcomes authors who have a story to tell, wisdom, perceptions or information to convey, a person they want to memorialize, a neglect they want to remedy, a record they want to correct, a strong interest that they want to share, skills they want to teach, and who consciously seek to make a contribution to society in an informative, interesting and well-written way. Proverse works with texts by non-native-speaker writers of English as well as by native English-speaking writers.

The name, "Proverse", combines the words "prose" and "verse" and is pronounced accordingly.

THE PROVERSE PRIZE

The Proverse Prize, an annual international competition for an unpublished book-length work of fiction, non-fiction, or poetry, was established in January 2008. It is open to all who are at least eighteen on the date they sign the entry form. Unusually for a competition of this nature, there is no restriction based on nationality, residence or citizenship.

The objectives of the Proverse Prize are: to encourage excellence and / or excellence and usefulness in publishable written work in the English Language, which can, in varying degrees, "delight and instruct". Entries are invited from anywhere in the world. Semi-finalists to date include writers born or resident in Andorra, Australia, Canada, Germany, Hong Kong, New Zealand, Nigeria, Singapore, South Africa, Taiwan, The Bahamas, the Peoples' Republic of China, the United Arab Emirates, the United Kingdom, the USA.

Founders: Verner Bickley and Gillian Bickley. To celebrate their lifelong love of words in all their forms as readers, writers, editors, academics, performers, and publishers.

Honorary Legal Advisor: Mr Raymond T. L. Tse.

Honorary Accountant: Mr Neville Chow.

Honorary Judges: Anonymous.

Honorary Advisors: Bahamian poet Marion Bethel; UK translator, Margaret Clarke; UK linguist & lexicographer David Crystal; Canadian poet and academic, Jonathan Hart; Swedish linguist Björn Jernudd; Hong Kong University Librarian, Peter Sidorko; Singapore poet Edwin Thumboo; Czech novelist & poet Olga Walló.

Honorary UK agent and distributor: Christine Penney

Honorary Administrators: Proverse Hong Kong.

Proverse Prize Winners Whose Books Have Already Been Published By Proverse Hong Kong

Laura Solomon, Rebecca Jane Tomasis, Gillian Jones, David Diskin, Peter Gregoire, Sophronia Liu, Birgit Linder, James McCarthy, Celia Claase, Philip Chatting.

Summary Terms and Conditions
(for indication only & subject to revision)

The information below is for guidance only. Please refer to the year-specific Proverse Prize Entry Form & Terms & Conditions, which are uploaded in April each year onto the Proverse Hong Kong website: <www.proversepublishing.com>.

The free Proverse E-Newsletter includes ongoing information about the Proverse Prize. To be put on the E-Newsletter mailing-list, email: info@proversepublishing.com with your request.

The Prize
1) Publication by Proverse Hong Kong, with
2) Cash prize of HKD10,000 (HKD7.80 = approx. US$1.00)

Supplementary publication grants may be made to selected other entrants for publication by Proverse Hong Kong.

Depending on the quality of the work in any year, the prize may be shared by at most two entrants or withheld, as recommended by the judges.

In 2015, the entry fee was: HKD220.00 OR GBP32.00.

Writers are eligible, who are at least eighteen on the date they sign The Proverse Prize entry documents. There is no nationality or residence restriction.

Each submitted work must be an unpublished publishable single-author work of non-fiction, fiction or poetry, the original work of the entrant, and submitted in the English language. School textbooks and plays are ineligible.

Translated work: If the work entered is a translation from a language other than English, both the original work and the translation should be previously unpublished. The submitted work will not be judged as a translation but as an original work.

Extent of the Manuscript: within the range of what is usual for the genre of the work submitted. However, it is advisable that novellas be in the range 30,000 to 45,000 words); other fiction (e.g. novels, short-story collections) and non-fiction (e.g. autobiographies, biographies, diaries, letters, memoirs, essay collections, etc.) should be in the range, 75,000 to 100,000 words. Poetry collections should be in the range, 5,000 to 25,000 words. Other word-counts and mixed-genre submissions are not ruled out.

Writers may choose, if they wish, to obtain the services of an Editor in presenting their work, and should acknowledge this help and the nature and extent of this help in the Entry Form.

KEY DATES FOR THE PROVERSE PRIZE
IN ANY YEAR
(subject to confirmation and/or change)

Receipt of Entry Fees / Entry Documents	[No later than] 14 April to 31 May
Receipt of entered manuscripts	1 May to 30 June
Announcement of semi-finalists	July-September
Announcement of finalists	October-December
Announcement of winner/ max two winners (sharing the cash prize)	December of the year of entry to April of the year that follows the year of entry
Cash Award made	At the same time as publication of the work(s) adjudged the winner / joint-winners of the Proverse Prize
Publication of winning work(s)	In or after November of the year that follows the year of entry

NOVELS, SHORT STORY COLLECTIONS
AND OTHER FICTION
Published by Proverse Hong Kong

If you have enjoyed *The Village in the Mountains* by David Diskin, you may also enjoy Philip Chatting's *The Snow Bridge and Other Stories* (2015).

**You may also like to read the following
(all titles in English unless otherwise stated)**

A Misted Mirror, by Gillian Jones. 2011.
A Painted Moment, by Jennifer Ching. 2010.
An Imitation of Life, by Laura Solomon. 2013.
Article 109, by Peter Gregoire. 2012.
Bao Bao's Odyssey: from Mao's Shanghai to Capitalist Hong Kong, by Paul Ting. 2012.
Black Tortoise Winter, by Jan Pearson. Scheduled 2015 / 2016.
Bright Lights and White Nights, by Andrew Carter. 2015.
cemetery miss you, by Jason S Polley. 2011.
Cop Show Heaven, by Lawrence Gray. 2015.
Death has a Thousand Doors, by Patricia Grey. 2011.
Hilary and David, by Laura Solomon. 2011.
Instant Messages, by Laura Solomon. 2010.
Man's Last Song, by James Tam. 2013.
Mila the Magician, by Zhang Jian. 2013. (English / Chinese bilingual)
Mishpacha – Family, by Rebecca Tomasis. 2010.
Odds and Sods, by Lawrence Gray. 2013.
Paranoia (the Walk and Talk with Angela), by Caleb Kavon. 2012.
Red Bird Summer, by Jan Pearson. 2014.
Revenge from Beyond, by Dennis Wong. 2011.
The Day They Came, by Gérard Louis Breissan. 2012.
The Devil You know, by Peter Gregoire. 2014.
The Monkey in Me: Confusion, Love and Hope under a Chinese Sky, by Caleb Kavon. 2009.
The Monkey in Me, by Caleb Kavon. Translated by Chapman Chen. 2010. E-book. 2010. (Chinese)

The Perilous Passage of Princess Petunia Peasant, by Victor Edward Apps. 2014.
The Reluctant Terrorist: in Search of the Jizo, by Caleb Kavon. 2011.
The Shingle Bar Sea Monster and Other Stories, by Laura Solomon. 2012.
The Snow Bridge and Other Stories, by Philip Chatting. Scheduled 2015.
Tiger Autumn, by Jan Pearson. 2015.
The Village in the Mountains, by David Diskin. 2012.
Tightrope! A Bohemian Tale, by Olga Walló. Translated from Czech by Johanna Pokorny, Veronika Revická & others. 2010.
Tightrope! A Bohemian Tale, by Olga Walló. Translated by Chapman Chen. 2011. (Chinese)
University Days, by Laura Solomon. 2014.
Vera Magpie, by Laura Solomon. 2013.

OTHER GENRES

We also publish in other genres, including autobiography, biography, children's illustrated books, educational books, Hong Kong educational and legal history, memoirs, poetry, teenage / young adult books, and travel. Other genres may be added.

WRITE TO US!

We are interested to read your response to
David Diskin's *The Village in the Mountains*
and any other of our publications.
Please write to our email address, proverse@netvigator.com,
giving us a few sentences which you are willing for us to publish,
giving your comments on this book.
If what you write is chosen to be included
in our E-Newsletter or website,
we will select another title published by Proverse
and send you a complimentary copy.
Please include your name, email address and mailing address
when you write to us, and state whether or not we may cut or
edit your comments for publication.
We will use your initials to attribute your comments.

FIND OUT MORE ABOUT OUR AUTHORS AND BOOKS

Visit our website
http://www.proversepublishing.com

Visit our distributor's website
<www.chineseupress.com>

Follow us on Twitter
Follow news and conversation: <twitter.com/Proversebooks>
OR
Copy and paste the following to your browser window and
follow the instructions: https://twitter.com/#!/ProverseBooks

'Like us' on Facebook: www.facebook.com/ProversePress

Request our E-Newsletter
Send your request to info@proversepublishing.com.

Availability
Most titles are available in Hong Kong and world-wide
from our Hong Kong based Distributor,
The Chinese University Press of Hong Kong,
The Chinese University of Hong Kong, Shatin, NT,
Hong Kong SAR, China. Email: cup-bus@cuhk.edu.hk

All titles are available from Proverse Hong Kong
and the Proverse Hong Kong UK-based Distributor.

We have stock-holding retailers in Hong Kong,
Singapore (Select Books), Canada (Elizabeth Campbell Books),
Principality of Andorra (Llibreria La Puça, La Llibreria).

Orders can be made from bookshops in the UK and elsewhere.

Ebooks
Most of our titles are available also as Ebooks.